She'd known something wasn't right, even suspected there might be danger, but she'd never expected this...

Juggling her briefcase and purse at her door, Kingsley searched her pockets for keys and inserted the house key in to the door lock. *Odd*, she thought, when it wouldn't turn. She tried it again, only harder. It still wouldn't budge. On a hunch, she tried turning it left and realized that the door was already unlocked. Had she been that distracted at noon when she had stopped home to back up her PC and give Isaac the disk to safeguard?

Pushing the heavy door with her hip, she eased forward. Street lamps provided the only illumination, the timer having failed to turn on her lamps. "Why not?" she grumbled into the darkness, pausing to let her eyes adjust to the gloom. "Pandora! Where are you, baby?"

She heard a faint noise somewhere nearby and froze, skin prickling. Some force drew her eyes left to the Chippendale mirror that faced her kitchen's entrance on her right. In the dim light her mind played a trick. Instead of a mirror she saw a framed portrait. She did not recognize the face and had no recollection of whom it might be. Before she had time to question the incongruity, the face in the portrait moved. A man. Big. Dark. Raising his arm. Instinctively she raised her hand to protect herself, but she was too slow. A horrible pain crashed through her head, turning everything black.

A tragic auto accident? No! The accident was staged, and young Doctor Ward murdered. But why? And by whom? The only witness, a DUI motorist, flees the scene. In the aftermath of Ward's death, and the media fascination, his widow, socialite Kingsley Ward, flees Philadelphia, impulsively accepting a job as VP of commercial lending at a small-town central Pennsylvania bank. But trouble follows her. She uncovers a bogus loan scam that leads her to suspect senior management. Throwing her life into further disarray, the anonymous witness to her husband's murder contacts her with compelling details about the killer's identity. Angry and frustrated, Kingsley vows to solve both crimes herself, risking her job, her reputation—and even her life.

KUDOS for *A Matter of Trust*

In *A Matter of Trust* by Nancy A. Hughes, Kingsley Ward's husband is killed and she flees the publicity and chaos left behind by his death, taking a job at a bank in a small town in central Pennsylvania. But it isn't long before trouble finds her again. Something isn't quite right about some of the bank's loans, and Kingsley believes she's uncovered a major fraud. But how far to the top does it go? And who can she trust? Being the newcomer/outsider, she doesn't know. But she needs to figure it out fast, as someone involved knows what she's uncovered, and they intend to see that she can't expose them. I like the way Hughes blends the subplots so that you can't tell which threat was related to which crime as she skillfully mixes romance, suspense, and mystery into one cohesive story. A really good read. I thoroughly enjoyed it.
~ *Taylor Jones, The Review Team of Taylor Jones & Regan Murphy*

A Matter of Trust by Nancy A. Hughes is a combination mystery, romance, and thriller. Kingsley Ward loses her husband in what she thinks is a traffic accident. Leaving Philadelphia after his death, she takes a job as a loan officer in a small town bank, only to discover that trouble doesn't only find you in the big city. She uncovers a loan scam that has her suspecting the top brass at the bank. Now, she doesn't know who to trust. If she tells the wrong people, her life could be in danger. But what about the new VP? Todd is equally new, so he's probably not involved in the scam and she should be able to trust him. Probably. Maybe. But what if she's wrong? Then it begins to appear that her husband's death wasn't an accident, but murder. Now she has two crimes to solve. Hughes weaves in a lot of different elements and ties them all together at the end. Very nicely done. If you like a good mystery with a touch of romance, you can't go wrong with *A Matter of Trust*. *~ Regan Murphy, The Review Team of Taylor Jones & Regan Murphy*

A
Matter
of
Trust

Nancy A. Hughes

Nancy A. Hughes

A Black Opal Books Publication

GENRE: MYSTERY-DETECTIVE/WOMEN SLEUTHS

This is a work of fiction. Names, places, characters and incidents are either the product of the author's imagination or are used fictitiously, and any resemblance to any actual persons, living or dead, businesses, organizations, events or locales is entirely coincidental. All trademarks, service marks, registered trademarks, and registered service marks are the property of their respective owners and are used herein for identification purposes only. The publisher does not have any control over or assume any responsibility for author or third-party websites or their contents.

Published by Black Opal Books http://www.blackopalbooks.com

DEDICATION

In Loving Memory of my parents
Jose M. and Elizabeth Shannon Arburu

Prologue

Early Autumn:

Exhausted from his first month as an ophthalmology resident, Andy kneaded his neck.

"Here, let me do that," Kingsley offered, kneeling on the couch cushion beside her husband. "I know it's overwhelming, but you've never failed at anything. You'll be excellent—just don't imagine doing it all at once."

Andy swiveled to smile at his wife. "I'm okay."

"Not really. What's bothering you?"

"It's nothing."

She worked at the knots in the core of his neck until he moaned softly. A wisp of a smile parted her lips. "I have great news." She waited for his undivided attention and only proceeded when he finally looked up. "I'm very late. This time I may really be pregnant."

Without turning, Andy patted the arms she had draped across his chest. "Are you sure? If that's what you want, I guess I'll adjust."

Kingsley stiffened reflexively. "Andy, I know how you feel, but you won't regret this. One little baby only replaces half of us."

He eased away. Rising to his feet, he pulled her into a brief hug, and then released her. "I guess you've earned this."

"Andy, I—"

She was tempted to lure him into deeper conversation, to coax some intimate dialog from him, but realized instinctively he had run out of words. On many levels, she appreciated his quiet, his introversion, his lack of bad temper—her visionary, bent on saving the sight of the world. He had been the one guy she'd dated who respected her mind and did not feel the need to compete with her on any level.

"I should go fill the gas tank," he said, sidestepping the issue. "And we're out of ice cream. You need anything?"

"I wish you wouldn't go out. It's pouring! Those old tires will never pass state inspection."

Andy put on his jacket and a forced smile. "This time next week, that faithful old Subaru will be recycled, tires and all. Who'd have believed it would make it through college and med school. Duct tape stock will plummet."

"Take my car—"

"The grammy mobile?" He shook his head at the thought of driving her old Lexus. "Bring you something?"

She shrugged. "No thanks."

"Give me a kiss—mmmm. I love you." He jokingly licked his lips and she melted.

She could have thrown herself at him, dragged him onto the couch, and torn into him, she loved him so much. But she had learned to let him initiate and allowed him to escape.

Andy ducked into his car, started the engine, and turned on the wipers that screeched in protest. He unearthed a towel from under the seat in case the defroster failed once again. Which it did. Scowling, he snagged the towel to wipe condensation from the windshield and tossed it nearby.

The engine stuttered as he backed from his space onto the deserted access road as black as his thoughts, past neighboring windows that pulsed bluish light.

Damn it, Andrew, what did you say and how did you say it? The least you could do is act supportive. She's been there for you a hundred times over. Kingsley, who could have had anyone, done anything, gone anywhere. Hitching her wagon to my star, urging me onward, willingly giving me time and the space. The spotless apartment, the checkbook in balance, the meals on short notice—

He skidded his rust bucket onto the secondary road, the idea of children gnawing his brain. Six billion people crushing the planet. When would religious fanatics put a check mark beside repopulate the earth? When would right-thinking people prevail over crooked despots who seized wealth for themselves, leaving impoverished women to have dozens of babies, hoping to raise one healthy adult?

Andy flashed to that volunteer trip, from which he had come home unable to sleep. He should research diseases or teach in a college. What good were glasses for people whose survival needs paled by comparison? Dad and Kingsley were right. He was entirely too sensitive, would be consumed by the futility of it all if he didn't focus on one worthwhile project for which he was suited and trained. Nobody died in an eye doctor's chair, and he could help developing nations if his trips were planned better.

He passed up the convenience store and the gas pumps, splashing instead onto the eastbound limited-access highway. Andy wished he'd been able to make her understand. She was articulate, he so tongue-tied. Why couldn't he explain his huge mental block about having children? His mind shot to that remote village—enormous scared eyes, distended bellies, near-fleshless limbs, flies on children's untreated sores as they lay on their death mats, too weak to struggle, too dehydrated to cry. He knew, deep down where he lived, that he'd been the wrong one to see it. His headaches were real, even though he suspected they were psychosomatic.

Ten miles later, he exited and crossed the overpass to enter the westbound highway. Rain pelted the windshield, demanding his utmost concentration.

One-quarter mile to the exit, right onto the overpass, back for the gas and the ice cream. He beat himself up a little bit further.

By the time you get home, you damn well better have the right thing to say. You know that she's right. And how would you feel if she finally gave up? Left you for somebody better?

Deep in thought, he approached the exit ramp, noting the red light at the top of the overpass. He took his foot off the accelerator, letting momentum glide the car toward the top of the ramp. That would save the few drops of gas that he'd wasted on his self-deprecating detour. As condensation crept up the windshield, he started to grope for the towel that had slid to the floor.

From nowhere, fierce headlights blasted his mirrors. They seemed close enough to touch his back seat. Inexplicably, his car gained momentum. He felt a thud. And another.

What? Who? A much larger vehicle was pushing him toward the overpass. *What the hell!*

Panicked, Andy stood on the brake with both feet and prayed that the light would turn green any second. Still red! And a fuel truck was barreling across the overpass. He'd T-bone it if he couldn't stop!

At the last minute, he cut a hard right, praying the overpass was wide enough to share the road with the truck.

Across the highway, an eastbound motorist had swerved onto the berm. *Way to go, idiot,* he cursed himself for the inattentiveness that had just caused him to miss his exit. *Whose shitty idea was it to change exit numbers to mile markers, anyway?*

His meeting had lasted entirely too long, and he'd been forced to follow slow-moving chickens who couldn't do more than forty in the rain. Where was he anyway?

He flipped open the armrest and extracted his new Garmin, a birthday present from his techie kids who were determined to bring him into this millennium. By the time he could figure out how to use it and just where the hell he was, he'd lose another half hour. He grabbed a Pennsylvania map from the glove compartment and opened it to his approximate location. *Aw, hell!* The next exit was ten miles away. Add to that ten miles back and another ten to the exit he had just passed and the distance to his destination—he glanced at his watch. *Has to be a better solution.*

Condensation fogged his windows, further decreasing his visibility. He powered all four windows down and up, the bristly fibers improving visibility. As he assessed the highway through the open driver-side side window, he noticed an idiot driving erratically in the far westbound lane.

A car that looked like a Buick sedan was tailgating a compact. Both cars pulled onto the exit ramp, so close together that little guy might have been towing big guy.

As they approached the top of the ramp, neither car slowed. Through driving rain that smeared his view, the motorist could see a red traffic light cut through the torrent. He powered down his window for a better look. "Slow down! Stop! You're going to get hit!" he screamed through the distance as the Subaru smashed into a truck with a horrible crash. The motorist reached into the back seat for his briefcase, fumbled it open, and grabbed his phone. "Come on! Come on! Come on!"

An eternity later he saw it. Low battery. He was about to jump from the car when a fireball exploded on the overpass. Simultaneously, he caught sight of that same Buick. Had the driver made a U-turn and backed down the ramp? *What the hell—*

Tires squealing and smoking, its driver floored the Buick back onto the highway and sped west, spraying a water-wall in his wake.

"Coward!" the motorist screamed into the storm.

Flashing red and blue pinpoints that materialized from the east must be two squad cars. Help was en route. A second later, a third responder flew past the motorist and made a U-turn through the grass median a quarter mile beyond him.

An awful realization occurred to the motorist: There wasn't a blessed thing he could do, and he'd had a couple of beers. And he'd be stuck here for hours with the overpass ablaze. The police would stop traffic on both sides of the highway, trapping motorists between exits.

Before the situation could escalate, he made a snap decision. After a quick U-turn, he drove west, wrong-way on the inner berm for a few hundred yards, and used the emergency connector to access the far westbound lanes. As he righted his car on the highway, he looked into the rearview. The entire area surrounding the overpass was engulfed in flames.

Shaken and unable to drive any farther, the motorist exited at his first opportunity. He passed up the pumps, even though he needed gas, and parked in front of the truck stop's diner. He sat, willing his heart and his blood pressure to settle.

Finally, he eased out of the car, the drenching rain cooling his sweaty face.

Inside the diner, to his right, were booths occupied by various good old boys enjoying a hearty country meal. To his left, a connector led to a store where over-the-road truckers could buy anything from snacks and CDs to hand tools and condoms. He pulled a tri-county map from a rack and a cold beer from a fridge. He unfolded the map.

"Y'all lost?" the sixty-something cashier asked, nodding at the map. She had tired eyes, wiry gray hair, and entirely too many pounds for someone so short.

He pointed to a small dot on a hairline road. "I need to go here without getting on the highway. Had enough of this rain."

"You're in luck. Take the secondary at the end of the gas pumps, turn right, and go about two miles. Turn right at the traffic light. You can't miss it. Oh, and don't let the cops catch you with an open bottle of beer."

He chugged what was left and dropped it into the recycling bin. As he exited the diner's double glass doors, he passed a huge man in the first booth by the window. "Done," the guy was saying into his phone. "Meet me tomorrow with the cash at—" He flicked a glance at the motorist and shielded his face and the phone with one beefy hand.

The motorist hurried to his car, circled to the pumps, and chose the one with the clearest visibility to the diner's exit. As his tank filled, he noticed a navy Buick parked near the door.

A brave man, he thought, *would look at the front bumper, check out the license, and call the cops.* But he felt anything but brave. He did not want to get involved. *Besides, there must be a thousand navy Buicks on the road, a favorite of guys like the man in the booth who don't fit in a VW bug.*

Maybe he could snap a picture of the license plate without being noticed. He withdrew his old Canon PowerShot Digital Elph from his pocket, pressed the on button, and swiveled the zoom button to its max. He was secreting the camera close to his body when the man in the diner exited and loped toward the Buick. The big man glanced toward the pumps just as lightning tore through the sky. At that precise moment the motorist took a shot.

The big man ducked into the Buick, starting the engine and the wipers simultaneously. Mr. Motorist busied himself, returning the gas nozzle and screwing on the gas cap, while averting his face and trying to look normal. When he dared steal a look, the Buick was lost in a curtain of spray, heading west.

❧❧❧

Kingsley felt a stab of pain and, going to the bathroom in hopes she was wrong, realized the stork would miss them again. She tried in vain not to cry, but she sobbed. She hated that Andy would be relieved, but she'd pitch it again, only better. They were, after all, still quite young and he wanted her to concentrate on her banking career. She mopped her eyes, blew her nose a third time, and took pills against the inevitable onslaught of pain.

Curled on the couch, she eventually dozed as the prescription painkiller took hold. Time slithered by. She lost all track.

In her dream someone was knocking. It sounded faint and grew in persistence, finally too loud to ignore. Groggily, she untangled herself from her afghan and went to the door. A hostile wind nearly blasted her backward.

"Mrs. Ward?"

Two uniformed officers, one young, one older, began to say something she couldn't quite grasp. The smell of wet hemlocks beside her front stoop, the bite and the dampness of the onrushing wind, their solemn faces, and the feel of strong hands that kept her from falling all blurred together. The screams, she realized later, must have been hers. Andy was not coming home.

Chapter 1

The Following August:

Kingsley commanded her stomach to stop churning as she approached her last rental option.

"Elegant. That's the character," the chatty realtor gushed about the small city's historic district. "Splendid examples of Queen Anne, German Gothic and Georgian Revival, Victorian Romanesque. And talk about craftsmanship. Notice the brickwork, the stained and beveled glass windows, and the exquisite carved doors. And there's the streetscape—mature trees, slate sidewalks, wrought iron fences."

Just. Shut. Up! Kingsley would have bolted, but she wasn't driving.

The realtor mounted the Victorian mansion's porch steps, crossed the veranda, and opened the carved walnut door. "The owner lives downstairs and rents the entire second as one apartment. I'm telling you, opportunities like these are downright nonexistent. Follow me."

Kingsley allowed herself to be propelled through a large foyer and up an ornate staircase.

After unbolting the door, the realtor entered a code on the security pad.

"This was once four large bedrooms," she said as she motioned Kingsley through the vestibule. She excused the narrow U-shaped kitchen on the right that sported no window but numerous cupboards. "Beyond the kitchen, on the right, you have the dining and living rooms. Look out these magnificent windows—hundred-foot oaks and your own parking place. Wonderful leaded glass built-in china cabinets in both of these rooms. Now, for the bedrooms."

She hustled Kingsley back toward the vestibule. "Opposite the kitchen, on the left is a spare room, great for an office or guests. Center front is a ceramic tile bath with both tub and shower. Notice the bathroom has two doors, one to this hall and one to the bedroom. Here is the best part." She directed Kingsley into the vast master bedroom. "Has its own dressing room and walk-in closet. And just look at that view! Can't you picture yourself watching the sunrise and those ancient maples change color this fall? Water, cable, and electric are included—great for heating these ten-foot ceilings. You'll never find charm like this in a condo. Now, there are two other couples scheduled to see it if you aren't interested."

"I'll take it. I'm starting a new job right after Labor Day."

The realtor grinned. "You bet. Would mister need to see it?"

Kingsley swallowed hard and just shook her head, unwilling to share her roiling turmoil with a stranger.

"Don't worry, dear. That state-of-the-art security system will keep out your ex and the creeps."

 espes

One week later:

You're really alone, Kingsley thought in the void's stinging silence. She eyed her new digs, trying to grasp the reality of her rash decision to flee Philadelphia. The movers had unpacked her kitchen, her china and crystal, and toted the refuse.

She wandered, studying the eclectic mix of Andy's and her contemporary style with her grandmother's antiques. Her heart ached to recreate her former nest, but her brain screamed that was one more delusion—that she'd never heal without a clean break.

They had celebrated Andy's graduation from med school and her MBA with their first real apartment and combed the Hickory Furniture Mart in North Carolina for bargains. How they'd laughed when their sense of scale failed miserably, barely leaving a footpath through their tiny Philadelphia apartment. Here, their treasures wouldn't furnish one of these rooms.

Kingsley lifted Andy's portrait from her grandmother's mahogany cloverleaf table. She traced his fine nose and the little dip in his lip and imagined its warmth. If only she had gone with him. She would have seen it. Warned him. If only...

The scenario replayed, as if by getting it right, time could rewind. If only she could cry, she might loosen that vice-grip knot that strangled her stomach. But she had exhausted her tears' reservoir months ago.

The phone jarred her reflection. "Sweetie, just say the word and we'll help you get settled." Her mother, Sarah Alderson, pitched it again. "It's an easy day trip."

"You've already been an enormous help resurrecting Grammy's furniture. I really must do this myself."

"Grammy would be tickled to know you're enjoying her things. You were her only grandchild and she loved you dearly. I'm just glad everything survived ten years in storage."

Stocking-footed, Kingsley padded carefully into the dining room. "Even with the expansion boards and eight chairs, a couple could waltz around the table without crashing into the buffet. Wait till you see her Persian rugs on these oak floors." She bent to stroke the rug's convolutions and sumptuous pattern.

"I know you were sad going through Grammy's things, but it did turn into a treasure hunt. 'Someone has to receive for another to have the pleasure of giving.' That's what she'd say. Now don't forget her cut glass and the Tiffany lamp are still in our attic." Neither mentioned stored wedding presents. "Honey, must you report to your new job so quickly?"

"If I don't, I'll lose my nerve." Kingsley could make out her father's voice, which was growing more insistent in the background.

"Your father is pestering me—"

Henry Alderson came on the line. "Why don't I come up on Friday and take you to lunch? Meet your new boss. Wouldn't hurt if I checked up on that little bank."

"If I show up with a wheel from the Office of the Controller of the Currency—" Her dad's insistence finally sank in. "What aren't you telling me?" she asked.

"Had a call from David Wentworth. More legal details about Andy's estate. Next time you're home, and we hope that will be soon, you'll need to talk with him yourself."

"What's it about?"

"Uncle David didn't elaborate. Evidently, it's personal."

She sighed. Of course she could call her godfather from

here, but just the thought of going it alone made her stomach clinch. "Will this ever end?"

"Just be patient—with your fresh start and with yourself. And, honey, if you ever need my help, on this or anything else, you've got it."

"Thanks, Daddy. Say goodnight to Mom."

They exchanged 'love you' and disconnected.

Kingsley forced her attention to the next day's challenge. She laid out a conservative suit, her favorite white silk blouse, and packed her briefcase with minimal necessities. Her reference books, framed diplomas, and professional materials could wait.

Crawling into bed, she sank into stacked feather pillows and tried to ignore the old-house noises and the whoosh of occasional traffic. She knew she was safe with the security armed, but that didn't stop the ragged loneliness that crept from its hiding places. She snapped on the TV and surfed to a *Law & Order* rerun. Somewhere between the police investigating crime and the district attorneys prosecuting the offenders, she fell asleep.

ೋ

Tuesday morning Kingsley aimed her grammy's old Lexus from the Historic District, imagining horse-drawn trolleys and buggies transporting the 1800s industrialists who built this neighborhood. *How priceless*, she thought, *in a country too quick to tear down and build something newer.*

Three-story brick and stone homes sported bay windows, turrets, dormers and mansard roofs, some with arched windows, ornate porches, and lavish landscaping. Others wore gingerbread beneath gabled eaves.

Approaching the highway, she merged south and into a

glorious morning that hinted of fall and clean slates.

Five miles farther, Kinsley exited into Keynote National Bank's corporate headquarters. She parked and hurried across the bank's grand plaza, absorbing the beauty of the boomerang-shaped building. Horizontal bands of rose granite and natural stone alternated with copper-pink windows that reflected cumulus clouds. Planters surrounded a towering fountain, spilling flowers that defied fall's intrusion.

Chimes announced the three-quarter hour.

She'd read that when Keynote outgrew its numerous small buildings, a large high tech firm had gone belly up, enabling the bank to grab this facility for its corporate headquarters, main branch, and back office operations. The aura of success was lost on nobody.

Kingsley had seen the ad for the position of vice president commercial lending in the *Philadelphia Inquirer* and impulsively applied with dozens of others. When the offer came, she grasped the chance to escape the depression into which she had fallen. Now, as she passed through the polished brass and ornate glass doors, she trembled.

Inside, a five-story atrium and tropical garden soared to a skylight that separated the Bank's main branch on the left from radiating corridors to offices on the right. As Kingsley crossed the marble atrium, she noticed a strange little man hiding behind the lush trees, palms, bamboo, and peace lilies. He was watching the teller line through the branch's interior glass wall. Where was security, she wondered?

Bustling bankers appeared to ignore the odd little man as they surged into the lobby. She followed them into an elevator that whisked her to Human Resources on the third floor.

After completing myriad obligatory forms, Kingsley hustled to orientation, where two dozen other newcomers enjoyed relaxed chitchat. Apparently, they already knew each other. Quietly she slid into a chair near the door.

A tiny blonde plopped down beside her, offering her hand and a smile that could melt tundra. "Hi! I'm Barrie. Managed to duck this thing for five months, but they nabbed me today."

A stocky man strode to a podium and flipped on a mike that squeaked overkill. Jeffrey Johnston, VP and HR Director, droned from time-rumpled notes, his limpid eyes connecting with no one except her. He seemed to glare straight into her soul. *My imagination*, she scolded herself.

"That man is a joke," Barrie whispered. "And that marketing video is ancient!" She groaned as he passed out mugs and lapel pins. Jeffrey labored through descriptions of every department. "*Banking for Idiots*," Barrie mumbled, and Kingsley, caught off guard, smothered a giggle. She stole a look at her companion's badge: *Barrie Brown, Assistant Controller*.

When Johnston announced lunch without giving directions, Barrie took charge and led the group to a neighborhood restaurant where tables had been reserved.

As the newcomers fell into common-ground chatter, Barrie steered Kingsley out of earshot. Kingsley smiled at the contradiction that was Barrie. She was blonde from her curls to her lashes. Even her eyes appeared golden. Her delicate features clashed with her outspoken nature.

While keeping her expression nonchalant, Barrie lowered her voice and got down to business. "If you're going to survive in this environment, there's stuff you must know."

"Such as?"

"Security problems, a power struggle's fomenting, no plan for succession—"

Kingsley studied the woman. "How do you know you can trust me?"

"—and we've got double trouble at the top. Ever hear of the Peter Principle? The late former president recruited our present CEO, Warren Kramer, as Chief Lending Officer. That was before the bank became a financial corporation. After the old man died, Warren was promoted to president, then CEO when the holding company was formed. He's honest, dependable, bright, and loved in the bank and community. But CEO material, he ain't.

"Doug Neiman, our president—he's the brains. At least he was until his wife's lengthy illness derailed him. He flew her everywhere for the best treatment. Finally, cancer free, she had hip replacement surgery, necessitated by the wreckage to her bones. She'd been watching TV, recovering from the surgery and asked for a glass of water. When Doug returned from the kitchen, she was gone. A blood clot. He's never recovered from her loss. Just goes through the motions.

"Below them, the jockeying for power is scary, even though nobody's qualified—not to head a bank of this size. Security is nonexistent. Ditto checks and balances to prevent fraud."

"Why are you telling me this? You don't even know me. I could be—"

Barrie snorted. "Heard you got tapped for the job. Checked you out. Insiders say you're smart but naïve, trusting, idealistic. Hey! Don't be insulted. I'm just saying, watch your back."

"What are you suggesting?"

"Document, document, document. Every transaction, loan AP, phone conversation. Take duplicates of anything that's suspect off the premises. And trust nobody. Except Margaret—you'll meet her directly. Oh! Follow up each client contact in writing with a return memo hitting key

points. Print out email directives from outside the department."

"You are one paranoid lady."

"'Once bitten...'" Barrie flashed her flawless smile, but
didn't elaborate. She rummaged through her purse for a
business card on which she added several numbers. "I'll
find you if you don't call me first."

"Barrie—should I have come?"

"You bet. There's a world of opportunity within those
walls and some of the nicest people on the planet. And the
customers—their work ethic and honesty are unsurpassed.
Yeah, you made a good choice. But if you find it's a bad fit,
move on. I hope you don't. I could use a cohort."

"It's a deal. And thanks for the warm welcome."

"Gotta run." Barrie gathered her stuff and gave Kingsley's arm a quick squeeze before darting for the door.

The restaurant, Kingsley realized, had nearly emptied.
She checked the itinerary prepared by HR: *Report to Loan
Division 1:30.* Retreat was no longer an option. Besides, she
was intrigued.

෴

Deep in Tioga County's wooded obscurity, a man
hunched over telephone books from the Pennsylvania Dutch
heartland. Smith, Jones, or Brown would not serve his pur-
pose. Columns of Moyers. Nope, not quite right. Dreibelbis.
Too catchy. Too bad—he rather liked it. Now Miller. He
tossed aside the Lancaster book and picked up Reading,
then Pottstown, and other central Pennsylvania directories.
Columns of Millers. Yeah, that would do. John Miller.
Common as hell.

He checked the calendar tacked on the rough-hewn wall.

He'd need a driver's license, proof of insurance, and car registration for the Erie job. After locking the cabin, he shuffled through fallen oak leaves that cushioned God's country. He unlocked his oversized garage. Entering his workshop, he scanned his choice of nondescript vehicles.

With a cordless screwdriver he affixed a stolen Ohio plate to his favorite LeSabre. He splashed the plate with traces of mud. Ohio—he realized his blunder. Two plates in Ohio. Two chances for prying eyes to realize something was wrong. Especially if the front plate was missing. Quickly he substituted a stolen Pennsylvanian plate and splattered mud in a believable pattern.

The new John Miller reviewed his action plan—convince the old holdout to sell that last parcel the Erie developer needed so badly. Collect the remaining fifty percent in cash from said client and ensure everyone's silence. That, he decided, included the client. He strode around his workshop contemplating weapons.

As his beefy hands configured his latest IDs, one of his cell phones rang. From exhaustive experience, he quickly analyzed the potential client, a nervous man trying to sound professional. He identified himself as a human resources vice president named Johnston from a bank in southeast Pennsylvania. He was in need of discreet service.

From the cell phone number the caller had chosen, Miller knew the banker had seen his ad in an obscure *Soldier of Fortune Magazine*. Technology was grand when it worked.

"I'll give you a number on which to reach me," the caller said. "Never call me at work or at home."

'...on which to...' Miller smirked to himself. *Book smart but* practically *dumb.*

"Our bank has hired a young woman whom we suspect will be trouble. I need someone with your credentials to flesh out her background and surface any, ah, vulnerabilities, if you get my drift. Are you interested?"

"Yeah, I can squeeze you in. It won't be cheap, though. What's the name?"

"Mine? Jeffrey…"

"No." *Idiot.* "The woman."

"Kingsley Ward. Kingsley Alderson Ward. She has recently relocated from Philadelphia. I'll run through her background for you, if that will save time."

And money. "I do my own research." A sly grin overtook Miller's face. Jeffrey Johnston had revealed a personality that begged to be used. Hell, what kind of an operation was that bank running anyway if this jerk was any example? Johnston could check out Ms. Kingsley Alderson Ward's vulnerabilities without Miller's assistance. Agreeing to take on the client, however, could lead to much bigger things.

And he was about to own a weak link.

"Give me a number where you can be reached," Miller said.

The HR VP complied. They disconnected. Two days in Erie should wrap up that business. And leave plenty of time to research one Ms. Ward. He also owed himself a few days R and R. Johnston and his little bank could wait until later.

Chapter 2

"W elcome! I'm Margaret Stiles," the bank's head of real estate lending said, identifying herself modestly. Her voice was near tenor, and her bifocals accentuated sparkling sapphire eyes. Everything about her was as neat as her crisp linen suit. "Nathaniel wants to meet with you before heading out to a meeting."

She guided Kingsley past lending's core of staff cubicles and junior officers' perimeter offices to the head's corner office. Twenty pairs of eyes followed her every movement, people some craning their necks. She focused straight ahead.

Nathaniel Frazier jumped to his feet, hand extended. "Welcome to Keynote! Sorry I'll have to make this brief, but it couldn't be avoided."

"I'm happy to be here," Kingsley said, taking the offered chair. She was struck once again by his resemblance to Colin Powell, although his hair was coal black and his nearly base accent betrayed Oklahoma.

"I'm delighted you accepted our offer. We're shorthanded and don't have time to train a new college graduate. That's why I pushed for someone who could step in and take over the commercial lending portfolio."

She felt a rush of relief. They really did want her.

"I'm afraid you won't have much of a honeymoon. We're at crossroads that will affect you directly and immediately. We have a new executive vice president, under whom lending will fall. His name's Todd Henning, Harvard MBA. He comes from a large Manhattan bank where he blazed quite a trail. You may no sooner get acclimated, than everything will change."

"I'll welcome the challenge."

"Good. Now the bad news, which I trust you won't repeat. Todd's arrival breaks the tradition of promoting from within, and he's rather young. I'm expecting resistance. If you get any unusual or conflicting orders from executive officers, bring them to me. You needn't get caught in the fray." Nathaniel studied her a moment. "Warren Kramer, our chairman and CEO, is a prodigious idea man. He's brilliant but quirky—carries the business plan around in his head, regardless of what's on paper. Be on the lookout for his directives and bring them to me. I'll let you know how to proceed."

He glanced around and lowered his voice. "A word about people. Margaret's a treasure, without whom we couldn't survive. Anything you need, just ask her. She has it, can find it, or knows who can. And I've never known her to betray a confidence or fail to go above and beyond the call of duty when we're in a bind. Also, your position was advertised in-house first. A number of people applied, none of whom have your credentials. I trust everyone will behave professionally, regardless of their level of disappointment. Still—"

"That's valuable to know."

Nathaniel rose. "We'll get together sometime this week. In the meantime, there are a few junior loan officers who have been pinch hitting with your predecessor's workload. Sorry I have to run."

After handing her off to Margaret, he hurried toward the elevator, leaving Margaret to orient her. She showed Kingsley to her new office. "The previous owners spared no expense," she said of the matching walnut desk, bookshelves, and credenza inside. The credenza, centered beneath towering windows, framed a panoramic view of the countryside. "When our executives wanted new furnishings, we were the lucky recipients of this."

Kingsley noticed four neat stacks on the credenza. "The most important things are on the left. When you're ready, Marle, your administrative assistant, can explain our procedures. One more thing—I made you a departmental cheat sheet—names and a little description. I know what it's like to be new. I took the liberty of tucking it into your belly drawer." She winked and was gone.

Kingsley sank into the soft leather desk chair and smiled when it fit her five foot eight frame perfectly. She swiveled toward the huge piles and grimaced. "That looks ugly!"

"You got that right!" A man in impeccable gray leaned on her doorframe. "The wife jokes that if she brought home another man, the kids wouldn't know the difference. That's how frantic we've been without Fred. I'm Roy, small business lending. Been covering the position with Manning Stoudt, another junior officer." He extended his hand, shook hers, and then flopped into one of her guest chairs.

"How long has my predecessor been gone?"

"About three months."

"I asked during my interview why the position was open. They said my predecessor left to pursue other interests."

Roy snorted. "That's a euphemism. He was here Friday, gone Monday."

"Was he a problem?"

"Hell, no. He was a knowledgeable, veteran lender whom everyone liked." Roy leaned his forearms on her desk and lowered his voice to a conspiratorial level. "Take a good, hard look at every loan that crosses your desk. Something's not right."

"Like…"

He straightened and rose to leave. "Just saying. Forewarned and all that. I'm right next door. No question too small." He gestured to the bank's letter opener that she was absently fingering. "Hey! Careful, those things are sharp."

Startled, she reflexively sucked the blood spurting from her left index finger. "One of those could take 'stabbing someone in the back' to a whole new level." As she applied pressure, she studied the implement in disbelief. That was one logo shop item she'd never give to a client. Returning the blade to its sheath, she dropped it into the trash.

Alone, Kingsley picked up the first client folder from the left pile. A renewal application. Next, a request to meet a prospect who made industrial batteries. Her brain kicked in as she dug through the pile.

There would be new forms, custom software, and procedures to learn, but she knew lending. Yeah, she could do this.

A stunning young African American woman interrupted her concentration. She was a willow, with dozens of cornrow braids poofed at the nape of her neck. "I'm Marle, your AA. If it's convenient, I'll explain our equipment."

Kingsley followed her into the cubicles where staffers attended to myriad details. Kingsley sat where directed, but Marle's phone clamored. "Give me a sec?" She strode to her desk and grabbed it.

A hush rippled over the workers as the elevator doors

opened, discharging a tall, gangly man. "Who's that?" Kingsley hissed to the girl at the next station.

"Frank Ziegler, the EVP who's going to take over some day. He's probably here to meet you." Since the man would pass within two yards, Kingsley stood and stepped into the walkway. Extending her hand she said, "Mr. Ziegler? I'm King—"

Ziegler glanced icily at her and, with a dismissing gesture, strode past her, leaving Kingsley not knowing what to do with her hand.

The girl giggled. "That's how he treats people he thinks don't matter. If you're lucky, you won't have much contact with him."

Driving home after work, Kingsley's mind staccatoed snatches of a day that, in retrospect, flashed by in bursts. Finally, she focused on something that Barrie had said. Kingsley had seen cameras in the branch, but as she moved freely from floor to floor, no one asked for ID or questioned her, a stranger, when she ran an errand on the fifth floor, which housed executive management and the controller's department.

There must be surveillance and a nerve center somewhere. Otherwise, what would stop a maniac from coming upstairs and shooting the brass?

Arriving in the Historic District, she was struck anew by its quaint beauty. She wrestled with her unfamiliar keys, stepped into her vestibule, climbed the stairs, and punched numbers into the security panel. A timer had dutifully fired up lamps, glowing their welcome. She sighed. Not bad for four days in residence.

For the first time in weeks, she was starving and pillaged her mother's stash of Tupperware containers. While turkey and barley stew heated, she swapped her suit for old jeans and a soft cotton sweater. Clothing would be easy if her observation of provincial bankers on a very strict budget was correct.

She evaluated her space and the huge amount left to be done. The stereo and computer would not hook themselves up, and the broad, north-facing windowsills cried for African violets. The walls needed pictures and she had to buy groceries. Removing cartons marked "take to bank" would make some clearance, but her books needed shelves.

The phone rang. "I've been thinking," her mom started. "Why don't you drive over Saturday morning and stay overnight? We could shop for your birthday, and go out to dinner."

Twenty-seven, Kingsley thought. She and Andy would have been buying a house big enough for a family. She had imagined her life as an exquisite tapestry, unfurled across a grand table, revealing the story of her charmed existence. A brocade odyssey, rich with magenta, sapphire, and velvety greens. Children would be pure gold. But fate had substituted black threads instead.

"…what do you say?" Sarah was asking.

"Sounds great, Mom."

"Then it's settled. We'll have brunch and go from there."

Kingsley laughed at herself. Mom still knew how to make her feel better. Always had. She glanced at Andy's picture and, with a sudden pang of guilt, realized she'd been too busy to think about him. She strained to imagine his voice, but the memory was fading.

Like a boulder dropped from a bridge into water, the initial impact had caused violent spray. As the waves dissipated, the ripples subsiding, the sunshine dried the bank. Remembering preserved the double-edge of pleasure and pain. Forgetting blurred both, but brought peace.

She could no longer choose. Andy was slipping away.

Her decision had been right—today bore that out. She couldn't remain, retracing the sameness and sadness, etching the familiar, yet isolating, routine until she couldn't climb out. She'd had to leave Philadelphia.

A knock brought her back to reality. Peeping, she saw two clean-cut men, colorfully casual.

"Hi. We're Michael—"

"And Isaac. We own the house next door."

Chain unfastened, she invited them in. Late thirties, perhaps early forties, about her height and similar as twins. Isaac presented a fresh apple pie, which instantly osmosed its tantalizing scent.

"We didn't want you to be without someone to call if you need a cup of sugar—"

"Or some muscle," the other finished. "Your landlord's a friend—told us you were coming. We've collected cards from our favorite markets, shops, and restaurants—the must-see local attractions."

"That's so kind. Thank you."

Michael produced a county map and a packet of brochures from the Visitor's Bureau. "Be sure to use this road map because the new highways aren't on the old ones. You don't throw wild parties, do you…"

"…unless you include the neighbors?"

She laughed, delighted to meet such nice people.

Michael glanced at his watch and announced they must go. *Saturdays*, she thought, examining the brochures after bolting the door. Day trips could fill in the gaps.

That evening as her newfound enthusiasm ebbed, she wandered the rooms aimlessly. When sleep finally came, she dreamed of a jungle and the odd little man who had been hiding among the bank's palms and peace lilies. Now dressed for safari, he laughed with delight.

Chapter 3

Arlene!" The bank's EVP Franklin P. Ziegler bellowed for his secretary. Hell, he missed that buzzer. If she didn't do the work of three people, he'd fire that woman. Her predecessor jumped at the slightest touch before her nervous breakdown and voluntary demotion to another department. Arlene simply disconnected the contraption on her first day, and every time facilities reconnected it, until he gave up.

"Arlene! Now!" They nearly collided as she entered his sanctuary. "Get Shirley immediately."

Arlene merely shrugged and placed the call. "She's on her way," Arlene called, collecting her tablet.

"We'll handle this alone," Frank said, dismissing the witness.

Shirley Granger, Senior VP for Branch Administration, Human Resources, and Marketing, scurried into the executive suite as fast as her narrow suit would allow.

Frank didn't look up. "Shut the door." She did. "Sit." Ditto. "I've been looking at our projections. We've got to cut fat. Employees are our biggest expense, so we'll target that first."

"Downsizing by attrition is well underway as employees retire or resign. And we're taking our time about replacing strategic vacancies. Staff is feeling the pinch, but so far we're handling it."

"Not good enough. Not fast enough. Here's what I've decided. Look for our most expensive employees—those who have reached the top of their salary bracket. Replace them with newcomers who will start at the bottom. Let's also target those who were grandfathered, which provide more benefits, vacation, and sick days. We can get away with fewer people that way."

"But that would eliminate our very best people. They're a valuable—"

"And we'll target people approaching their vesting date before they become more expensive."

"Does Warren know about this?" Shirley asked of the bank's chairman and chief executive officer. "And what about Doug?"

"CEO Warren isn't interested in details. And Doug, while still president, is so consumed by his wife's illness and death that his mind isn't on the bottom line." Lacing his long manicured fingers and bending toward Shirley across his ornate desk, he riveted her eyes. "Profit's the only thing that counts around here."

"What about lawsuits? Our HR manual clearly states that employees be given a chance to respond to disciplinary problems. Many of these people have spotless records."

"Screw it. Hell, Shirley, Pennsylvania's an at-will state. They work at our convenience. We can fire them if we don't like the way they wear their hair. Or for no reason, as long as we don't trigger discrimination issues. Let 'em sue. We can bury them in money."

Shirley opened her mouth and then closed it again.

"Look, Shirley, you don't have to like it. I'll speak to Jeffrey Johnston myself. Let's cover ourselves this way." Frank leaned back in his leather chair, focused on the ceiling, and stroked his deep red silk tie by gently running his thumb down its underside. That tick caused the embroidered navy reptile near the bottom to ripple, as if it were prancing. "Get an employee letter together. Tell them 'Our independent consulting firm has recommended that we realign our human resources to better maximize our capabilities. Some positions will be eliminated, but we will retrain our fine employees whenever possible for the exciting new positions that our progressive ventures and technology are creating.' There. That sounded good, didn't it?" He gave himself and his tie another stroke. "Get marketing to fluff it. Let me see it first, but put it out under your signature."

"I don't remember our hiring an independent consulting firm," Shirley said as he grinned slyly. "Can we retrain from downsized positions?"

"What we can do is save a ton of money in salaries and benefits. Look, Shirley, because of merger mania, there's a pool of qualified bankers we can get cheap. They'll be so grateful, they'll work extra hours without complaining about what they've lost." Frank rose, looked at his calendar, and bellowed for Arlene to call Jeff in HR.

Shirley, dismissed, retreated to her own office on the first floor. Her eyes fell on her Persian rug and her $500 raincoat on its brass stand. She felt that her soul had been bought, but where else could she, who had risen from summer help, duplicate this job without any college? And weren't all corporations alike?

This was the real world and how profits were made. She'd be naïve to think otherwise. Shirley phoned the marketing director and passed down the assignment.

Meanwhile, Frank, ensconced in his shrine, tasted the power breakfast and found it delicious.

ര⁄ൟ

Frank Ziegler loped off the elevator, missing nothing. "I heard a phone ring more than once," he accused no one in particular before throwing Jeffrey Johnston's door open. Two seated employees leapt to their feet and fled.

Frank snapped the door shut and grinned. "Your boss, Shirley, has been told. What do you have for me?"

Jeff opened a desk drawer and produced an inch-thick computer printout on which he had made numerous marks. "Here are the ones we've targeted. If they're over fifty, we'd better throw them a bone. Include a hold harmless agreement. Maybe six months' salary."

"Make it two. Give it to them on a Friday. Let them have only fourteen days to think it over. By the time they can get onto an attorney's calendar, they'll be out of time. How many can we drop?"

"Ten percent."

"Make it fifteen. Eliminate ten full-time positions. Let's drag our feet about replacing the other five that are strategic. If we wait a few months, we'll save a bundle. The others can work overtime—won't cost us anything since they're salaried, not hourly. Now then, I want to target a few troublemakers."

Frank skimmed Jeffrey's list. "Good. You've got that mailroom manager. When we attempted to mail our credit card statements too late for the customers to avoid interest charges, he howled and emailed Warren. I'd counted on several months' interest before customers squawked. Get rid of him. Oh! And her," he said, adding a pencil mark. "She was injured when her boss insisted she help with their move. Herniated disk. Sheer stupidity on the boss's part, but she's filed a complaint."

"Won't she sue if we fire her?"

Frank grinned as he stroked his tie. "Got someone who will swear she did it gardening, hauling fifty pound bags of potting soil."

They reviewed their action plan. Jeffrey would approach the victim's desk with a carton and rental security. The victim would be given a five-minute rundown of supposed offenses and a supervised half-hour to collect personal stuff before being escorted off the premises.

"Has Fred Macmillan, who headed commercial lending, given us any trouble?" Frank asked.

"He signed off—took the severance. I still think that was a huge mistake. That man hit his goals. We ended up paying a shit load of money for Kingsley Ward." Frank glowered at him. "Sorry, Frank. Nathaniel Frazier was adamant about her credentials. There was no way to get around Nathaniel, since he's our token black senior officer. If I were you, I'd leave Lending alone. Nathaniel Frazier mints money."

"I want that Ward woman watched very carefully. She's going to be trouble. You are on top of it?"

"A work in progress."

Frank thumped approval on Jeffrey's printout. "Employees are our single largest expense. Whack that down and our yearly earnings will be exceptional."

The two exchanged satisfied smiles. Frank loped to the elevator, scowling at anxious staffers who scrambled out of his wake.

ероен

Chairman and CEO Warren Kramer popped into Frank's

office so quietly that Frank jumped. "Come. I've called an executive committee meeting in the boardroom."

Frank glared at Warren's exiting back and snapped his leather folio shut. Grudgingly, he trailed Warren into the boardroom that was shrouded in eerie silence.

"Doug has something important to share with us," Warren began after everyone was seated. "I want you to hear it together. The rest of our employees will be notified later." Before continuing, he rose to close the door. Everyone shifted uncomfortably.

The head of operations mouthed to his neighbor, "Bank being sold?"

His coworker shook his head no.

Doug rose slowly, scanning the faces of his colleagues, looking too tired and old for his fifty-eight years. "After much introspection, deliberation, and prayer, I've decided to retire at the end of the year."

A collective gasp escaped from the group.

"In my thirty-three years as a banker, the best twenty have been spent right here, watching us evolve into a modern financial institution. I never thought I would want to go anywhere else. I deeply appreciate everything you did for me during my wife's illness." He cleared his throat. "When our minister said we should give our children both roots and wings, I never thought they'd fly off to California permanently."

A chuckle broke the tension.

He took a ragged breath. "My children are deeply involved in their careers, don't plan to move back, and are nagging relentlessly that my grandchildren need me." He paused to look around the room. "What has also piqued my interest is SCORE, their local Senior Corps Of Retired Executives. Heading this effort will enable me to help youngsters get started while I can still share my knowledge. Give back."

Saddened, stunned faces circled the table, as each struggled to comprehend the impact of losing the one person who ably bridged the gap between their mercurial chairman and senior management.

Blood began throbbing in Frank Ziegler's ears. As third in command, he had watched Warren grow older, knowing that when Warren retired and Doug moved up, Frank would become president. But with Doug out of the picture, Frank's career was fast tracked. Why, he could be chairman and CEO in just two more years! And just fifty-two now—

Frank flashed to how he had outlasted them all, starting as a teller, going to school part time, earning a two-year business degree and keeping up in his field. He had put up with all manner of subjugation, paid his dues, humbled himself and groveled when appropriate.

And learn, oh, how he'd learned Keynote's ways. He could compete with the best. Was the best.

But unlike reclusive Warren, Frank planned to be recognized nationally. What an exquisite hand fate had dealt! *Calm*, he commanded himself as he steeled his expression.

The meeting digressed into informal chatter until Warren called them back to attention. "Doug was good enough not to spring this on me. He, the board, and I have given a lot of thought to succession. The bank would be in a precarious position without a strategic plan."

The group stole knowing glances at Frank, the man to whom this concept was foreign.

"I have a second, important announcement. Some of you have already met the newcomer in our midst." Eyes shifted to the dark-haired man seated at the bend of the table. "Todd Henning is a local boy who left for college, then found New York more exciting. Todd is joining us to be in charge of technology, operations, lending, and some of our new initiatives. Todd's experience has considerable breadth. Frank," Warren said, turning his attention to the executive VP, "I'm going to ask you to orient Todd."

Frank gave Todd a fatherly smile and nodded agreement.

"Finally, the board has decided to add a second executive vice president position."

Frank's insides lurched again. His position as the only EVP was being divided in two. It would take two to replace him. Frank tried desperately to control his expression, although, in his mind, he was jumping to his feet, thrusting his fist in the air while shouting, "Yes!"

Frank barely heard Warren's concluding remarks. "This is 'insider information.' When we're ready to release it, you'll be briefed first."

∽∾∽

Dolly Ziegler, Frank's wife, was surprised to see her husband home early and in such a great mood. Long ago, he had dropped any pretense of civility unless he had an ulterior motive. Mostly, she stayed out of his way. She seized this rare opportunity to hit him with a request.

"The blood bank approached the Women's Club about critical shortages and their need for a local business to host a blood drive. They'd like to use Keynote's lower level because it's big enough to handle the traffic."

She was watching him hopefully, in that begging way that he hated, dreading his rejection, which would mean facing her club empty-handed.

Following him into the kitchen where he poured scotch and hunted crackers, Dolly rattled the carefully rehearsed details until he cut her off. "Tell them we'll participate. Just make damned sure I get the credit."

"I'm afraid dinner isn't ready yet—"

He waved her off, striding toward his study. Door locked, he clicked on the desk lamp and unlocked the drawers. Lovingly he extracted the bank's annual report, flipping to the dog-eared executive salaries even though he knew them by heart. There it was!

He jumped up and paced, relishing the figures. He made $200,000 plus perks. Nobody wanted to hear about taxes, social security, numerous other deductions and obligations that shrank the figure considerably. Plus there were the requirements of his station—the cars, club memberships, custom clothing, and endless charities with hands in his pockets.

As president, his salary would jump to $500,000. Half a million bucks! To chairman, $750,000, not counting bonuses, stock options, 401(k) and pension contributions. Here, in turn-of-the-century rural Pennsylvania, that money was huge. The status was dizzying! He thought of his wife and her late parents' wealth, all tied up in trusts for her and their grandchildren. How he wished they could see him now.

Frank flopped into his chair. Head tilted, he closed his eyes. When, as a child, was he first aware of how poor they were? Was it his clothes? His mother's repetitious "We can't afford it"? The places other kids went that he couldn't? He hated his mother for not telling him the truth—that his dad was a drunk and a gambler. Everyone knew except him. As he got older, the teasing got nasty. His hurt grew to anger then rage, fueling dreams of revenge.

Picking on Frank had ended abruptly when the eighth grader grew a foot, bulked up, and beat the school bully nearly senseless. Nobody crossed him after that, but they didn't like him much either. Had it not been for the coaches and teachers who challenged him productively, he would have landed in prison.

Dolly, the shy daughter of the community's leading family, held the key to his future. While juggling part-time community college and an entry-level bank teller position, Frank had spent hours courting her father, feigning interest in his advice. Dolly's father knew of his background, but saw the fire in his belly.

When Dolly's older brother died overseas, Frank edged into the void. In time, he won over the father. Frank had done very well for himself, although his acceptance into the community was largely due to her father's connections. From him, Frank had learned the power of charming everyone whom he needed to use.

His crucial error was discounting Dolly's mother. That she had prevailed wasn't evident until the will had been read.

Among the changes he would make as the bank's new chairman: fire the Ivy League upstarts Warren had hired.

As the clock chimed seven, he envisioned his picture, accompanied by the article about his promotion, above the fold in the Sunday newspaper.

Chapter 4

Kingsley's phone interrupted her scrutiny of a prospect's loan application. "Kingsley, hey!" Barrie bubbled. "Lunch at the diner? If we go at twelve-thirty, we'll miss the main onslaught but they'll still have dessert."

Upon entering the restaurant, Kingsley found Barrie talking to the waitress. "If you order the special chicken Caesar, she'll have it out here before you can hang up your raincoat."

"With an ice tea, please." Kingsley settled into the booth and the pair exchanged chitchat like old classmates. "What a beautiful ring. Is it an heirloom?" Kingsley asked.

"It was my eighteenth birthday present from my grandmother. I was the oldest granddaughter. It was a family tradition."

Kingsley thought of her own Grammy with a rush of appreciation.

"Actually, I came very close to losing it."

"Here at work?"

"No, my ex stole it." Barrie paused when the waitress interrupted with their salads.

Looking closer, Kingsley realized the stone was an em-
erald, several karats with no inclusions.

"How did you get it back?"

"I should have seen it coming—his departure, I mean.
There was more and more space in the closet." Barrie took a
bite, chewed carefully, and swallowed before continuing.
"I'd gone to the shore with my girlfriends. When I got back,
he was gone. A week later I realized my ring was gone too,
along with my diamond studs. I was furious."

"What did you do?"

"I have a dear friend who's a cop. I asked him to sneak
into the bastard's new apartment, toss it, and retrieve my
jewelry. He turned me down."

Kingsley watched a smug grin overtake Barrie's face.

"Instead, he taught me to pick locks. First I got really
good with that pick. Even though my ex practically lived at
the hospital, I was sure I'd end up in jail. Getting in was
easier than I thought—a simple Kwikset, no deadbolt or
alarm. Bet he thought he was losing his mind when he
found my stuff missing. If you ever need an expert lock
picker, I'm your gal."

"And they let you work in a bank!"

Barrie checked her watch. "Their homemade pies are
fantastic. There's time."

"After sitting all week, I shouldn't. I don't have a gym
yet."

Barrie dug in her purse. "Here's two complementary
passes to my fitness center. Very nice people, great equipment, and trainers who know how to coach women. Don't
put it off. Call them today."

಄಄಄

That evening, the fitness center blazed with lights, its

parking lots jammed. A lovely redhead with soft hazel eyes greeted Kingsley at the front desk.

"Why don't we start with a tour?" Dawn suggested. They wandered past state-of-the-art treadmills, ellipticals, cycles, and steppers that hummed to upbeat music. Another room held CyBex and Strive equipment. Lifters hefted free-weights. A group of women and two older men were doing the Life Circuit, although socializing seemed the agenda. Body Pump, yoga and a spin class engaged participants in separate gyms.

Kingsley cut short the pitch. "Where do I sign? I've seen enough."

"Great. Let's do your body comp. Based on your goals, I'll design a program for you." Taking her into a small private room, Dawn started a chart. Weight? 118. Taking her measurements, Dawn was surprised by Kingsley's thirty-six-inch bust, camouflaged by her baggy shirt.

"According to the computer, you have eighteen percent body fat. That's excellent." She took Kingsley's pulse and resting heart rate and made notes. "What are your goals?"

"I want to get strong, be healthy. I sit for long hours. I have trouble sleeping and thought this would help. It's very important that I not lose weight."

"You may actually gain as you develop lean muscle."

Kingsley sighed.

"Hey, trust me. This is going to be fun. Besides, with your model proportions and beautiful face, I bet you'll meet lots of guys. If I had those auburn curls, 7-Up-bottle-green eyes, and flawless complexion, I'd be dripping in men. But—forgive me for sounding rude—you look entirely too tired and sad for a twenty-six-year-old. You came to the right place. Now, let's set you up with a trainer. Elaine's excellent and available if you have time."

Later in the locker room, Kingsley luxuriated in the oversized showerhead's pulsing massage. She reveled in the anonymity that newness afforded. When she finally emerged from the gym, the parking lot was nearly deserted. Her car looked abandoned, way out in the lot. Instinctively, she reached for her keys as she hurried to close the great distance.

Halfway, she heard the acetate swish of somebody behind her. Realizing hers was the only car out there, she picked up her pace. The footsteps closed quickly. Reaching into her pocket without breaking stride, she found only tissues but no pepper spray. The farther she walked, the darker the empty lot grew. She panicked, adrenaline coursing through her body. Even if she ran, she wouldn't have time to unlock the door, jump in, slam, and lock it before being overtaken.

"Stop!" a man's voice directed.

Mustering her courage, she whirled, feet planted to face her aggressor, the key her only weapon.

The tall figure froze and put up one hand in surrender. "I'm terribly sorry. I didn't mean to frighten you." He lifted the other hand from which something dangled. "You dropped these."

Kingsley's gaze darted touch basfrom his face to his hand. Her driving gloves! The last "S"—Surprise—that Andy had given her. Forcing back tears as emotions collided, she bobbed her head as she reached for the gloves.

"These fell from your pocket back there in the hall," he said, motioning toward the side entrance. "I couldn't catch you."

She stole another look. He was quite tall, six-two or three, broad shouldered and slender with light, wide-spaced eyes that dominated a rather square face. His hair was dark, short, curly, and damp. In a black warm-up suit and black sneaks, he blended with the asphalt when he turned to gesture.

"This really isn't the best place to park in the evening." His deep, slow-paced voice did not patronize. "There's a much better area on the opposite side that's lit by the highway's mercury vapors. Just be careful pulling onto the highway because there's a blind spot coming up the hill."

Kingsley struggled to regain her composure. "I'm sorry that I—"

"No, I should have called you from back there. Said something intelligent like, 'Gloves! You dropped your gloves!' I just didn't think."

She turned them over and smoothed the soft leather. "Really, thank you. Most people wouldn't have bothered, and I wouldn't have had any idea where I'd lost them. That was very nice of you, really. I'm sorry I was so rude. Thanks for the tip about parking. I'm new here. Don't know my way around yet." She knew her rattling sounded dumb.

"I'll let you go. Got your keys?"

She nodded, noticing he had stepped back a few paces while she unlocked the door. The stranger motioned for her to start the engine and, when she did, he waved and turned. As she rolled through the lot, she saw him striding toward the opposite lot, hands in his pockets. She exited, pulse finally settling. Stopped at the red light, she smoothed on her gloves, even though it was too warm to need them.

•••

Late the next afternoon, Kingsley noticed Marle's frantic motions for her to pick up on line two. "This is Paul Yocum," a pleasant voice began. "I understand you're my new account officer. I'm sorry to bother you so soon after your arrival, but I have a little problem."

"That's perfectly all right. What can I do for you?"

"My bank statement shows a $20,000 draw against my business line of credit, but the money didn't show up in my checking account. More to the point, we didn't request the draw. I'm sure there is a simple explanation, but I thought I'd better call and find out."

"It sounds like an error was made in posting your account. I'm very sorry. This can easily be reversed, along with any charges that might be attached. May I meet with you personally?"

"I don't want to put you to any trouble, but I'd be delighted to give you a tour. I've been a customer for over twenty years. Your people have always been a valuable asset."

"Would Monday morning be convenient?"

"That would be great. Let me give you directions to the plant."

As soon as she hung up, she jumped from her chair to find Marle. "Where would I find Paul Yokum's file?"

"That would be Wire Products, Inc. I'll send for the forklift."

Kingsley laughed. "Just the current material."

Marle motioned Kingsley to where active client documents were organized alphabetically. She extracted a fat accordion folder and handed it to Kingsley. "That'll keep you in bedtime reading. He's one of our biggest clients. Besides, he's a major shareholder."

Kingsley thanked her lucky stars for inheriting this part-time college student whose goal was business law. She'd overheard Marle placating customers and was told she didn't believe in mistakes.

Kingsley opened the folder and thumbed through the pages, noting that Manning Stoudt, a junior loan officer, had handled transactions since her predecessor's departure. Common courtesy said she should talk to Manning before meeting with Paul Yocum, but Manning's office was dark. No wonder. It was past five o'clock on a Friday. She decided to touch base after meeting with Paul. The idea of hitting the road again prickled her with excitement. As she closed out her first week, she felt reborn.

ತಿಲ

Saturday dawned crisp with a trace-scent of fall. Wrapped in thick terry, Kingsley made coffee and carried it back to her bedroom. Elbows propped on the sill, she watched squirrels rocket through towering maples and oaks that showed traces of red. Eastward, sunrise glowed on centuries-old slate roofs. She drank coffee and beauty in equal proportions.

By the time she had dressed and awakened her car, the sun had climbed in a periwinkle sky. Heading south, she passed Keynote and felt a tingle of excitement. I do belong somewhere, she thought as the Lexus flew solitarily east on the Schuylkill Expressway. She merged south onto the Blue Route and exited at St. Davids.

Kingsley navigated back roads to her parents' secluded property, bordered by limestone walls piled by early settlers who had once cleared the land. Yesteryear squirrels had planted the oaks that now interlocked lofty canopies.

She scanned fall's progression, remembering the smell of burning leaves. Her father had lit a small pile for his daughter's edification, the practice now prohibited by environmental law, which he said must be respected. But what she cherished most was the time he lavished on her, his only child.

Sarah Alderson met her on the front porch before she could thumb the brass handle. "Sweetie, you made such good time. Freshly baked coffee cake, strawberries and peaches, fresh-squeezed orange juice, Irish Cream coffee—how's that sound?" Arm in arm, Sarah drew her daughter inside. "Henry! Come!"

Kingsley paused in the grand foyer as her father crossed the upper gallery and took the curved staircase two at a time. Fresh from his jog and a shower, his hug smelled of his signature cologne.

They headed into the kitchen behind the large dining room that fronted the right quadrant of Aldersons' Georgian mansion.

Pesto slipped into the room, meowed and rubbed against her legs.

Kingsley gathered her silky long-haired tuxedo cat that gazed adoringly from iridescent eyes set in a perfect white face. "Hey, fellow. How's my baby?"

"You can't have him back!" her mother teased.

Kingsley had adopted the kitten when she was sixteen, and then left him at home during college. Pesto transferred his affection to Sarah, for whom it had been love at first sight.

Henry barely tolerated the creature that loved to torment him, although the women caught him cooing baby talk to the cat. All three kept up the pretense.

When they'd finished brunch Henry cleared his throat in his trademark segue to serious stuff.

Here it comes, Kingsley realized. *Lingering business about Andy's death that he'd alluded to on the phone.*

"David Wentworth's had recent dealings with the heating oil company's attorneys. He wants you to call him today. I've left his card by the phone in the library."

Setting her linen napkin beside her plate, she decided to get business out of the way. Positioned behind the foyer, the library with its floor-to-ceiling bookshelves had always held comfort and solace for her.

She noticed the ladder had been slid near the oldest volumes where her mother kept Grammy's first editions and rare books. Kingsley smiled, remembering how she could always predict where the dinner table conversation would lead, based on that ladder's location.

"Find it?" Henry called.

She nodded to him as she settled into her father's desk chair.

"You'll be okay?"

"I'm fine, Dad, but will you please stay?"

She dialed the number, and when David picked up, she put him on speaker.

"Here's where we stand," C. David Wentworth said, after the three exchanged pleasantries. Uncle David, her dad's college roommate and her godfather, took his loyalties very seriously. "The night that Andy was killed, the driver had been on the road fifteen hours. Forensic testing confirmed that his log sheet was altered. No drugs or alcohol were found in his system. But, as you know, since he died at the scene, no criminal charges are pending against him. The company's liability, however, is another matter all together."

"I read speculation that he had fallen asleep at the wheel," she said. "But how could that be? The driver had to be awake to negotiate the turn onto the overpass. Could the traffic light have malfunctioned? Given both drivers a green?"

"We'll never know because the light was destroyed in the fire. The company's attorneys want this settled as quickly, quietly, and cheaply as possible. They have insurance, but not nearly enough for this type of negligence. You could win a substantial settlement in or out of court, if you want to pursue it."

"I researched the company, a family-held business for three generations," Henry interjected. "Their business assets could be fair game. But you should know they provide dozens of jobs and have contributed generously to the community. That the young adult children could take over the business now is at risk."

"I need to know how you want to proceed, Kingsley," David said. He ticked off some numbers.

"I have no interest in bankrupting this family. I have a good job and the trust Grammy set up for me. And no amount of money will bring Andy back. I want to settle. Be done with the whole sordid business." She realized she'd been clawing at her fingers, more an entrenched nervous habit than from a fresh eczema attack.

"On another front," her godfather said. "I had a call from the Philadelphia police. Just a heads-up, mind you, but there may be a new development surrounding the circumstances of Andrew's death."

Kingsley stiffened and leaned forward in the chair.

"A person claiming to be an eye witness to the accident has come forward."

"What? How! And why now? It's been almost a year!" She shook her head. "No way some publicity monger who read all the papers is going to get his fifteen minutes at our expense. Do Andy's parents know about this??

"I understand that the Wards got the same information."

"That's just cruel." She blinked to discourage tears of rage that such blindsiding threatened.

"I agree," David said. "With your permission, why don't I ask the police to direct any further information to me personally? If anything materializes that needs your attention, I'll let you know."

Kingsley, willing her anger to settle, took some deep breaths. "Did the police attach any credence whatsoever to this so-called witness's story?"

"No. His story didn't match the evidence, and besides, he had just worked his way through a DUI. The cops suspect he'd been drinking again. And that would account for why he didn't come forward at the time. Once they realized he was under the influence, he'd have lost his license forever. Perhaps lost his job. Gone to jail."

Agreed on letting David handle the details, they finished the call.

"Sweetheart, I am so sorry."

Kingsley batted her hand in her father's direction, dismissing his need to console her.

"You all right?"

"Sure, Dad."

"Your mother's been talking nonstop about taking you shopping for your birthday present. She has something special in mind. But of course she'd understand—"

As if on cue, Sarah tapped on the glass pocket doors, wearing a mischievous grin.

Kingsley took a deep breath. "Sounds like the perfect antidote, Dad."

After shopping and dinner, Henry lit a fire and they sank into the living room's overstuffed chairs.

"First fire of the season." He smiled contentedly, having succeeded in making it draw. "That should warm you up."

Kingsley smoothed the butter-soft sleeve of her new leather jacket and thanked them again for her extravagant present.

Mother and daughter exchanged grins, both relishing their lovely day.

"I'm exhausted," Sarah concluded. "You two can talk shop until midnight if you want, but I'm going to bed."

Once her mother was out of earshot, Kingsley seized the opportunity to pick Henry's brain. "Do any rumors of a power shakeup at Keynote reach you guys at the OCC?" she asked, hoping his position at the Office of the Controller of the Currency might provide insight. "I heard that the analysts are concerned that our lack of succession means that Keynote could be sold, sooner than later. And I just got there."

"I can't imagine what Keynote's board has been thinking," Henry said. "That Warren Kramer and Douglas Neiman would go on forever? Word is that senior managers below them are vying for power without anyone being really qualified. Except for one, and who that is, I'm bound not to repeat. Evidently he's controversial, but I didn't hear why."

"Bet that's Frank Ziegler. He is so rude. I can't imagine what life will be like if he takes over."

"Forget your feelings. Focus on your goals. Some of our best leaders aren't very personable. They have to be tough to make shrewd decisions, especially when business survival's at stake. I hear the bank's hiring talent—brought you in, didn't they? And Bill Henning's son, Todd. What's your impression of him?"

"No idea who Mr. Henning is yet, or what he'll be like. I'm just hoping he's not a clone of that man Ziegler. Did I make a mistake going there? Could I be out of a job?"

"Customer-contact employees like you bring in money. With your credentials, you're pretty safe. In the event of a takeover, duplicate back-office staff would be downsized. Branches in the same locale would be merged, eliminating some staff. The surviving bank would cherry-pick from that talent pool at the top. But new owners typically don't need the resistance and bad habits that former disgruntled executives bring to the table."

"What about your friend's son—Todd Henning? Would he be out?"

"They'd be smart to retain him. If he's like his dad, he could turn things around, but only if he's in a position of authority. But it may be too little too late." Henry took a sip of his brandy, and smiled at his daughter. "Not one word, or this confidential source dries up. Besides, I could be dead wrong. Don't let my opinions sway your decisions. Just keep your head down, mouth shut, and hit those goals." He looked intently into her eyes. "One last thing—watch your back! Be damn picky about whom you trust."

Chapter 5

Sunshine bounced off Paul Yokum's painted cinderblock office walls that were lined with photos labeled *Wire Products History*. The no-nonsense metal cabinets and battered oak furniture fit the slender man with merry eyes and thinning gray hair. His mission seemed to be putting Kingsley at ease.

"I'm a big fan of your bank," he said, motioning her to a seat across from his desk, which was piled high with paperwork. Paul pointed to a picture of a shed surrounded by chain-link fencing. "That's the company's birthplace. I'd installed lots of fencing—pools, yards, warehouse perimeters. One day my little boy needed a guinea pig cage, which we made ourselves. Pretty soon we had orders for kennels and humane traps that led to my first patent." He chuckled, looking at an eight-by-ten picture of his family. "My wife gave me an ultimatum—get out of the wire business or get out of our yard. I hadn't thought of myself as 'in the wire business,' but her demand forced my first expansion. To make a long story short, I kept outgrowing sheds and garages, needed assistants, raw materials, sales, service, transportation, and so on.

"Finally I realized I needed a real plant. I thought I'd saved up enough down money, but none of the banks would give me the time of day. Enter Warren Kramer, who was in charge of your lending department back then. I showed him my business plan, expecting the usual rejection. Know what he said?"

Kingsley was fascinated. "No, what?"

"That I wasn't asking for enough money! That most new businesses fail because they were under-capitalized. He calculated projections in his head and told me my plan was sound. He even noticed that my inventory was needed in weeks, not months. Adjusting that helped my cash flow. That was twenty years ago. The rest is history. Come, let me show you." When they entered the plant, he pointed to a red painted line. "That's where phase one ended. Today we just do fence products here, but three other locations make everything from supermarket carts to animal enclosures."

Paul showed her where the wire came in from the adjacent rail line, was stored, transformed, and shipped out. She noticed that he had a smile and personal word for every employee whom he knew by name. Arriving back at his office, he motioned her to a chair. "I believe in being a good neighbor. Before we built, we met with community leaders to learn their objections. I thought the challenge would be building on farmland. Know what topped their list? School buses! The parents were worried that the increased traffic would endanger their kids."

"What did you do?"

"We promised to schedule our shifts to begin and end when the children weren't coming and going. Even the police were pleased about that. We need these people. They have a great work ethic and are so loyal. You saw our daycare. The children come to work with their parents, catch the school bus, and then return here. My turnover is zilch!" Almost as an afterthought, he approached the bank's error. "I made photocopies for you"

"I'll look into it immediately. Of course, your account will be corrected. If it turns out to be anything out of the ordinary, we will pursue it rigorously. I'll get back to you by tomorrow, at the latest."

As she drove away, Kingsley felt uplifted. Bankers who gave great customer service could make a real difference in people's lives. Her respect for Warren Kramer expanded exponentially. Now, however, she had her first problem to solve.

"All quiet here," Marle reported as Kingsley swept into the office. "I'm straightening out some misapplied payments, reversed a delinquency, approved a few overdrafts, the usual stuff."

Second week on the job, Kingsley thought, and everything's under control.

"Nathaniel wants to see you."

Kingsley glanced reflexively toward his far corner office, dumped her coat and briefcase in her office, and grabbed a tablet and pen. Nathaniel's secretary motioned her into his office where she was offered his nearest guest chair. He rose, but didn't sit down again until she was settled. "Sorry to make you cold call," he said. "Clients just don't get any better than Paul. I miss the direct dealing. How did it go?"

Kingsley brought him up to date. "Must be a back-office error," she added, defending some unknown person or function.

Nathaniel began shaking his head before she had finished. "Can't be. This happened right here. May I see the paperwork?" She handed it over and waited, but he didn't react. "Why don't you leave this to me," he said, voice neutral, and then changed the subject abruptly to other matters that would affect her.

Much later, back in her office, Kingsley was roused from concentration by murmuring outside her office. Catching Marle's eye she mouthed, "What's up?"

Marle slipped into her office and flicked her eyes suspiciously across lending's core toward the far side. "Jeffrey Johnston—he and Mr. Frazier just went into Manning Stoudt's office and closed the door."

"Is that unusual?"

"Jeff had a carton in his hand."

"What does that mean?"

Marle put her index finger below her left ear and drew it quickly under her chin, making a scratchy noise in the process.

Kingsley was horrified. What if this small mix-up had cost Manning his job? How serious could it have been anyway, especially if someone just entered the wrong account number? The client wasn't upset, and the error was swiftly reversed. While the workstations prickled with artificial busyness, Kingsley tried to refocus on business.

A short time later, an angry man darkened her doorway, feet apart, clenching and unclenching his fists. "Thanks a lot! You really screwed me over."

Manning Stoudt, she instinctively knew. "I'm sorry. I would have talked with you first, but you'd already left."

He wasn't listening. "Our AA has my numbers. You should have just called. It was an honest mistake. Wire Products, Inc. is filed behind Wireless, Inc. I grabbed the wrong number in haste. You have no appreciation for how busy we've been. I had it fixed before you got back. You shouldn't have interfered."

"Interfered! Paul Yocum had a legitimate concern and

deserved immediate service. And that's what he got." She resisted the temptation to pull rank, knowing his anger and resentment might screw up every loan he touched for the rest of the day. She softened instead. "I do appreciate the haste a challenging workload can cause and what you did to keep things afloat. I had no idea I'd caused any trouble."

Manning exhaled, hands thrust in pockets, and studied the wall. "Sorry I yelled. It's just—when I saw Jeffrey Johnston showing up with his box—thought I'd have a heart attack."

Again, the box. "Why don't we get together tomorrow and go through the files that you've worked on. You can share your concerns, okay?"

"Okay. Tomorrow." He exited abruptly, no doubt to go drink his dinner. Her gut said, *Don't ask Nathaniel what happened.* If there's anything she needed to know, she'd be told.

ᘒᘖᘒ

Jeffrey Johnston strode into his office and snapped the door shut. Gingerly, he extracted a paper from his leather portfolio and dropped it into a UPS mailer. Next, he went to the personnel files to pull Manning Stoudt's information. Quickly he chose several sheets and discreetly photocopied them. After returning the file and shutting himself in his office, he added the still-warm copies to the mailer, and grabbed his personal cell phone.

"Miller? See what you can learn about Manning Stoudt. His prints are on the yellow sheet. I'm including some background material. Call me on my cell phone—never here at the bank. And never leave messages."

As Jeffrey hung up, he recalled the look on Manning's

face when he showed up with that empty box he had used to deliver forms on Two. The junior loan officer thought the box was to clean out his desk. Jeffrey wasn't sure how he managed to keep a straight face.

ⱌↄⱌↄ

Frank Ziegler studied the bank's organizational chart, considering the areas he'd assign to Todd Henning. Technology, fine. As long as Frank could pull up what he needed, how it worked did not interest him.

Private banking—handholding the wealthy. That he would keep. The trust department was on shaky ground. Give that to Todd. If he did well, Frank could take credit. If he failed, it was Todd's funeral. Frank wondered how long it would take to discredit this latest intruder.

Arlene knocked on his door, only opening it after he bellowed. "Todd's here to see you."

"Send him in." Frank slipped on his fatherly face as he shoved the chart into a drawer. "Todd, welcome," he said in a silky voice, pumping Todd's hand and motioning for him to sit. "Henning: that sounds familiar. Did Warren say you grew up around here?"

"Yes, although my parents retired to Arizona."

Frank wracked his brain for the name then remembered a boy who was a sophomore when he was a senior in high school.

"Gregg Henning! Was he your brother?"

"My cousin, although he was more like an uncle. He left for college the year I was born."

Frank tried to conceal his surprise. *How old is this guy anyway?* He was handsome, clean cut, impeccably groomed, unlike the locals who bought suits at the outlets. "What made you decide to apply to our bank? Did you want to come home?"

"Actually, I didn't apply. Warren recruited me."

Frank swallowed hard. He wasn't consulted! It was just like Warren to act independently. Doug had been so preoccupied with his wife's death. *Surely an oversight...*

"I've been thinking about your orientation," Frank said, changing the subject. "I'd like you to spend some time with our department heads, then we can discuss your assignments."

Todd looked slightly perplexed, but merely nodded.

૯⁄ঙ৲৩

On Thursday, Kingsley motored beneath the tunnel of magnificent elms that led to Warren Kramer's country club. Inside the lobby, fresh flowers spilled from an enormous urn set on an antique marble-top table. A Mozart oboe concerto seeped unobtrusively.

"Mr. Kramer is expecting me for lunch," she told a woman in a smart black suit, white blouse, and black walking shoes.

"Right this way." She escorted Kingsley to an elegant private dining room where a large round table had been set with white damask, china, and crystal.

Warren Kramer, his back to the door, rose to greet Kingsley. It couldn't be true! But it was—that strange little man she had seen hiding in the atrium garden to watch the tellers.

"I'm so glad you could come. Please sit down," the gentleman said, holding the chair to his right. He introduced four other newcomers: the technology vice president, a board member, the director of marketing, and a branch cluster manager. "As soon as Todd arrives, we'll order our lunch. Please have anything you like. My wife is especially fond of their seafood," Warren said kindly to Kingsley.

She couldn't help notice his rumpled suit, having protruding white cuffs with fray whiskers. His water-combed hair explained the rumor that staff called him "slick" behind his back.

"Ah, there you are." Warren rose to greet his last guest.

"Good afternoon," a vaguely familiar voice said, as the man approached the chair on her right.

Turning, she was horrified to recognize the man from the fitness center who had found her gloves.

"I think I've had the pleasure of meeting everyone, except this lady," he said smiling at her.

"Todd, this is Kingsley Ward, our new head of commercial lending. Kingsley, Todd Henning is our newly promoted executive vice president."

All during lunch, Kingsley couldn't imagine what this confident man could be thinking. Still, he asked questions that she could answer easily and never mentioned the circumstances under which they had met. Finally, she decided he didn't recognize her.

After all, it was very dark and she'd been a damp, rumpled mess.

Chapter 6

Kingsley's new boss, Nathaniel Frazier, lobbed a distress call to her from the Midwest. "My mother's gravely ill. I caught the last flight to Tulsa last evening. Could you cover the department head meeting for me tomorrow? I'm to report on lending's fourth quarter projections—anything that could derail our end-of-year goals. My secretary has my notes, which staff can flesh out. Oh! The doctor's here. So sorry. Extend my apologies. Gotta run."

Kingsley stared at the receiver in disbelief. Department head meeting, she had heard, was a bastion of senior management from which only cursory information leaked. Panicked, she sprinted toward Nathaniel's secretary who unearthed a memo covered with squiggles. "I'll transcribe his chicken scratch if that will help but…Good luck! He usually wings it."

Gathering Margaret, Roy from small business lending and Tim, the head of specialty lending, she laid out the challenge. "We don't need to report on our good loans—that's in the system—but what's in the pipeline and what might go bad. Could your people combine a list of loans you might book by the end of the year? Please estimate the odds of booking each loan—twenty-five, fifty, seventy-five, and a hundred percent."

Roy chuckled. "Let me guess. We'll eyeball it and then take a stab?"

His joke, while unscientific, helped Kingsley relax. They were good people who seemed unperturbed by the assignment. Perhaps she'd survive.

She plunged ahead. "I'll need your Watch List in four sections: classified loans that we're keeping an eye on, critical loans with more than significant problems, nonaccruals, and finally charge-offs, the latter being those that will go belly up by the end of the year."

With no more concern than if they'd been asked to send out for pizza, they disbursed to the task.

That evening, Kingsley, Margaret, and Marle assembled the big picture, proofed, and duplicated the reports. By ten, Kingsley had twenty copies ready for the meeting, stacked on her credenza. Twenty more she took home, just for backup. If she died overnight, Margaret would represent lending for Nathaniel.

The following morning, Kingsley arrived way too early. When she flipped on her light, she immediately saw the empty spot on her credenza. Staring, she started to sweat. She counted the extras that she dumped from her tote, collected them, and took some deep breaths. Rattled but determined, she took the elevator to Five, white knuckles gripping the handrail.

She had chosen a light gray banker's suit that just cleared her knees, a simple white blouse, and a narrow gray and lavender silk scarf. She had clipped her hair severely at the base of her neck with a black lacquer barrette. Wispy bangs she had slicked down with gel. But, as her temperature rose, ringlets escaped at her hairline, her nape feeling dangerously damp.

Minimal requirements she demanded of herself, *Don't sweat, cry, throw up, or wet your pants. Just get it done, then escape.* Stepping with confidence she did not feel, she closed on the boardroom. Its opulence oozed its comfortable status.

A secretary showed her Nathaniel's seat where she sat stiffly and tried not to fidget. She stacked her reports on the table to her left, wishing she could hide behind them. Instead, she opened her leather portfolio and clicked open a pen to scribble nonsense, as if she were capturing a brilliant inspiration.

As she awaited the arrival of others, she recalled her childhood Saturdays spent in her father's Philadelphia office. Ensconced at a tiny table, she would draw pictures while he worked, pretending she was a banker, too.

"Picture yourself as you'd wish and you will grow into that role," he had said.

No, she would not fail.

As senior management filed in, the grandfather clock in the hallway chimed eight. Todd Henning arrived, smiling and greeting each one with a personal comment before taking his place at the head of the table.

Kingsley hoped it didn't show that she blushed when he remembered her name.

Relaxed in his element, Todd made some announcements and called on Shirley Granger to report on HR and branch administration, followed by the head of technology.

"Kingsley Ward is covering for Nathaniel. Kingsley, will you please update the others on what's happening with his family?"

Kingsley told them what little she knew, emphasizing his apology for departing in haste.

"I doubt that Nathaniel had time to prepare his report," Todd said, "and you certainly aren't expected to do so yourself with so little notice. Please ask him to email us when he returns."

"But I am prepared—" Her voice sounded squeaky. She cleared her throat.

"Oh. Go ahead, by all means."

All eyes shifted toward her, the room very quiet.

She divided the reports in two piles, sending half each way around the table. "Page one is my summary, followed by short individual reports on our four departments. The bottom line for each is bold faced and brought forward to the summary sheet on page one." She timed a pause as they flipped through the pages, then reviewed the highlights and her conclusions. "The additional pages include our projections and concerns. The underscored comments are Nathaniel's. The last pages are appended to support my summary." She paused, looking up, afraid that she'd rattled too quickly.

The boardroom door flew open abruptly. Frank Ziegler entered, grabbed a chair, and wedged himself beside the head of finance. Todd appeared not to notice, although all eyes were focused on Frank, who had bent to the finance man's ear.

"Does anyone have any questions for Ms. Ward?"

Kingsley stole a glance at Todd and admired his calm. He was a lot younger than most at the table, yet seemed to have earned their respect. The head of finance, a member of the executive committee who invested the bank's money and managed the budget, half raised one finger.

"We'd like your opinion on our loan loss reserve," he

said, referencing the money banks must set aside from income to cover loans that go bad. "The examiners think our figure's too high. Since you're supposedly the expert, you tell us who's right."

Kingsley looked at the little man, whose very thin face was dominated by a narrow hooked nose that seemed to be pulling his close-set, unsmiling eyes together under one continuous eyebrow. Frank pierced her with hostile eyes.

"If you'll turn to page six," she responded as papers shuffled around the table, "you'll see we anticipate charging off no more than fifteen percent by the end of the year."

"So you're saying the figure's too high? To what would you recommend a lower figure?" He'd narrowed his eyes to slits, glaring unblinking at her, the outsider, turning his head but not his eyes to catch a whisper from Frank.

"I've noted the quality of our loans. It appears we've been sufficiently conservative to minimize foreclosures."

"Young lady, you're not answering my question."

The others shifted in their chairs.

"I'm not qualified to answer the first part of your question—whether the loan loss reserve figure is too high or too low as a percentage of total assets. Your experts have to decide that from a balance sheet perspective." She scanned the faces for approval from those who understood and from the others who just needed assurance that she was knowledgeable. Frank whispered again.

"And you're doing what to ensure that fifteen percent is enough? We don't need any year-end bombshells."

"We do all we can to ensure the quality of the portfolio: Pay strict attention to our guidelines for booking quality business; keep a balance between quality and quantity; watch our clients' progress carefully; but, most importantly, give them excellent service to help them meet their goals and avoid problems."

The man opened his mouth to keep going, but Todd interrupted. "Does anyone else have a question for Ms. Ward?" Frank stood up. "Frank?"

The man simply batted his hand as he exited. Todd thanked her again and then turned to the next Head.

Kingsley took notes mechanically, congratulating herself for simply surviving. She tried not to stare, but couldn't help noticing that Todd's eyes lit up his face. He did have other features—a very straight nose and a mouth that turned up at the corners that made him look pleasant, even when frowning in concentration. *Task at hand,* she scolded herself. When the meeting adjourned, most hung back to banter with him. She escaped, knowing she was out of her league and grateful that it was over.

ↄ〜ↄↄ

Adrenaline still pumping, Kingsley made rounds, heaping thanks on those who had helped build the report. As she passed Marle's desk she remembered the missing reports. "Would the cleaning crew ever throw out papers on my credenza?"

Marle scowled. "They're not to touch any surface that hasn't been cleared. I'll call housekeeping if you're concerned. Your timing is good—they make their weekly visit tonight."

"No, that's okay." Perplexed, Kingsley returned to her office and searched it again, but the twenty copies were nowhere. As she was refilling her waste paper basket, she noticed Todd approaching her office.

Jumping, she smoothed her skirt over the black lace that

had escaped at her hemline and pulled on a professional expression.

"Got a minute?" he asked, directing her attention to the copy of her report that he held in his hand. "This report is excellent. I hardly expected it."

"I'll pass that along to our staff. They're awesome. They really scrambled for me."

"I apologize for Tom's insolence. I should have cut him off sooner. He was out of line."

"As a newcomer, I expect to be challenged. The head of finance did ask some good questions."

"At numbers, the man is a genius, but he's the first to admit that he's no good with people. The bank's lucky to have his talent. But you handled him well."

"I don't need sugar coating, but if he ever calls me 'young lady' again—"

Todd laughed and started to leave. "I just wanted to say thanks, Ms. Ward. You did a great job."

"Kingsley. It's Kingsley," she said, immediately feeling silly.

☙❧

Kingsley stayed late Wednesday evening to make up for Monday's emergency. She killed the fluorescents, opting instead for two brass lamps that she'd brought from home, one on her desk, the other on the credenza. *Better*, she thought as she dropped Jimmy Buffet into an old single-disk player. As she massaged cortisone cream into her rash-riddled hand, she idly wondered if she could ever wear rings again. Pulling the seal from a carton of yogurt, she kicked off her shoes, settling cross-legged on her cushioned leather chair. Sixty plus emails demanded attention. Most were

FYIs, which she digested and then deleted, but two screamed for immediate answers.

"Anybody here?"

"Just follow the music," she called to the voice as she typed the second reply. When Todd appeared at her door, she jumped, knocking her spoon onto the floor.

"I'm sorry," he said. "Maybe I should tie a bell around my neck." He was coatless, but a striped burgundy silk tie was still perfectly knotted. In spite of the hour, he looked like he had just showered and put on new clothes. "I'd hoped to find someone who could hunt up a document. That's not all you're having for dinner, is it?"

Although his easiness calmed her somewhat, she struggled to act nonchalant as she retrieved her spoon from under the desk. "What file do you need? I'll try."

He handed her four stapled pages. "When I made my request, I used the wrong title—department instead of division."

She looked at the pages and saw what he meant. "I recognize this. When do you need it?"

"Well, actually, tomorrow morning at seven-thirty, I'm afraid—"

"If you want to sit down, I'll pull it up. Let me see..." She opened directories, scrolled through documents until she found what he wanted. "Here, come and look." He circled the desk to scan the screen.

"That's it. Could you print it?"

Kingsley scrutinized further. "Wait. I think we have something newer." She called up another spreadsheet. "Would this work?"

"Even better!"

Kingsley pushed print and got up to fetch it. Todd stepped out of her way as she swung her chair back to re-

trieve her shoes. She caught herself, feeling unprofessional—again. "I spent several hours on concrete today. One of
our manufacturing clients is building a huge addition. Since
nobody's here, I thought—"

"After six, dress code doesn't apply." He snapped a
glance at his watch. "Eight forty-five. Leave them off."

She folded her trouser cuffs up by one turn, then padded
out to the printer. "You better proof this."

"Looks fine to me," he said, barely taking his eyes off
her face, which she felt redden.

"Oops. Look at page three, column C, near the bottom'"
she said. "See the XXXX? The printer does that when the
number doesn't fit in the space." Returning to the PC, she
scrolled to the cell, selected it, and reduced its font by one
point. "Let's try that again." She printed that page and returned, smiling with renewed confidence. "How many copies?"

"Twenty."

"Our photocopier makes duplicates, collates and staples.
Fast."

"Great. That just leaves a covering memo, which I'll
have to write in the morning. I'm afraid I haven't learned
how they set it up."

"I bet it's a template—that would be stored on the F
drive." She worked back through the directories but
frowned. "I don't have access, but if I log off, you can log
on with your password." She rose to offered her chair,
which he took.

"I'm in. Now what?"

She reached around his arm for the mouse, scrolled
through directories, opening and closing anything that
looked promising, their faces inches apart. His after shave—
it was wonderful but she couldn't place it.

"I know what you're thinking," he said, quietly.

She jerked back.

"'What's he doing in charge of technology if he can't find a document?' Problem is, I don't know where they put it or what they called it." He flashed a smile that showed flawless teeth as he quickly returned to the screen. "That's it—the memo letterhead they designed for me. Now I can do it myself."

"Just save as after renaming it so you don't overwrite the template."

Dumb, dumb, dumb, Kingsley smacked herself. A kid would know that. She took the report to the copy room and watched while the machine spit out the pages. She returned with the stack to find that he'd finished his memo.

"Could you proof this for me?"

As she scanned the screen, she was aware that he'd turned to watch her. She backed up a little, trying to concentrate, but realized she didn't know what she'd read.

"Look at the time—it's nearly ten. I've squandered your evening, but—could you do one more thing for me?"

"Sure. What do you need?"

"Please call me Todd. I'm too ordinary for 'mister' or 'sir.'" He gathered the reports. Thanking her again, he sauntered toward the elevator.

She grinned. Good thing she stayed, but ordinary? Well hardly!

঩৩঩

Warren Kramer entered Frank Ziegler's office so quietly that Frank jerked, nearly slopping his coffee.

"Your invitation." Warren presented it with a flourish. "We'll be making that very important announcement." He savored each word, shuffled a few dance steps, then winked at Frank. "This bank will rise to new heights."

In spite of hating Warren's theatrics, Frank's pulse rate took off.

Alone, Frank slit open the envelope, addressed in calligraphy to Mr. and Mrs. Franklin P. Ziegler. The honor of their presence was requested for cocktails, dinner, and dancing to honor retiring president Douglas Neiman at the country club, Saturday, October 14. Frank knew that's when they would announce his promotion! That soon! He caressed the raised script with a fingertip and thrilled at the tactile sensation. The next fifteen days would be the longest of his entire life.

Chapter 7

Early sunshine backlit the maples to transparent gold. Rummaging through her neighbors' brochures, Kingsley retrieved the Hawk Mountain piece. Founded in 1934, it was the world's first refuge for birds of prey—a 2,380-acre nature preserve, touted as the United States' best observation point for autumn raptor migration of 17,000 hawks, eagles and falcons. The migration timetable noted that the first weekend of October was the time to see Cooper's hawks, sharp-shins, redtails, redshoulders, golden eagles, northern harriers, ospreys, peregrine falcons, merlins, and American kestrels.

I'll hike it, she thought, as she pulled on cargo pants, a soft cotton tee and flannel shirt. Laced into LL Bean Day Walkers, she paused, trail gloves in hand, to study her naked ring finger, the rash finally healed.

Till death. They were parted. She'd better get used to it. Her engagement ring with its pear-shaped diamond had been Andy's grandmother's, the wedding ring new, just for her. She passed on the diamond, but slipped on the band. *Just a little while longer*, she promised. Emerging into the invigorating air, she felt a rush of euphoria.

Kingsley headed north. One hour later, she turned into the sanctuary. She gasped. Hawk Mountain was pristine and majestic. She approached the visitors' center, whose façade of 440 million-year-old sandstone and new western cedar blended with hemlocks and mountain laurel. She wandered through the native plant garden protected by Benner Deer Fencing. She was so engrossed reading plant labels that she failed to notice the tall man approaching.

"Imagine running into you here." Turning, she recognized Todd Henning, who had traded his wing tips for boots. "Were you thinking of doing the trails?"

Recovering, she showed him the map. "South Lookout is three hundred yards down that path…"

"And the view is spectacular, although I haven't seen it since I was a boy. Doubt that it's changed very much."

She traced the map's dotted route with her finger. "I'm thinking of trying the River of Rocks Trail. It's described as 'a six-hundred-foot vertical descent—a challenging four-mile loop that leads to a periglacial bolder field on the valley floor.'"

"That's not for inexperienced hikers, but it's well worth the effort. Mind if I tag along? I might need someone to go for assistance."

They walked to South Lookout to gaze at the forest's undulating ridges of maples and oaks, beeches and gums afire in their fall wardrobe. Leaving South Lookout, they followed orange blazes painted on rocks through mature rhododendron, laurels, firs and hemlocks. They scrambled up steppingstone boulders to the North Lookout with its panoramic seventy-mile view of the ridge-and-valley province of the central Appalachians.

A volunteer, who was documenting bird sightings, pointed north excitedly. "Over there—a bald eagle!"

Sharing a boulder and her binoculars, they saw sharp-shinned hawks circle in kettle formation.

"Look way down there," Todd said, directing her gaze. "There's your River of Rocks."

They retraced their steps to enter the trail to begin their descent.

"Listen," she said. They stopped. "It's so quiet you can hear acorns crash and leaves plop."

He smiled, first at her then around in awareness, taking a deep breath. They identified maples and oaks, beeches and gums, sassafras and tulip poplars as they headed through boulder-strewn stretches that challenged their balance. Finally they came to the River of Rocks with its millions of sun-bleached, VW-sized boulders. They perched on a flat overhanging ledge to eat lunch.

"When was the last time you ate at a restaurant with this kind of view?" he asked, unzipping his backpack.

Kingsley shrugged out of hers and pulled off her gloves to fish out her sandwiches. "This one's smoked turkey and that one's ham and cheese. I have tomatoes, lettuce and pickles in a separate bag. Take either one, or half of each."

"A traveling deli. I'm really impressed. Let's see—the bachelor's version—peanut butter—natural of course—on wheat, apples, bananas, trail mix, cupcakes. Want to share?"

"Chocolate Tastykakes! My favorite. You're on." She stole a look at his face. Now his eyes looked deep blue under brows that weren't heavy in spite of his shock of dark hair. His features were symmetrical, his upper lip line entirely too nice for a man. The jut of his forehead and square of his jaw saved him from looking too pretty. His lingering tan said outdoors. She forced herself not to stare. He seemed so relaxed away from the bank that she forgot about rank. "What made you decide on Keynote?"

"I wasn't looking for change. While at a banker's conference in San Diego I met Warren Kramer at, of all things, the urinals in the washroom. He came right up to me, introduced himself while I wracked my brain about how I was supposed to shake hands."

Kingsley laughed, picturing Todd with safari man.

"Later, we sat in the lobby to talk. I could tell by the pointed questions he asked that he had researched my background. What a mind he has! But you know, his suit pants and jacket didn't match, nor did his socks."

Kingsley spoke of his hiding among the plants, but wondered if that had been wise. Todd was, after all, executive management. Sounding critical of executive management was professional suicide. He smiled reassuringly, however, saying that he'd seen it himself.

"He's like a lot of brilliant people who are oblivious to practicalities. After San Diego, he asked for a meeting—convinced me that at a large bank I would always be a specialist, but here, I could move ahead faster, broaden my knowledge. He pursued me until I accepted."

"Is it radically different?"

"Working for him will be a challenge. Senior officers have stacks of Warren's brainstorms that draw them away from their duties. But he's respected as a good, decent, honorable man, which is refreshing. So many aren't. He does, however, stray from reality, which may account for abuse in the ranks. It's too early to tell." He frowned slightly. "I shouldn't have said that."

"Said what?"

He grinned and rose to gather his things. They circled the River of Rocks, then began the steep ascent. Losing her footing, she lurched, but he caught her as if she were weightless.

Stamina flagging, they stopped more frequently, rationing water.

"How's this for perfection?" she asked, as they entered a chapel-like grove of twenty-foot rhododendron, bisected by a small stream that nourished ferns and mosses.

They sat in its enclosing protection to recharge for the steepest ascent.

"I'm curious about something," he asked. "I hope you don't mind my asking about your being here alone. Doesn't your husband like hiking?"

She glanced at her gloveless hands, unprepared for the question. Of course he'd have no way of knowing. "I'm not—He isn't—He died in an automobile accident last year."

He looked taken aback. "I am so sorry. I didn't know. How did it happen?"

"He—" Silence hung awkwardly for a moment. "I'd rather not—I'm not—"

He came to the rescue. "Hey! The sun's dipping over the mountain. We'd better get moving. They'll get downright nasty if they have to come find us with flashlights. If I'm starving, you must be too," Todd said once they were back at the visitor's center. "I spotted several diners on my way up the mountain. Care to join me?" She hesitated. "Look up. That turkey buzzard knows that you're weakening. He's circling to grab you for dinner."

"That's silly," she said but looked up anyway, laughing at her gullibility.

"I'm parked over there—the black one." He pointed to an Explorer. "Why don't you follow me down the mountain? I promise to stay near the speed limit."

✧✧✧

The mom-and-pop diner with no curb appeal belied the heavenly aroma inside. They ordered hot roast beef sandwiches, fries, coleslaw, and coffee from laminated menus with clipped-on specials.

"I'll never be able to eat all that," she said of her turkey-sized platter. He merely grinned as she proceeded to demolish it, hardly speaking. "I can't remember being this hungry."

He beckoned the waitress to refill their cups and to order dessert. "She'll have ice cream on her pie," he instructed the waitress, changing the subject before she could protest. "You asked about challenges. Frank Ziegler, he's one. It escapes him that I report to Warren, not him. He's opposed to a number of projects we need to tackle or upgrade before the competition sweeps us away. Then there's our image in the community. We're doing so little."

"Community relations? Now that interests me."

"If we're going to be the predominate bank, we need to be community leaders—get involved in local issues. We don't have a volunteer committee. The corporate giving program's a mess, yet the employees are such caring, family people. The potential is there."

Kingsley remembered Paul Yocum's experience building his new plant, reiterating Paul's story in detail. "If he ever has a disaster at his plant," Todd hypothesized, "he has already built in good will."

As their conversation meandered without any dead spots, she was struck by its comfort. Finally she said, "I don't handle questions about my husband very well, but I'm trying. Back home, the sympathy and kindness were welcome at first, but—" She paused, glancing at her hand. "I know I should take off my ring. It's protection or fear, I suppose."

"How long has it been?"

"Almost a year."

"That's not very long. I'm sure it still hurts. Healing takes time. You must be kind to yourself." His eyes had grown solemn, gray.

"Friends say, 'you're young, you'll find someone new,' as if I could snap in a replacement battery. Moving made sense. I love my work. The people are great. Driving in every morning, just thinking about what will unfold—"

"Bankers." He chuckled. "We're born, not made. I'm glad that it's working for you."

She nodded. "I'm not just saying that because of your position."

"Forget about that. I'm really just people. I'm glad you told me. And you don't need to apologize."

"It shouldn't have happened. He just went for ice cream." Kingsley's mind flashed a picture of Andy in his rain jacket, smiling, then gone. "I was so angry. He was a fine person who didn't deserve it."

They were silent a moment before their eyes met.

"It will get better," he said quietly.

She warmed to his kindness, his ease, and perspective. He wouldn't have dragons plaguing his life. Lucky man.

"You mentioned Paul Yocum," he said. "Nathaniel said that you'd had a mix-up with his company. Something about Manning Stoudt?"

She sighed. "Manning Stoudt helped pick up the slack while Keynote was short handed. No doubt he was working too fast with too little sleep. He intended to make a draw from Wireless, Inc.'s business line of credit but got Wire Products, Inc. by mistake. Manning was furious because I went to see Paul, Wire Products's owner, although it was an excuse to get acquainted. I couldn't believe it caused such a flap."

"Are the companies near each other?"

"Just in the file cabinet. Geographically, Wire Products is in York County, southwest of Harrisburg. Wireless is up here in Schuylkill County—Deer Lake."

"I didn't think we had commercial loan customers this far north. You said Deer Lake?"

"It's on the main drag, or in a small industrial park."

Todd shook his head thoughtfully. "I've been looking for an old stone farmhouse to renovate. Just last week I was all over this area. I can't for the life of me recall a customer in that location. And Deer Lake is a tiny community."

"I know he said Deer Lake."

Todd shook his head slowly again. "I scoured the area with a realtor, thinking of everything from groceries to a gym. I scrapped the idea because it's fifty miles from the bank." He grinned challengingly. "Just how sure are you that it is Deer Lake?"

"I checked the computer."

"Would you care to place a small bet? If you can pro- duce Wireless, Inc. in Deer Lake, I'll buy you dinner at the restaurant of your choice."

"And if you win?"

"You cook one for me."

"It's a deal." They shook hands on the bet she felt sure she would win. "Let's see—I'm partial to seafood."

"You're pretty confident—"

"The expensive kind, like fresh lobster that must be flown in. This will cost you."

He only laughed.

Back in her apartment, she dropped her gear and col- lapsed on the couch. Glancing at the clock, she realized she'd just spent the entire day with a man for the first time in a year. And the day had been fun.

Chapter 8

The next morning, Kingsley braved a new church alone. Colored light streamed through ancient stained glass, its solemn beauty stirring her soul. Massive bells pealed from the brownstone tower, and the choir swelled hymns from her Anglican childhood. After the service, friendly parishioners coaxed her to attend coffee hour.

But by late afternoon, inky clouds blotted the sun, diminishing her spirit. Evening deepened with relentless rain pinging her windows. She hated the shroud of diminishing light, feeling downright forlorn.

As darkness edged into her soul, she resisted the urge to call someone, anyone, opting to retreat into a backlog of work.

She startled when the phone rang.

"Hey, whatcha doing?" Barrie—Ms. Bubbles.

Kingsley laughed, picturing the anything-but-dumb little blonde, curls all askew. Kingsley told her of Saturday's adventure for which she was now doing penance.

"That's bizarre, running into him. You know, Kingsley, he could be a stalker. But he is gorgeous, if you like the dangerous type. Have you checked out his eyes? They're changeable. I bet you could figure his moods."

"Barrie, forget it. It was just a chance meeting. Besides, even if in-house dating weren't fraught with problems, he outranks me in my own chain of command. It was just a nice day."

"Sweetie! He really could be a stalker with a dark, mysterious past. An obscure burial ground in upstate New York." She giggled. "You could be next. Any mysterious bulges in his pockets, other than what you'd expect?"

"Stop! Please."

"Okay." She sighed. "I have something for you, if you're going to be home."

"Sure. Join me for shrimp chowder, fresh rolls, spring mix salad, and tomatoes from the deli."

Barrie arrived in a dripping, hooded raincoat. As she stepped into the vestibule, Kingsley noticed something moving at her neck—small, black and white, all ears and big eyes. Opening her coat, Barrie produced a four-month-old kitten.

"Good heavens, wherever did you find her?"

"I thought she looked just like that picture of your cat, Pesto, that's on your desk. You said she's at home with your folks? This little vixen needs a home. Owner's kid is allergic." Kingsley looked at the beautiful white face surrounded by long glossy black fur. "The resemblance is amazing."

"She's been spayed, has her shots, but no front claws. However, her days are numbered unless she is placed quickly." She shot Kingsley a cherubic smile. "I just knew that you'd want her."

"I don't have any food—"

"No problem. Got some in the car."

"What about a litter box? It's Sunday evening and—"

"Got Pandora's box too."

"Pandora?" Kingsley laughed delightedly as Barrie handed over the warm little kitten, which promptly attached itself to her neck. "I think I've been adopted."

"Here's the number of her former parents. They said to call. Well, what do you think?"

Kingsley stroked Pandora's beautiful face, running her fingers behind velvet ears. Pandora purred as she snuggled in. "I think we're in love."

"Back in a sec." Barrie disappeared and returned with supplies. "Wait until you see this contraption," she said, following Kingsley's direction to the bathroom. "The litter box has a motorized rake, which sweeps after she steps out. It's supposed to work well with clumping litter." She released the kitten, which tentatively began to explore her new digs while the girls uncorked wine and warmed their supper.

"What's your plan for winning this Wireless bet?" Barrie asked after Kingsley detailed the challenge.

"Since Wireless Inc. is in our system, the rest should be easy. I'll pull the documents from central file, then I'll check product details. I'll call, pretending I'm a customer, and ask for directions. I don't know how far I have to go, but somewhere, there's a lobster with my name on it."

Barrie smirked. "Oh, he is so clever. Bet he's behind the Wireless mix-up just to get into your pants."

ഇരുഇ

At seven-thirty Monday morning, one hour before the official day began, Todd went to Human Resources. The office was empty. Feeling a bit sheepish, he pulled Kingsley's file. Behind the bank forms were her transcripts from Penn,

listing her name as Kingsley Alice Alderson, and from her
MBA program at Wharton as Kingsley Alderson Ward.
Married in between. He scanned her academic record,
mouthing "Wow." Back in his office, he phoned a colleague
at her former bank. "Why did she resign?"

"Sorry, Todd. I can only tell you her reasons were personal. Why don't you ask the newswire to research the archives? You can piece it together. Can't give you any details—it's illegal these days."

"That's okay, buddy. Thanks for your help."

That evening Todd opened the bulky package prepared
for same-day delivery by the service that the bank used. The
clips started with an article from a community monthly—
seven pounds, two ounces, twenty-one inches, daughter of a
prominent family. He smiled. In the next clip, she was a
beautiful five-year-old, curls to her waist, kissing a smaller
child while handing her a teddy bear. She'd been delivering
Christmas gifts at a homeless shelter with thirty volunteers
when the photojournalist captured the essence of giving.
The next clip, six months later, reran the photo, the photog-
rapher having won an award.

The next article included a quote from her father urging
people to remember the shelter's mission, that many other
children had volunteered.

He scanned school age activities, heavily weighted with
community involvement—up on a ladder, down in the
trenches, walking for this cause or that with her family. Was
it her family's position or that face? For some reason, she
drew attention.

At fifteen, the clips changed abruptly. The society pho-
tographer had captured her dancing with her father at a
charity ball that he had chaired, while her mother was heading another event across town, the theme being service, a

family affair. He studied the photo that already showed a lovely young woman taking her place.

He refilled his mug then picked up a stack of small clips—plays, honors, awards, National Merit, class officer, graduation, followed by college. *My god, she's been arrested—for what?* A demonstration without a permit involving a blind person denied civil rights. The next clip showed charges dropped, the matter settled in favor of said blind person. *Good for her.*

He read her engagement announcement to Andrew J. Ward, son of Dr. and Mrs. Ward, premed at Penn, followed by her wedding photo. Even the newspaper's grainy halftones couldn't diminish how beautiful she was. Next her MBA, honors, and her first job.

With all that he'd seen, he realized he'd only gone through one fourth of the packet. Then he saw why. The horrible accident, engulfing flames and twisted metal— Kingsley's worst nightmare captured on film. So horrendous that nearby trees burned hot enough to melt the overpass. Obits with photos, candids of the families, and the growing obsession with Kingsley. From various tabloids, shots of the funeral, her head up, face frozen, eyes somewhere ahead on the ground.

It didn't stop there. A tabloid photo of her leaving the morgue with her father. The story said she'd insisted on seeing him, in spite of his horrific injuries. The uproar that followed—the clerk's being fired for selling confidential details. Public interest fueling creative stories with old archival photos followed by speculation about criminal and civil charges against the heating oil company. One last photo of her, climbing the steps, briefcase in hand, returning to work. Then nothing.

Regardless of whatever reason she'd given her employer

or even herself, he knew. She had fled. How long could they keep her? She seemed well adjusted, but one never knew about private hell. He thought of her playing Jimmy Buffet that evening she'd located his document and jumping to kill it before Jimmy suggested they get drunk and screw.

Did he feel sorry for her? Anyone that brave didn't deserve pity but admiration and protection, the latter he instinctively knew she'd refuse. Feeling ashamed for violating her privacy, he committed the clips to his shredder.

ფოფ

Late Monday, Kingsley approached central file, but not before verifying Manning's location. No point freaking him out. Flipping through the Ws, she found Wertz Group, Windows Unlimited, Wire Products, Inc., followed by Woodworker Supplies—but no Wireless, Inc. The file must be in his office.

At five, she heard Manning tell the girls he was leaving. Nonchalantly, she paused at his door. Finding the file in plain sight hadn't been realistic, she conceded, shaking off her disappointment. She returned to her work, losing all track of time. How dark it became! She looked at her watch and then scanned the outer office. Everybody was gone home.

Why not search? she reasoned. *Little Lobster, you're mine. No, make that Big Lobster.* Turning left, she walked the square between the outer offices and the core of cubicles and filing cabinets. Lending was deserted. She circled again, one quarter round, to Manning's office where she made a cursory inspection in the dim light. She checked his bookshelf and surfaces, but drew the line at opening drawers.

Finally, she spotted a box under his desk. Crouching, she

moved it into the light and lifted the lid. A shaft fell on the title—Wireless, Inc. Quickly she scanned the first page. The owner's name was Mark Young. The mailing address was Orwigsburg, its physical location being Deer Lake. And they made electronic devices. All right!

Before she could read any further, she heard the swoosh of the elevator door. Quickly she replaced the file and slid the box under the desk. As footsteps approached and still on her knees, she returned Manning's chair to its position. The footsteps passed the reception area, closing on the turn where she crouched. Stooped to a crawl, she turned right into the walkway, turned left, duck-walking the passage toward her own office.

She heard a switch snap. Turning she saw the glow in Manning's office. She prayed that he hadn't heard her. Slithering into her office, she felt for her jacket, briefcase, and purse. In the dark, she quietly exited.

Safe in the stairwell, she chided herself. *Who's in charge of commercial lending anyway?* Tomorrow she'd simply track down Mark Young and Wireless, Inc. If Manning was guilty of sloppy documentation, so what? A junior officer's displeasure should not intimidate her. Still, she prickled. There was something off about the whole situation. She thought about Todd and grinned. She'd won the bet. Now, where should they go and what should she wear?

Tuesday, she dialed information for southern Schuylkill County and asked for the number of Wireless, Inc. The operator searched briefly, momentarily coming back on the line.

"How do you spell that again?"

Kingsley patiently did.

"There's no such listing," the operator said. "Might it be known by a different name?"

Kingsley was baffled, but hadn't learned anything else from the file. "Will you please try Mark Young?"

That produced a hit, which she wrote down. She dialed. When Mr. Young answered, his reaction was that a tele-marketer had caught him. Kingsley quickly explained her mission—to locate the owner of Wireless, Inc., in Deer Lake.

"Never heard of it." Mr. Young sounded toothless. "Who'd you say you were?"

She tried to explain but, when he remained baffled, she described where the business might be. "Nope. Sorry, young lady. Never heard of it and I've lived here for eighty years."

The old man hung up.

Kingsley tried to shake off a creepy feeling. Bet or no bet, she should pursue it. Considering her options, she tapped into the computer's loan files to locate Wireless, Inc. There it was with particulars about the loan. It wasn't large: $200,000—and the principal's name was Mark Young. The only explanation she could think of was that Manning had entered the wrong name or address or even the county. What a screw up! She'd better take a hard look at every ac-count that he had touched since her predecessor Fred's de-parture. Her lobster was swimming away.

Chapter 9

Kingsley pinned eighty pounds on the Maxicam rower. Grabbing the bar, she braced her feet and scooted back to position. *One, two, three*. She pulled, concentrating, wrists level, as the bar slid on its retractable cable. *Four, five, six—*

"That's a lot of weight."

Jumping, she lost the bar, which sprang back with a horrible clang.

"I'm sorry. I didn't mean to startle you," he said, sweeping the gym for reproach, but the Saturday diehards were too bent on their workouts to notice or care.

"Make some noise next time," she half-scolded.

He stooped to her level, pale gray gym shorts, sleeveless tee darkened with sweat at the solar plexus, his skin shiny, hair damp. Frowning he looked at her weight stack. "I was saying, that's a lot of weight for someone your size. You could get hurt."

"I can do it. I want to be strong. Besides, it's just one or two sets of twelve reps."

"How about trying three or four sets at forty pounds? Sixty max. May I?"

She nodded.

He pulled the pin and reinserted it. "Go ahead." He stooped and put a finger on her spine. "Don't lean back, or it's ineffective." He stood and backed up. "Pull your shoulder blades back—there, you feel it?"

She looked up, but he'd focused on her hands and her feet.

"That's better form."

Halfway through the fourth set of twelve, she stopped. "You're right. I feel the burn." She glanced down the line of other machines. "I suppose the same principle applies." She reached for her chart to study her trainer's directions. "She agrees. Guess I'm doing this wrong."

"Not at all. It's your workout. That chart's just a guide." He wiped his forehead on his towel and then glanced at the clock. "Well, gotta go. Can't go to meetings all week without doing the paperwork sometime. Oh, by the way, about our Wireless bet. From your silence, I figure I won."

"Our computer does say Deer Lake, but I struck out trying to trace it. I think someone screwed up the address. I can't justify digging further."

"Italian."

"What?"

"I like Italian. Maybe spaghetti or manicotti."

"You're declaring yourself the winner?"

"Yep. How about this evening?"

Kingsley scrambled for an excuse, but couldn't fabricate one fast enough. "Are you Italian?"

"No. Does it matter?"

"I don't cook Italian for people who are, and I never cook for gourmets."

"Good. I qualify. But seriously, I won't hold you to it." He smiled easily, unthreateningly, and then started to leave.

Such a nice man, she thought. And he had won—sort of. She called after him and he turned around.

"I'm not conceding, but I'll cook if you bring dessert."

"I'm sure I can find a bakery somewhere. Where and what time?"

She described how to navigate the one-way streets and how to avoid the tow-away zone. When he turned toward the locker room, she couldn't help notice women's heads turning. Slender, well proportioned, strong, but not bulky. And a great butt. His damp clothes, she realized, smelled of Tide and that unusual scent that she couldn't place. Italian. Okay. That would be easy.

That afternoon, Pandora stuck by her heels.

"This isn't a date. It isn't," she explained to the kitten as she tore five different market-fresh greens, covered them with damp paper towels and refrigerated the bowl. She popped the stems from bite-sized mushrooms, which she stuffed with Salino's sweet sausage. With fresh parmesan grated and bread wrapped in foil, she browned meat and scraped it into the saucepot to simmer in her aunt's home-made sauce.

"Would we have held out for lobster?" She grinned at the kitten. "Absolutely, with a kitty bag."

Kingsley scanned her red wines, chose a Nissley's Chambourcin and calculated how long it would take it to reach fifty-five degrees. She disliked warm wine and he wouldn't dare scold her.

She studied her walk-in closet. "What goes with black cat hair?" she asked Pandora, selecting a two-piece velour slack set and chunky jewelry.

Somebody knocked. An hour early! While framing something witty to excuse her old jeans, tee, and bare feet, she opened the door.

It was Isaac, her next-door neighbor, looking pathetic.

"Kingsley, I've locked myself out. Michael's late. Could I use your bathroom?"

She pointed the way down the hall. "Watch out for the kitty litter box."

Pandora, intrigued by his tassels, kept pace with his loafers.

"Hey, thanks a lot," he tossed over his shoulder as he hurried back out.

She dressed deliberately, dabbing on makeup while Pandora watched from the vanity counter. Kingsley adjusted the faucet to a drip. Pandora chased drop after drop, licking her paw in between.

As Kingsley was finishing, she heard a knock. That would be Todd, right on time. Halfway down the hall, she heard a great splash, followed by frightened cat noises. Running back, she found a sodden Pandora scrambling out of the toilet.

Neither had noticed that Isaac had left the lid up, which was Pandora's usual route to the floor.

Disoriented and flailing, Pandora projectiled into the clumping kitty litter. Kingsley yelled "Just a minute!" at the door while grabbing her frightened pet. Holding her closely, she flung open the door.

Todd stared at them, plastered with litter, and broke into uncontrollable laughter. "I can't wait," he finally said when he was able to breath.

"I think I need help."

"Understatement!"

They closed themselves in the bathroom, spread a large towel on the floor, and dusted, brushed, and pulled off what they could while Pandora struggled and yowled. Finally, while Kingsley immobilized her, Todd used Kingsley's manicure scissors to gently snip off what was fused to her fur.

Having done their best, they released the terrified kitten. Pandora tore down the hall, disappearing under the bed. Kingsley looked at her clothes in dismay.

"Why don't you change, and I'll shake this mess into the dumpster?" he volunteered.

By the time she finished dressing—again—Todd had located the vacuum was sweeping the floor.

"This is not how I usually entertain."

"I think your litter level's a little low," he alliterated, pleased with his joke.

"You've earned a drink." She directed him into the kitchen. "If you like scotch, there's Glen Fiddich, which Dad says is good." She picked up the wine that he'd left on the counter along with a bag of Macintosh apples. "This looks wonderful. Open it for me?"

While he fixed drinks, she microwaved the stuffed mushrooms, lit the burners to boil fresh pasta, and warmed the sauce.

"How about tossing the salad for me? The wooden bowl in the fridge—dressing is in the cruet beside it. Oh, by the way, if the cops pull you over and you test positive for drugs, tell them it's Aunt Susan's poppy seed dressing. I'll only share the recipe if they let you go."

"What have I stumbled into?"

Street lamps backlit the dining room windows, spreading an aura of yesteryear charm. They ate slowly, warmed by the food and the wine, finally edging toward more personal topics. Glasses refilled, they moved to the couch. Todd nodded toward Andy's picture, still prominently displayed. "Is that your husband?"

She squirmed. The portrait was such a permanent fixture

that it was almost transparent to her. She hadn't considered its intrusion on a new relationship. Should she have removed it temporarily? Her brain failed to produce the right thing to say.

"I understand about loss. I was married once," he was saying, which jolted Kingsley back to their conversation. "I thought it was forever. Perfect. We were opposites, which, I thought, was supposed to be halves of a whole. She was compelling—always surrounded by men vying for her attention. Socially, I'm reserved. I didn't presume to approach her and was flattered when she pursued me. In retrospect, I was unprepared for aggressive women, especially those who could play me. She pretended to want the things that I thought were important. She'd done her research. My family and friends were so snowed. That is, in the beginning.

He took a sip of his drink. "After we were married and I launched my career, she became restless and demanding. Our life—I—was too dull." He paused, took another swallow of wine, then set his glass back on the end table. "I thought she'd be happy if we started our family, but she had endless excuses. I was excited when she became pregnant, and disappointed when she miscarried. Afterward she insisted she needed space—that we buy a weekend retreat in the Poconos.

"I would have done anything to make her happy, to revert to happier days. To make a long story short, she was incapable of fidelity—used the retreat to entertain men indiscriminately. I'll always be grateful to my best friend Randall, who risked our friendship to tell me the truth. I'd trusted her—had no idea.

"I had a chance meeting with her doctor. Turns out she'd had an abortion and, because of the timing, it couldn't have been mine. I confronted her. She just laughed and called me a dinosaur. The lawyers wrapped up what never was. I'd tried to work at the marriage. Never did figure out where I failed." He fell silent.

"Some people just aren't meant to be together," she said. "Unfortunately, it isn't obvious at the time. Maybe people who live together first have the right idea, although that wasn't my family's way."

He nodded absently. "Yeah, mine either, but I was their champion for doing what was expected to hold up the standards. You know—oldest child, setting an example. Problem is, I'm comfortable with that role. Maybe dinosaur fits."

"May I ask you a question?" she asked solemnly.

"Sure."

"What were you intending to do with that bag of apples?"

Caught by surprise, he laughed so heartily that Pandora darted from under the couch and streaked down the hall.

"Pie, but the bakery sold out. I couldn't find the frozen shells in the grocery or the stuff that goes in it. This is as far as I got."

"Then we'll make one. Come on—you can peel while I make the pastry."

Over hot pie and Green Mountain coffee, she shared what she'd learned of the Wireless matter, omitting any details that screamed unprofessional. He listened intently. Although he offered no comment, his face took on a hardness that raised her guard.

"What's your plan?" he asked.

Her mind shot a replay of the Manning—Nathaniel—Jeffrey Johnston with the box episode and the angry fallout that followed. In spite of the evening's congeniality, she felt it was best to downplay her concerns. "I've concluded it's a

minor clerical error, which staff can correct. Chasing obscure details isn't what they pay me the big bucks to do.
You win—and that ends my involvement."

His easy smile relieved her enormously.

With that, the matter was dropped. He glanced at his
watch and then began picking up glasses and plates. "We'd
better beat up on your kitchen or you will be up half the
night."

"Everything will be thrown in the dishwasher before you
get home. Besides, you paid the cleanup detail in advance,
thanks to Pandora." She flecked a speck from his navy
suede-cloth shirt.

"If you're sure…"

"I insist." He put on his jacket, grinning. "Thank you.
This has been fun. You're a good sport and a very good
cook."

"I'm so glad you came. It's been too long time since I
entertained."

As he was leaving, he gave her arm a quick squeeze before descending the stairs. He turned once to wave.

Pandora crept from under a chair, meowing as she
brushed against Kingsley's leg. She stroked the poor kitten
and returned to the kitchen to find her a tidbit and finish the
wine.

"We've got to improve our ice breaking routine." She
grinned at her pet. "On second thought, we couldn't have
planned that any better."

⁃∽⌒∽⌒

Kingsley and Margaret munched sandwiches, perched on
the bank's fountain wall, backs absorbing the Indian summer sun. "How do I track down a company if both owner

and address are wrong in the system?" Briefly she told Margaret the story, omitting the part about searching Manning's office and the bet. Both, she felt, would be awkward to explain.

"There's a possibility you haven't considered. Suppose there is no such company?"

"There has to be. The account number is on our staff's summary sheet. Funds have been moved uneventfully, albeit in error, from one company's account to another."

Margaret shook her head. "I meant to say it's possible that the company exists only on paper. That the loan is bogus and the company fictitious."

"I don't see how that's possible. The way commercial loans work, the paperwork goes in two different directions, with checks and balances in place. I think it's a paperwork error."

"Can you get a look at the file?"

Kingsley caved, telling Margaret about Manning's box and nearly getting caught.

"You didn't!" Margaret laughed after digesting the information. She then became serious. "Why on earth would he keep a file under his desk except to hide it, if only temporarily? That's weird. If you truly suspect something bogus, you should ask our fraud or loan review department to get involved."

"What if I'm wrong? What if Manning's just sloppy or ran out of room on his desk? I've already caused him enough trouble. Making a false accusation could be a career-ending move for me."

"You're not meddling. You're conscientious. Do what you think is right. Just be careful. If I can help in any way, just let me know."

Throughout the week, no matter how late Kingsley worked, Manning stayed later.

Chapter 10

Frank dressed carefully in his custom tuxedo for his big evening, which had finally arrived. He admired his reflection in his black patent shoes and practiced his smile in the powder room mirror. He slipped on gold cuff links and his precious Rolex. When he caught sight of his wife, his smile faded.

Dolly was emptying the dishwasher in floor-length black crepe and stocking feet. Frank glared disapprovingly as she dragged the hem through the dog's water dish. "You're not going to wear those shoes," he said, pointing to the black pumps waiting in the corner.

"They're comfortable for dancing," Dolly justified meekly.

"In the first place, they're shot. Wear the black satin ones. Besides, I'll be too busy working the room."

Dolly closed the dishwasher door and tried to slip past him. Frank grabbed her arm. "Let me look at you. I've never liked those earrings. What's wrong with the diamonds I bought you?"

"These were Mother's. They bring me luck," she said of the gold four-leaf clovers with emerald-cluster centers.

He dismissed her with a hand wave and let her escape. "Hurry up or we'll be late," he called after her, reaching for his black dress raincoat. Rain threatened again, and he didn't want water to spot his satin lapels. "Not that coat," he scolded as Dolly reached for her London Fog. "Wear the fur."

"It's too warm. Besides, fur just isn't acceptable. The animal rights activists—"

"—weren't invited," Frank retorted. "Now remember. You know nothing about the bank or my business. Whoever we're sitting with, let them do the talking. What you say reflects upon me."

Frank never conceded that she had taught him the finer points of etiquette when he was still flipping burgers. She put on the fur.

৩৩৩

In the country club's ballroom, the elegant crowd mingled while servers butlered hors d'oeurves and drinks. When dinner was announced, bank officers distributed themselves among the town's gentry and board members. Frank eyed the tables set with fine china, crystal and vases that spilled minuette roses, freesia, lisianthus, baby's breath, and English ivy. Noting the lack of a head table, he hustled Dolly toward the most influential guests.

Finally, as they sipped coffee and cordials, Warren rose and tapped the mike, asking no one in particular, "Is it on?" The room became quiet. "This evening we honor Doug Neiman. This evening's for you, Doug. My thanks to the younger Neimans who sneaked in from California and kept their mouths shut."

After the chuckles subsided, Warren referred to his notes,

summarizing Doug's impressive accomplishments, his leadership at Keynote, the profits he'd nurtured, the value to the shareholders, and the community. Media photographers slinked into position while TV crews hugged recorders to their shoulders.

Frank passed his linen napkin over his brow. While he wouldn't begrudge Doug his moment of glory, he hoped this wouldn't go on forever. He fidgeted while community leaders shared anecdotes that brought gales of laughter and tears.

Cameras flashed. The head of the United Way presented him with a plaque with heart-felt compliments about making a difference. Reporters took notes on the press release and backgrounder that marketing had provided.

Finally, Warren, and Shirley presented a hand-made bentwood rocker that bore the bank's logo.

"We will be forever grateful to Doug for leaving the bank in good shape. It would dishonor him and our stakeholders if we didn't plan a smooth transition. Doug will help through December, after which we'll embark on a new era. Incidentally, Doug, I hope you can stand two more months of partying."

When the room quieted, Frank realized Warren was settling into his big announcement. Frank squirmed.

"At this time, it is my pleasure to announce Doug's successor. This is an important position because it's a succession slot, barring the unforeseen, to the chairmanship. This individual will have a seat on the board of directors. He also will stand in for me as the need arises. In case you hadn't noticed, I'm getting older too. I'd like to introduce that man who is no stranger to our town."

The photographers edged closer to the podium. Frank eyed them, hoping he could control his face. *Look perfect in print*. That he'd remember his humble yet stirring comments.

"A local bank needs local leadership. Someone who knows the culture, the community, its needs, and its customers. A person recognized in banking circles for his education, experience, and community service."

Frank smiled. Payoff time. Every word hung like a perfect, captive snowflake. But Warren mentioned Harvard University, followed by affiliations that Frank didn't have. The press would get it all wrong! He, the new president, would be humiliated by the idiot who downloaded the wrong bio sheet! How would he straighten that out?

While a dozen thoughts fought for space in his head, the name was announced. And it wasn't his!

"May I present William Todd Henning, III."

In total shock Frank looked up to see Todd approaching the podium to shake Warren's hand, a dozen strobes flashing. In the ensuing commotion, Frank bolted and disappeared.

After Warren's command to strike up the band, Dolly prayed she didn't look as pathetic and abandoned as she felt. She was relieved when Shirley Granger came over to chat, complimenting her on her Mother's cloverleaf earrings. Finally, Dolly spotted Frank motioning to her from the lobby. He was holding their coats.

She had never seen Frank quite that angry. As they rode home, every attempt at polite conversation only made matters worse. The subtle significance of quasi-business functions escaped her, yet she knew a lot was transacted between cocktails and dessert. Maybe that had gone badly.

Finally, when she commented about that nice young newcomer who would become the bank's next president, he yelled at her to shut up. She cowered, relieved when, upon entering their home, Frank strode into his study and slammed the door. Dolly slipped off to bed and, awakening at five, realized he hadn't been there. She tossed for another hour, thinking, and made a decision.

಼ఌ಼

Sunday morning, Kingsley scanned the *Philadelphia Inquirer*, followed by the local paper's business section. Stunned, she studied Todd's picture accompanying Keynote's announcement.

What a difference a week made! She thought of him on her bathroom floor, snipping Pandora's fur with her manicure scissors. He'd peeled apples for their pie, ate at her table, and let her glimpse his private failure.

A pang of regret, of letdown, of being a lonely outsider blindsided her.

Why couldn't he really be an ordinary guy? Soon he would hold the bank's most powerful position. Even a casual relationship would be suspect. Reigning in her emotions, she rationalized.

She wasn't looking for somebody special. Not now. Not yet. It was too soon. Besides, she was too conservative, too conflicted, too unaccustomed to fast, which a man like him would expect. Nevertheless, she left the paper with its photo exposed, glancing its way from time to time.

಼ఌ಼

Monday morning, Frank was lying in wait for Warren when he arrived.

"Morning, Frank. Great party Saturday night, wasn't it?

Doug was so touched." Warren was smiling, recollecting. "Pretty exciting news for the future of the bank, too, wouldn't you say?"

"How could you do this to me! That was my job, and you didn't even tell me. I was completely blindsided!"

"Frank, I thought you of all people would be pleased. With Doug leaving, my being so close to retirement, and global changes happening overnight in our industry—we need help if we're going to survive. We must consider all our stakeholders—shareholders, customers, our employees and their families, the community, the—"

"What about me? I've worked, slaved for this bank since I was a teenager—been here longer than anyone, even you. That was my job. I earned it. Nobody knows this bank better."

Warren stared at Frank and then at his hands. "You've done exceedingly well for the bank and yourself. Why, you're the third in command. That's pretty impressive. I thought you were happy with your job."

"Of course, but—"

"Frank." Warren took on a fatherly tone. "You've spent your entire career here, it's true. You do know this bank inside out. But that's one of your challenges at this point. People who stay in one place too long can acquire a colloquial perspective." He broadened his reference as if to dilute the sting. "We've become inbred, which can reinforce obsolete habits in the culture."

"But to bring in this…this kid…over me. It's humiliating. Everyone knew I was next in line. It looks like a demotion, a loss of confidence."

Warren smiled. "We are getting older, aren't we? When we were his age, we thought we were old. Our world has changed so dramatically. We need not only fresh ideas, but leaders who cut their teeth on technology or ran with open arms to embrace it. We need to work smarter."

"But I command excellent people who do all of that. Just look at the new vice president of technology. He can run circles around anyone we had previously. He was my recruit."

"He reports to you, right? Do you understand what he's doing?"

"I know that he understands. He has wonderful credentials. That's why we hired him."

"Do you know what initiatives to instruct him to undertake and how to evaluate the results? We need to lead top down, but we've allowed ourselves to become bottom up. We can't let the bank be run by middle management. The responsibility of the CEO and the board is to make global decisions and give global directions."

"And you think I can't do that? That this outsider can do it better?"

"Todd graduated at the top of his class, both in undergraduate and graduate school. He's been out there, learning from the big boys, yet he has hometown roots. The odds of our finding his unique qualifications were extremely small."

"You should have told me—"

Warren lowered his head. "I'm sorry, Frank. It didn't cross my mind that you'd be offended. I think of you as, well, anchored." He thought a minute before broaching another subject. "We have another challenge. Perhaps this is a good time to bring it up. The board members and Doug have some...issues...with your management style, which have nothing to do with Todd's appointment. Turnover is a concern. Our board members are hearing too many customer complaints about inexperienced employees. I'm puzzled myself. So many new faces, strangers manning our branches.

What's happened to our culture that we can't keep experienced employees? I've seen the numbers. It's costing us a fortune in inefficiency, recruiting, and training."

"I don't understand that reasoning—"

"And morale. It's lousy. Employees are scared, making mistakes because they're overworked, unappreciated, and distracted. I'm getting an earful from managers. Then there's the debit card. It took forever to put it in place."

"We had to recruit expertise, research it, select an outsource firm to run it, market it—"

"But I'd been bringing that up for years. You should have been pestering me about it. We were last in our territory to launch it, which cost us customers."

"So what is it you're trying to tell me?"

"I hadn't planned on having this discussion just now. We're going to be evaluating our products and services, do some tweaking in our organizational chart. We need to consider how best to maximize Todd's talents and utilize yours. We are initiating a search for a second EVP. Our growth simply demands that. And we'll proceed with what's best for the bank. Continue your current assignments until we make some decisions. There is, however, one thing you can do now. One of the comments that has surfaced entirely too often is that people are afraid of you. I'm sure they don't appreciate the level of your concentration or the weight on your shoulders. Perhaps you're preoccupied. Perception, unfortunately, is reality. So maybe you could, ah, lighten up a bit?"

Warren's secretary was making frantic motions from the doorway. "I'm sorry, Frank, but we're going to have to continue this some other time. I'm late for a meeting. Please accept my apology for my insensitivity on Saturday. You are an asset whom we wouldn't want to lose."

Frank retreated into his office. Lose him? Just what did that mean? For the first time in thirty years, he felt at risk. He'd better do something quickly. He picked up the phone and dialed Jeffrey's extension. "Have a minute? No, I'll be right down."

Frank stormed from the elevator, feeling everyone's eyes. *Damn*, he thought. *How can you control employees without fear?* Stalking into Jeffrey's office, he snapped the door shut.

Jeffrey looked up. "Saw the newspaper, Frank. Tough break."

"That plan we discussed two weeks ago about terminations? Scrap it."

"It's already done. I intended to call you, but you beat me to it. I had a directive from Shirley Granger. As head over HR, she was summoned to Warren's office. I'm to prepare a report about every employee who resigned or was terminated within the last year with a detailed explanation."

"What brought that on?"

"Remember the mentally challenged fellow who ran the copy center? He got his fourth straight Most Valuable Employee award in the employee balloting?"

"Yeah. We targeted him because he was making double what we could pay a high school dropout."

"Turns out his father was a major client who read Warren the riot act. Closed all his accounts and took some colleagues with him. Warren is furious. There's more, Frank. Shirley's departments may be reporting directly to Todd, not you, although that decision's not final."

"But no one knows branch administration better than I do. That's where I got my start."

"Shirley hasn't had any real clout, but that could change. However—" Jeff paused for effect. "I have something valu-

able for you, if you're interested in scoring fast points." He
motioned upstairs with his thumb and extracted an envelope
from his desk drawer. "Here, take a look at this. Our former
head of commercial lending, Fred Macmillan, suspected
something wasn't right about Manning Stoudt. He was right.
Seems Manning falsified his credentials."

Frank stared in disbelief at the papers in his hands.
"How'd you get this?"

"Used a PI named Miller who ran an ad in a soldier of
fortune magazine. He's very good. Absolutely discreet. My
consolation present to you, my friend. Do with it as you
wish."

For the first time since Saturday, Frank felt like smiling,
his fertile mind cranking possibilities. With the envelope
tucked under his arm, he strode through HR, smiling and
nodding pleasantly at puzzled staffers. *Regroup! Regain my
power*. Frank stabbed the elevator button six times before
the door managed to close. Once back in his office on Five,
he snapped his door shut and eased thoughtfully into his
custom leather chair, his blood pressure finally settling.

He ticked through his problems and rearranged their pri-
orities. Eliminating that Henning intruder could wait. That
would take thought, perhaps outside intervention. Capitaliz-
ing on Jeffrey Johnston's excellent information should be
implemented immediately. *I'll do it*, Frank thought, as the
flawless plan was born, fully grown. He returned to the elevator that whisked him to One.

Frank barged into the branch, having first noting that no
one was spying on him from the atrium garden. How that
silly man rose to be president and CEO of any bank con-
founded Frank.

He flopped uninvited into Branch Manager Connie Davis's guest chair to lay out part one of his plan. "You've

been selected for a special pilot project for our high-net-worth customers," he launched without a greeting or segue.

"Really! I appreciate—"

"These customers have better things to do than run errands. We want their relationship manager to do the running for them. We're keeping this new service very quiet because, if word gets out, our second-tier customers would be offended."

"I certainly appreciate that—"

Frank sliced her with a don't-interrupt-me glare, raising his voice slightly. "Here's an example: When we close a loan, the customers needn't come into the branch to sign for the business checking account. The account officer can get their signatures. By personally delivering the checkbook and debit card, the banker gets one more face-to-face contact and another opportunity to cross-sell them to other products, like CDs, insurance, et cetera. We'll assign one hand-picked teller as the point person."

"Certainly! I'd recommend—"

"I've chosen Juanita Rodriguez. Not only is her work excellent, but it also shows our commitment to promoting minorities. When the occasion arises, expediting these transactions will be her top priority."

"Is this a promotion for her?"

"It'll certainly be a plus on her record." Frank gave his tie a long, sensuous stroke as he smiled just a trifle.

Reptile, Connie thought, masking her disgust.

"I'll go over the details with her personally, although there are no new skills to learn. I just want her to be ready for action."

"And you say this is confidential?"

"Totally. Just you, Juanita, and myself, except, of course, for those executives who are tracking the experiment. I'll report to them personally. If this succeeds in expanding their business, we may broaden our definition of qualified customers. The service, however, will always be circumspect—never advertised."

Abruptly, he got to his feet and started to lope toward her door.

"Frank?"

He turned, impatience rising.

"High-end customers talk with each other. From non-profit boards to their wealth management people to their golf buddies—word gets around. People like them count on their peers' experiences and recommendations."

He batted his hand. "Not your concern."

"One more thing?"

He braked again, swiveling his head without making eye contact.

"I hesitate to ask this, but there have been rumors. What happens to this special project if Todd Henning is put in charge of branch administration's chain of command? Should I talk to him?"

Frank jerked, scowled, his face heating, then checked himself with a patronizing smile. "That rumor is wrong. You'll work directly with me." His voice softened slightly. "And remember—we wouldn't want the executive leadership to think you've gone chatty. Your professionalism will be noted as 'executive assistance above and beyond' on your permanent record."

She smiled involuntarily. "That's nice, but I'm not in line for a promotion. I'm topped out of my salary range unless, of course, there's a promotion or new position."

"Just between you and me, a new cluster manager position is being created that will include this main branch and two others. I'm only too happy to compensate employees who play ball—that is cooperate—with me. You know, for the added work and responsibility."

"I would appreciate your recommendation. Sir?" she called after his exiting back. He turned. "I'll shepherd your elite private banking service as you described."

The minute Frank disappeared through the atrium, Connie clapped once, grinning foolishly. Cluster manager? That hefty raise would pay for her pool.

Later that day, Frank met Juanita in a remote back-office conference room. The diminutive teller appeared to be awed and flattered by the assignment from the executive vice president. Frank studied her—so lovely, with soft brown curls, deep-set black eyes and flawless Castilian complexion. She was just the right blend of professionalism and subservience that customers with entitlement issues demanded. And she seemed to grasp her assignment intuitively. Frank returned to his office to set the wheels in motion.

♥ॐ♥ॐ

Connie welcomed Warren Kramer in from the atrium garden where he'd been watching for twenty minutes. He paused at her doorway, hands folded, waiting politely for an invitation to enter. "Just touching bases. Anything you'd like me to know?" the chairman asked.

"I appreciate Frank's special interest in our branch. Having someone who really, really understands branch banking makes our jobs so much more productive." She avoided the corporately incorrect easier. "He takes special interest in our tellers' challenges. Don't you think that's unusual for someone in his position?"

"Such as—"

"When we extended our hours, he predicted that some

part-time employees would prefer working three to seven. We polled our employees to learn who would be interested in those hours. Sure enough, by taking that slot, those who had spouses who worked first shift didn't need baby-sitters."

"I didn't know that." Warren nodded slowly, elbows on chair arms, mouth resting on his steeple-like fingers. "I appreciate you input, Connie. You've just helped me make a difficult decision."

Deep in thought, he rose, nodded to the teller line, and disappeared past the atrium garden. Connie made a mental note to repeat this conversation to Frank. Perhaps she could also afford a vacation.

Chapter 11

H e's taking a personal day," someone volunteered to Kingsley's casual inquiry about Manning's dark office. As Wednesday wore on, Wireless prayed on her mind. At last, one by one, offices darkened.

"Anyone still here?" a voice called.

"I am," Kingsley answered.

"Turn off the photocopier and coffee pot when you leave."

"Will do. Good night." Alone, she gave it more time. Next she checked the opposite half of the building. Even that was deserted. Opportunity beckoned.

Without turning on Manning's light, she pulled back his chair and looked for the box. It was gone. Carefully, she rummaged through his desk drawers followed by his credenza. Nothing.

Then a plain gray box, stashed in a shadowy corner, caught her eye. Inside, she found the Wireless file. Tucking the file under her arm, she hurried toward the copy room.

She placed the Wireless file on the floor beside an empty legal file folder. Because of the papers' varying sizes, she was forced to insert the pages manually, rather than use the faster batch feed, which might jam the pages. As soon as the light scanned, she snatched the original, inserted another and grabbed the copy, taking no time to read, but concentrating instead on perfecting her rhythm.

Once finished, she straightened the originals, placing the Wireless file inside the larger folder that now also held her copies. She snapped off the light and was about to leave when she heard the elevator doors. She froze. *Just wait*, her startled senses whispered.

Could it be Manning? Had she remembered to turn off her light? She was sure that she had. She'd even taken the precaution of taking her briefcase and coat to her car, keeping only her keys. Her mind raced annoyingly. *Stop! Get a grip!* Hidden by darkness, she heard Manning's voice.

"Someone left on the lights and the coffee pot is on."

Damn, she thought. A long pause followed.

"Nobody's here."

A second man said something she couldn't make out. Peering out as the footsteps retreated, she saw Manning's light flicker across the tall cubicles. How long could they talk? Should she sneak out? If she did, she couldn't return the Wireless file. What if he found it was missing? Wait. Better wait.

Kingsley strained to hear their conversation, but couldn't make out any words until the second man's tones became ugly and threatening. As civility degenerated, she picked out some words. Cooperate. Fraud. Prison. Had Manning been caught, or had he caught someone?

"Not an option, you idiot. You'll take the fall alone since there's no evidence to implicate me. Just do as you're told."

Kingsley shrank into the copy room's interior.

The voices began moving, the footsteps returning back toward to the elevator.

Don't breathe, she thought. *They'll be gone in a minute.*

But the footsteps passed the elevator, rounded the corner, and headed her way. She'd be discovered unless she found a quick hiding place. She'd overheard them. They'd know!

She looked frantically around the dim room. The photocopier only cleared the wall by six inches and the adjacent wall held open bookshelves. Piles of unshelved duplicator paper weren't high enough to conceal her. As the two men drew closer, she panicked, then noticed the metal cabinets against the front wall. Ever so quietly, she tried the door and peeked in. Empty! She squeezed in and eased the door shut.

Within seconds, the light snapped on. Shafts blinked through the cracks as two figures walked back and forth. Legs—all she could make out was banker slacks. The photocopier's lid lifted, closed, the machine whirred and the unidentified voice said, "I need this," and "no, not that one."

Kingsley didn't dare breathe. They were making multiple copies of—what?

She began to feel sweaty. Could they smell her body lotion? Her hair spray? Know someone was there? Trying to stay calm, she distracted herself, counting the times they hit the start button. Five, twenty, sixty-five, ninety-four.

"Damn thing's out of paper."

"Hit this button here." The paper carrier elevatored down and opened. She heard paper rip, something go thunk, followed by the apparatus engaging, moving back to position. One hundred five, one-twenty, four more, and—it stopped. Finally they snapped off the light.

She remained motionless, ears straining, until she heard the elevator door close, taking both voices with it. When the elevator did not return, she dragged her cramped body from its hiding place, still hugging the folders. She stole through the darkness and replaced the file in its box, which hadn't been moved. Stealthily, she slipped down the back stairwell.

Through the cracked exterior door she saw no one. With a rush of relief, she hurried toward her car, drained, her mouth parched. The crisp autumn air quickly chilled her damp body. Locking herself in her car, her eyes swept the lot. It was deserted.

Once home, Pandora punished her with reproachful eyes.

"Poor neglected baby," Kingsley cooed, scooping her up. "Will a gourmet treat and spring water appease you?" Leaving Pandora to relish her supper, she dumped her rumpled suit on the dry cleaning pile. She decompressed in a hot shower; food could wait. All she wanted was a tumbler of wine and a peek at the papers.

On the dining room table, she reassembled the file. Wireless Inc.'s mailing address and its owner were as she remembered. The documents appeared to be legitimate. There was a financial statement including balance, income and expense sheets, a projected income sheet, collateral analysis, and a credit report.

The bank's forms for the loan approval and credit write up were included and signed by Manning Stoudt. The amount of the loan, $200,000, was within his $500,000 lending authority.

Other documents, including the note, security and loan agreements, and financing statements looked fine. She concluded, with disappointment, that there was nothing unusual.

As she turned the last page, she found something odd, a plain sheet of white paper listing nine eight-digit numbers, each followed by 500000. Looking closely, she realized they were dark blue and not from the black-ink photocopy machine. Also the paper was slightly different. Could she have put her copy in his file? She panicked and quickly re-examined each photocopy, praying he wouldn't notice one single discrepancy. She looked at the numbers again. Something clicked. Account numbers—that's what they were.

She tore a slip from her grocery tablet, onto which she copied them to check against central file in the morning. Then she hid the page of blue numbers. Pandora jumped onto her lap. "If you'd lend me one of your lives, I could risk returning this to Manning."

Pandora stretched close to her face, nuzzling her with fishy lips, Kingsley's sins having been forgiven.

"What did I hear and, more to the point, what should I do about it? Maybe I misunderstood. Maybe it's none of my business. Whom can I trust?"

Pandora just yawned and curled up on her lap.

⁌⁌⁌

Kingsley opened her eyes the next morning to bright sunlight and jumped out of bed. Seven thirty! She should be at work. She dressed hastily, shoved yesterday's mail into her briefcase, and dashed out the door.

Halfway downstairs, her security alarm screamed. After fumbling with locks, she killed the racket, and phoned the security company. Sitting on her haunches, looking quite innocent, was Pandora, having set off the motion detectors.

Kingsley eyed the panel and realized she needed remedial training to set windows and doors without the motion detectors. Against her will, but having no choice already being late, she locked her door again without resetting the alarm and raced to her car.

It wasn't until late afternoon that she went through the mail. Between the phone bill and a cousin's postcard was a letter from her family's attorney. She read and reread David Wentworth's letter detailing the settlement proposal from the heating oil company. It would net seven figures. All that would be left of that exquisite man was cash and memories.

She remembered what his advisor had said on his graduation day from medical school: "Good luck, kid. Go save the world." She stared at the figure. What would Andy say?

She tried to conjure his opinion and hadn't a clue. She reached for a tissue and blotted her eyes.

"Is it that bad?"

Kingsley looked up and saw Todd in her doorway, wearing a black suit and a sympathetic face. He could have just come from the funeral.

"What are you doing here?" Instantly she regretted her harsh tone and rude choice of words. "I'm sorry."

"I have a meeting with Nathaniel in a few minutes, but I'm early. Thought I'd stop by and see how things are going."

"Do sit down, please."

"Anything you'd like to talk about confidentially?"

"I shouldn't have brought my personal mail to the office. There's a letter from my family's attorney. Accepting the settlement money feels so obscene. What am I supposed to do? Blow off my job? Shop? Travel? Engage in riotous living?" She folded the papers with shaking hands.

"If he were alive and could do anything with it, what would it be?"

"I've been trying to imagine. He didn't have debts. His parents are wealthy and lack for nothing. Andy chose ophthalmology because he wanted to help people who didn't have access to eye care. As a kid, he used to collect old eyeglasses for Lions International. The Lions send them to developing countries. His goal was to help people who might not otherwise be treated. He even dreamed of opening a free clinic. Now it won't happen."

"You could make part of that dream come true."

"How?"

"Instead of accepting the money outright, you could set up a trust or foundation in his memory. Our trust department handles that sort of thing. Use the income for scholarships for deserving students who share his dream. Or help underwrite the cost of the Lions program. I'm sure that costs plenty."

Kingsley looked up at him. "You're right. The only thing that makes sense is to put it to work."

"You'll need to talk to your accountant. With proper planning, you can prevent Uncle Sam from taking too big a bite."

"It's a lot of money. I want to use it properly." She handed the letter to Todd, who read it and handed it back. If he'd whistled or said anything flip, she'd have been disappointed, but he did neither. "You're a good person. Thank you." She smiled appreciatively at him and glanced at her watch. "Nathaniel's probably back, and I've detained you."

"Kingsley? It will get better, but you've got to give yourself time. Meanwhile, you have the resources and confidentiality of the bank at your disposal. If I can help, let me know."

After he left, she decided to call David's office to put it in motion. First, she stopped to speak with Nathaniel's secretary. "I hope Todd wasn't late for his meeting. I'm afraid I held him up."

"What meeting?" She frowned, flipping through her calendar pages. "Nope. Nathaniel's in Boston, and Todd didn't stop."

"I must have misunderstood."

☙❧

Kingsley closed her office door, punched nine for an outside line, and dialed her godfather's number. "Uncle David? I'm looking at the check. It's huge! An excellent plan to honor Andy was brought to my attention. I'd like to get your reaction when there's more time. I'm not very objective when it comes to Andy."

"Of course, dear. I'm at your service."

"Something else. Now that I've calmed down, did I hear you correctly? Would you please repeat what the police said about an eyewitness to Andy's accident?"

His sigh kindled her apprehension. "Well, ah, all right, for what it's worth. A man who identified himself as a salesman from Virginia told Philadelphia police that he'd been wrestling with his conscience for months. He'd been making a loop through the northeast, homebound on one particularly stormy fall evening. He thought he saw a car push another car into the path of an oncoming fuel oil truck at the top of an on-ramp. He said that the driver made a U-turn on the ramp and sped away just before a fireball exploded on the overpass.

"The caller said that he had convinced himself that what he witnessed was an illusion caused by lack of sleep, poor visibility, disjointed concentration, and so on. Several weeks later he was driving on that same four-lane again. Construction on both sides of the highway had reduced traffic to single lanes. He realized it was the same location where he'd seen the accident. He was shocked to see that the traffic jam was caused by construction of a new overpass.

"He searched the Internet for accident reports, and that yielded the details of your husband's death. He found no mention of a second car or a police investigation into the matter. It was unclear who was at fault because there were no witnesses, and neither driver survived. It had been stormy, late, a Sunday—there must have been a break in the traffic because the witness didn't remember seeing any other cars." David cleared his throat. "Kingsley, the police have some questions if you would be willing to talk with them."

"I don't know what I could tell them, but okay. Do you have a name and a number?" She jotted it down, and they disconnected with promises to touch base.

Kingsley rolled back from her desk, swiveled her chair and studied fall's progression beyond her floor-to-ceiling window walls. The glorious reds, vibrant oranges, electric yellows, and brilliant burgundies were fading, leaves trickling in the windless air like tiny parachutes. In their absence, elegant mature hemlocks and white pines took center stage.

She identified river birches by their ruffled bark, visible for the first time. She rose, paced a small circle, then resettled into her chair. She scolded herself to relax. Following up on crank calls was routine police procedure. She reached for the phone.

That the police were eager to interview Kingsley was underscored by the offer to drive from Philadelphia at her convenience. At six p.m. that evening, Kingsley heard heavy footsteps ascending the stairs to her apartment. Pandora lifted her head, froze, bolted into the bedroom, and tore under the bed.

Kingsley opened the door.

A slender man, no more than five nine, introduced himself while holding a gold shield for her inspection. Even though she had no idea what his ID should resemble, she liked that his face looked sincere, tired, and sympathetic. "Come in," she said, motioning him through the vestibule and toward the living room.

He smiled, as if remembering a familiar joke. "Interesting setup—kitchen, then living room, and then dining room beyond it."

She relaxed. "How would you ferry the turkey past the living room to that back corner?"

"I'd drop the damned thing halfway onto the carpet." His face sobered. "Thank you for seeing me. Did your attorney fill you in?"

"As well as he could. He probably told you that he's a civil attorney. Our association is personal. Besides being my father's best friend, he's my godfather. He takes that very seriously."

He nodded. "Without wasting your time, let's get to it."

She motioned for him to sit on the couch, and she sat in her angled channel-back chair. He placed a manila folder on the coffee table from which he withdrew a grainy five-by-seven-inch black and white photo of man's face. "Have you ever seen this man before?"

She looked, squinting at a grainy wash of black, gray, and dirty white pixels of a man's profile. "Is that the man who called you?"

"No. This man may be unrelated to your husband's accident. Please. Take a close look. Do you recognize him?"

She shook her head without answering and shrugged. "I don't understand—"

The detective explained what a motorist believed that he saw on the ramp, emphasizing the word *believed*. And that he'd seen a car matching that description at the nearest truck stop. "A surveillance camera mounted behind the gas pumps captured this photo of a man in the background. He was approaching a car that resembled the eye witness's description."

Kingsley looked at the photo again. "He could be anybody. The picture's so dark, and too blurry, in fact, to notice any distinguishing features." A thought occurred to her. "Why would they still have surveillance footage after all this time? I thought places like that reused them every, what—twenty-four hours?"

"Got lucky. A batch of them, destined to be replaced, were pitched into a box that ended up on a shelf instead of in the trash. The owner's off-site. Employees didn't know who had the authority to pitch which stuff. So there it sat." He put the photo away. "Mrs. Ward, did your husband have any enemies?"

She smiled, in spite of herself. "Of course not. Andy was a kind, gentle soul bent on saving the eyesight of impover-ished people. His entire life had been rather...what's the word for it?...Reclusive? Passive? Circumspect? He's the last person in the world to tick anyone off."

"Did he have any bad habits? Gambling, for instance?"

"No. Never. We went to the casinos once and, after fif-teen minutes, he said he'd seen enough and we left. His idea of gambling was investing in the stock market, and even that made him nervous. He let his father's investment coun-selors choose conservative mutual funds for him."

"Did he owe anyone money?"

"No. His folks are old money, and his father owns a thriving medical practice. He comes from a culture that gives money away. But he is—was—very frugal. Believed in living on current income. Didn't touch his trust fund, ex-cept for his college tuition, for which it was intended."

"Who would benefit from his death?"

"I can think of who won't—the patients he'll never cure. The causes he'll never champion. The expenses he'll never cover—"

"That's not what I meant. He won...if that's the right

word…a prestigious fellowship that, as one person phrased it, was a career-maker."

Kingsley bristled. "He did not need a career-maker. Not with his grades, class standing, and community service. I have his transcripts, vitae, and certificates of appreciation right here in a box if you'd care to see them."

"Let me rephrase. And I don't mean to sound flip, but what lesser mortal will benefit by now receiving Dr. Ward's fellowship?"

"I haven't followed his former colleagues, so I haven't a clue."

"Did he say, before leaving your apartment, that he was going to meet anyone?"

"He was just going to fill the gas tank and buy ice cream." *Buttered almond, his favorite.* Chocolate was hers, but the detective wouldn't be interested—

"Why do you suppose he was on that exit ramp? Aren't the nearest convenience store and gas station located before you come to the highway? Isn't it close to your complex? Why do you suppose he'd been on the highway?"

She shrugged. "Maybe he just wanted to take a drive, clear his head. He had been rather withdrawn. A volunteer trip to a third-world country left him depressed. I think he felt overwhelmed."

The detective rose and handed her his card. *Just like TV,* she thought. *And now he'll say…*

"Ms. Ward, if you think of anything else, please give me a call. Thank you for seeing me." He started to walk toward the door.

"Wait a minute! Detective, what do you think happened? You wouldn't come all the way from Philadelphia months later if you didn't think that salesman's call was significant."

"Just following up."

As he turned back to the door, Kingsley could have sworn he looked troubled, as if she'd verified the salesman's account. *But of what?*

Chapter 12

The next day, Kingsley could not drag her concentration back to her work. Instead she kept staring at the check. No matter how many times she scrutinized it, the number didn't change. She thought of the detective. Who would benefit from Andy's death? A: another deserving candidate for Andy's fellowship, or B: a disgruntled loser who hoped to capitalize or get revenge. The latter was ridiculous, although she could research both possibilities from the same source.

She left work early enough to get home before five. She entered her apartment, dropping her briefcase in the foyer, and hurried into her study. Four-thirty—she was in time. From the far reaches of the closet floor, she dragged the archive box that contained the contents of Andy's desk. She'd not had the heart to examine it earlier, but now—

Among two dozen file folders she found the one neatly labeled in his hand: *Fellowship*. Copies of his application, supporting material, and the award letter were stapled in chronological order. On top, as she hoped, was the name and contact information for the trustee who had announced his award.

She dialed. The soft-spoken gentleman who picked up on two rings turned out to be the benefactor himself.

"Kingsley, how nice to hear from you. We are all so terribly sorry about your loss. Your husband was a fine man who is greatly missed. How are you doing? And what can I do for you?"

"I know how busy you must be, but if you have a few minutes I could use your advice. I'd like to set up a trust in Andy's name. But how could I screen worthy candidates?"

"I can tell you how we do it. We are a private foundation that is well known in our extremely narrow sphere. Potential candidates send us a letter. We send them our guidelines, an application form, and a list of relevant documentation to accompany their submissions. Our volunteer committee that represents a cross-section from our field reviews qualified applicants' vitae, puts them in some semblance of order, and conducts interviews. I'd be happy to send you blank copies of our forms." He chuckled. "You're welcome to steal our ideas."

"Thank you. Please do. That would be very helpful. You said you're private foundation?"

"That's how we're incorporated. A private foundation, such as a family trust, is taxed at a much higher rate than a public foundation. An option for you is to donate your funds to the latter as, say, the Andrew Ward Jr. Fund of the XYZ Community Foundation. If they agree, you could serve on a committee to review the candidates. The downside is that you wouldn't have control over who gets the grant. We deal with the taxes by making sure that, beyond operating expenses, we donate one-hundred percent of our net investment income to our Fellows. It's our practice to keep those expenses to thirty percent or less. That's the gold standard for 501(c)3 not-for-profits. Last year we donated ninety percent. A good CPA could help you navigate your options."

"I'll do that. By the way, may I ask who received the fellowship in Andy's place? I'd like to send a personal note of congratulations and well wishes. I'd hate to have a promising young doctor feel that 'there by the grace of God...' Mention that Andy himself would wish them well."

"I'd be happy to get in touch with our Fellow, although I'll need her permission to give you her contact information."

"Her?" Kingsley smiled. "I like that. So, was she the runner up?"

"Let's see." From the sound, the doctor was thumbing through pages, occasionally licking his finger or thumb. He must be looking at forms like those in Andy's folder. "Actually, just between us, she was our fifth choice. There was a problem with number two. Given the passage of time, number three joined the military, and number four embarked on a PhD path in genetic research."

"Without disclosing her name, can you tell me a little about her?"

"Give me a second—ah, here's the committee's summary. 'An outstanding candidate.' Her combined grades weren't like Andrew's—I'd never seen anything like his before. I suppose you know he never got a B in his life—but she'd worked twenty hours a week throughout undergraduate and medical school. Still came out near the top of her class. It goes on, 'Her passion for macular degeneration dove-tailed nicely with our interests.' She'd amassed huge student-loan debts. She had a single working-class parent—you get the picture."

"And the runner up?" The doctor paused so long that Kingsley thought she'd lost the connection. "Hello?"

"I'm sorry. I was just thinking about what I could legally say."

"That's okay. I didn't mean to put you on the spot. I was thinking I might consider him as a candidate myself."

"No! You don't want to go there. That is, um—can I absolutely count on your discretion?"

Kingsley rose from her desk chair, nerves tingling. "Yes. Absolutely."

"After Andrew received the Fellowship, I had a blunt letter from this applicant's father's attorney that bordered on threatening to sue. I fluffed our declination letter, normally sent to unqualified applicants, detailing the qualities of the chosen candidate, but without naming Andrew. Number two came up short, although I didn't say that. An idiot could have read between the lines by reading about this year's Fellow. I thought that was the end of it."

"It wasn't?"

"After Andrew's death, Number Two made an appointment, supposedly to pitch his case again. I made a decision to not hold a worthy candidate responsible for his father's bad behavior. He showed up with his father and attorney in tow. It quickly became apparent that this was the father's cause. The son oozed spoiled brat. When I started suggesting alternative programs, the father got defensive and then downright nasty."

"What was the attorney doing all this time?"

The doctor snorted. "He was as cowed as the kid. Kid? At twenty-six, the candidate, a recent med school graduate, had been an adult—supposedly—for eight years. Every time the father raised his voice, the attorney touched his client's sleeve and said soothingly, 'Sid, calm down.' Or, 'Now, Sid.' I finally suggested they leave."

"I'd still like to meet the son. He might benefit enormously if he could disengage from the father."

Kingsley waited, accustomed as she had become to his long thoughtful moments. "It's against my better judgment..." A long pause. "But if there's a risk that your path might intersect with this obnoxious family..." Pause.

"I promise, I'll never quote you."

"The father's name is Sidney Paul. Son is Thomas. Thomas S., probably for his father."

Kingsley eased the conversation to a close after leaving her contact information to receive the proffered application forms, should she adopt them for Andy's trust. "Thank you so much for your help," she added, promising to keep in touch.

She disconnected. Hurrying into the living room, she opened the drawer where she'd dropped the detective's card. She dialed the cellphone number he'd added. After five rings, it went to voice. Disconnecting without leaving a message, she redialed five minutes later. That time he picked up immediately.

"Detective? You asked who might benefit from my husband's death. This is a long shot—and please don't quote me—one Thomas S. Paul's father was angry when his son was turned down—twice—for Andy's fellowship."

"Ms. Ward, we questioned Thomas in the presence of his father and their attorney. Father and son were in Manhattan for a Broadway performance with several other people the night your husband died."

She sighed. "I thought I had something."

"Thanks anyway. But if anything else occurs to you..."

഻

Sarah Alderson sat perched on her long-legged stool,

adding a few lines to her sketch as Pesto, who had curled near her feet, roused, stretched, and lifted adoring eyes to his mistress. Getting impatient, he started meowing nonstop. Sarah let her moccasin drop to gently rub his head with her toe. He stretched to meet her, knowing if he sprang onto her lap, he would be banished.

Sunshine streamed through Sarah's east-facing wall of patio doors. Those to the south and west overlooked flagstones that fronted her English garden, back dropped by woods. She spent hours cultivating her soul-feeding gardens, which now were spectacular as hemlocks, hollies, and mums replaced their deciduous brethren for attention.

Sarah's specialty—garden flowers in water colors and oil—adorned her line of greeting cards, stationery, and accessories, which were sold in specialty shops throughout the Northeast. Pesto frequently peeked from the roses and hydrangeas.

"I still think an anniversary service sounds like another funeral," Henry said as he entered her studio.

"You can't really blame the Wards. They're deeply religious," Sarah said, picking up where they'd left off at breakfast. "Imagine how we'd feel if we lost Kingsley."

"Losing their son is an unending heartache, but Kingsley has to move on. She sounds very happy with her new job and apartment. There's that familiar lilt in her voice that's been missing so long. And aren't we hearing a lot of new names?"

"She told me she did plan to attend." Sarah got down from her stool, filled a two-gallon can, and began watering the potted plants by the patio doors. He waited.

"Henry, all her life she's been soft-hearted and kind. She'll attend if she thinks it will help the Wards, regardless of whether it's painful."

"We'll go, but—"

"If you're so opposed, you talk to her."

"I'll see if I can stop by for dinner." He paused for a minute to admire Sarah's work, then wandered upstairs to his library's solace. *A visit alone without Sarah*, he thought. *That Wireless matter needs exploring. What has she unearthed?*

He'd know better if he could study her face, see what she wasn't saying. And they would discuss the Wards. She was a great cook and would whip up something special for him. He made the call.

⌔⌖⌔

"I've decided to go," Kingsley told her father while putting the finishing touches on dinner. "But not for the reasons you think. I'm expending far too much energy fabricating excuses and feeling guilty. Besides, I have to consider their feelings."

"Your mother's not going to like that."

"Tell her it's just for this year. Closure. If it becomes a yearly tradition, I'll visit some other time. I couldn't have asked for nicer in-laws. Attending is the least I can do."

Henry considered his daughter's aura, hoping she had dislodged herself from that frozen, dark place in her mind. It had been rough and raw with jagged lurches. But she'd made a wise decision, much as he'd hated her relocation. His eyes swept her space, which was cozier, more like her and less like Andy. He smiled at his daughter.

"This is Basmati rice," she said. "A friend's teaching me to cook Indian. After you try it, you'll never want to eat instant rice again. First, you sauté cumin, cardamom, cinnamon, bay leaf, and mustard seed in oil. You add the rice and water and then boil it until wells form. Ah, there, see the wells? Now smell it—rather like popcorn, wouldn't you say? Now we reduce the heat, cover and simmer it for ten minutes. Perfect."

In between watching the rice, she kept an eye on lemon salmon cooking on the George Foreman grill. "Toss the salad for me, will you? Dressing's in the door of the fridge. Pick something you like. And open the wine—the white—behind the juice. Here's the corkscrew."

"Yes, ma'am."

Kingsley turned up the stereo and danced from hall to sink, giving her father a spin en route. After they sat down, he steered the conversation from banking in general to hers in particular, edging closer to the topic of interest. "Tell me about this Manning Stoudt person," he said.

Much to his delight, she cut to the chase. "The paperwork's in order, but the situation doesn't make sense." She told him what she'd seen in the file, including the list of blue numbers, but left out how she had found it.

"If you're suspicious, why don't you tell your supervisor?"

"I got Manning into trouble for a routine error that shouldn't have caused a big flap. I don't want to be responsible for getting him fired. And I don't know Nathaniel well enough to understand what drives him.

Henry scowled. "Sounds like Nathaniel over-reacted."

"On the other hand, it's possible that the loan is fraudulent. I have to be very sure."

"Why don't you turn it over to your internal controls?"

"Dad, I overheard a conversation between Manning and another man who's also involved."

"Who is he?"

"That's just it. I didn't see him or recognize his voice. It could be anyone in the organization, even someone from loan review."

"Keep your ears open. Hearing that voice may give you direction. But, honey, leave the sleuthing to the professionals, okay?"

"I hear you, Dad. I'll be careful."

෴

Kingsley entered the blue list's numbers into lending's database and, one by one, a corresponding loan appeared. All were recently booked by Manning and all for $500,000. Of course, she thought, grasping what 500000 meant. There was nothing unusual, although none showed any recent activity. The companies, their principals, and addresses had nothing in common from their locations to the nature of business.

At ten, Margaret popped into Kingsley's office. "Are you coming? We'll be late."

Kingsley pulled herself back to reality. "For what?"

"Officer's meeting. Starts in five minutes.

"That's Thursday.

"This is Thursday."

Jumping from her chair, Kingsley grabbed her portfolio and a pen.

"Take the stairs," Margaret said, steering her. "The elevator will be swamped."

They emerged in the lower level, a vast open space of composition tile floors, beige walls, and an acoustical drop ceiling. Suspended from metal tracks, colorful marketing posters displayed the latest promotions and advertised an upcoming blood drive. Two hundred folding chairs faced a makeshift stage.

"Over here." Barrie waved to Kingsley and Margaret as Warren and Doug took their places on stage.

Warren welcomed them, thanked them for their hard work, and then introduced the new officers, starting with Todd and working his way through the chain of command. After a typical state of the bank summary, Warren beckoned to the controller, who expounded on charts, graphs, and tiny figures that covered twelve pages they'd found on their chairs.

Doug reported on the bank's progress during the first three quarters. Kingsley noticed many officers' vacant stares, as this report was old stuff. Even she, a six-week veteran, knew most of it. Division heads took turns, all of whom talked much too long. Margaret tapped her watch and Barrie crossed and recrossed her legs.

After the meeting finally wrapped up, senior officers dragged chairs and regrouped for informal meetings. A large group from Five, including senior officers from off-campus locations, headed collectively behind a white fabric screen. As Kingsley passed toward the elevators, someone's voice stopped her cold. That was it! The way he pronounced his vowels, the slur, like his tongue was too big for his mouth.

Motioning to Margaret and Barrie, she whispered, "Who's that talking?"

The girls listened, unable to distinguish one voice from another over the din. There was no way to circle the screen without crashing a high-level executive meeting. The exiting crowd forced them to keep moving downstream or be trampled.

At lunchtime, Kingsley ransacked lending's central file for the folders that corresponded with the blue list's numbers. Not finding the first, she looked for the second, and

then the third. Halfway through, she suspected she wouldn't
find any. And she was right.

Looking over the cabinets and cubicles, she could see
Manning's office was dark. "He in?" she asked the administrative assistant whom he shared with two other junior officers. She looked up and groaned.

"Don't I wish."

"Why? What's up?"

"That guy's driving me nuts. He's booking loans right
and left. Makes customer calls all day, pops in and out
without sharing his schedule. He comes in at night and
works till all hours. Next morning, there's this humongous
pile in my in-box, plus my regular work. Like I'm his private secretary. I did not just say that." She sighed in annoy-
ance and looked up at Kingsley. "Can I do something for
you?"

"Just had a quick question for him. Any idea when he'll
be back?"

"You can catch him tomorrow. I can tell him you're
looking for him when he phones in."

"No! Don't do that! I mean, I have other ways to get the
same information. By the way—does he work on the week-
ends?"

"No, thank goodness. If he did, Mondays wouldn't be
worth living."

Thanking her, Kingsley returned to her office to think.
She had searched Manning's office for the Wireless file after the new account numbers were entered into the system,
yet she couldn't recall seeing those files anywhere. She had
to find them.

Chapter 13

Dolly unlocked her back door and lunged for the phone.

"Mrs. Ziegler? This is James Martin, your new trust officer. I'm sorry to bother you. Are you well enough to talk with me for a minute?"

"Why, yes, of course."

"Your husband said when I called previously that you weren't well and should not be disturbed. He said he handled the family business and to use his bank number. That he'd pass along anything you needed to know."

"I haven't been ill. Are you sure it was Frank you spoke to?"

"Why, ah, yes."

"I don't understand why he'd say that."

A lengthy pause followed.

"Perhaps I should start over. I'd like to meet you personally to review the details of the trust fund your parents set up for you. I could come to your home or—"

"No! You can't do that! I mean, do you have an office?"

"Yes, of course. I'll give you directions."

That afternoon, James Martin met Dolly in a private conference room. The trust officer wasted no time to get to the point. "What I've found that's unusual is there's no record of any direct dealings with you." He motioned to several bulging accordion folders on the table. "A dozen trust officers have handled your account since your parents' death, and three bank mergers exasperated that."

"It's ironic that you should call me today. I need to figure out if I can afford to live on my own. That is, if it comes to that."

James stared at Dolly, who was fingering the trim on her shabby suit's cuff. "Ma'am, I don't know what your lifestyle requires, but you're a wealthy woman."

Dolly's eyes shot up. "I wouldn't call $2,000 a month allowance wealthy."

"That's not entirely correct. You're also entitled to the earnings from this trust plus two percent of the principal if you need it. Didn't you know that?"

Dolly gulped. "How much is the principal?"

"Six million dollars."

Dolly gasped, hyperventilating, blood draining from her face.

James jumped to his feet and called for someone to get her some water.

"I—I don't understand," Dolly stammered, her hands shaking so violently that a small wave of water splashed onto her skirt. "It's such a shock. Are you sure? Are you positive? How do I access the money?"

"I recommend that you deal directly with us, rather than having our bank send papers home for your signature as my predecessors did."

"I don't remember signing anything. Wait. Frank hands me a pen and say something like, 'Tax return. Sign here.'"

"The trust also handles your taxes, household expenses,

and more. Are you sure you never saw these?" He pulled samples from the huge pile. "Real estate taxes, personal property taxes, electricity, gas, sewer—"

"Wait a minute!" Dolly got to her feet and leaned over the table. "That can't be right. Frank rants about the great sums he pays."

"Look at them, Mrs. Ziegler. Please."

Dolly riffled, identifying their new slate roof and the wrap-around porch on their Victorian mansion, the sand blasting and repointing of their brick, and interior renovations. All of that, she knew, Frank said he had paid. In fact, he'd pitched quite a fit. "But how?"

"How are the bills paid? Recurring expenses, like the taxes and utilities, come directly here. Everything else is forwarded to your husband." Dolly tried to think of bills that were missing, but everything was there. "Maybe we should look at your children's file."

She peered, fearfully, as if the papers might bite her, at a time capsule of her children's lives—dance lessons and football camp, private schools, and college. Frank had claimed credit, and, worst of all, her children had never known of their grandparents' generosity.

"What's he been doing with his money?" she asked, grappling with the incomprehensible. "If only I hadn't signed over the house."

James eyebrows shot up. "What did your father's will say about it?"

"I never read the will. Frank insisted on taking care of everything. I was too upset about their untimely passing. Having no business background, I was grateful that he was willing to take on such a burden."

"I think you should check with your father's attorney. His name's here somewhere. Here it is—Elliott Cunningham. Would you like to call him? I can give you some privacy."

"No! Please stay and help me."

When Elliott Cunningham came on the line, James hit the conference button. "He left the house to his daughter 'for use in her lifetime,'" Cunningham said. "Upon her death, it passes to her children. Should none of them want it, the house is to be donated to the Library Association, with fair market value being transferred from the trust to Dolly or her heirs. He stipulates that it cannot be given, sold, or inherited by spouses."

"But, but—my husband had me sign it over to him."

"I don't know who drew that up, but it's not worth the paper it's written on."

Dolly sank back in her chair. The parting conversation between banker and attorney blurred to a buzz. "Mrs. Ziegler?" She jolted back. "We can explore this in depth when you're ready. For now, I suggest you open a new account at a different bank to receive your income. If you're expecting trouble at home, you might consider renting a post office box for bank correspondence. And retain an attorney who specializes in these matters."

∽∾∾

Dolly managed to keep it together until she pulled into her driveway. Once cocooned in her own kitchen, she dissolved into tears. All that money. All those years. The lost opportunities. The lies. Had Frank really been that desperate? Hated her so? Or was he just greedy and selfish?

She cursed her parents as well for miserably failing their dutiful daughter. Too numb to think, she sank into a wingback by the fire but got up and paced, sat, but jumped up again. Mechanically, she picked at some clutter and sorted the laundry. Absently she checked pockets for tissues, matchbooks, golf pencils, and paper clips before isolating the dry cleaning pile. From Frank's black suit pocket, she pulled a note from someone named Juanita.

She reread it several times, not understanding. Finally she shoved it into her pocket.

Dolly poured sherry, gulped it, and poured another. At least Frank wasn't home. Could she confront him? Would he hurt her? Kill her when he found out what she'd learned? And he would know, sooner than later, when the bills stopped coming to his office. She lurched when the phone jangled, knocking her glass to the floor. It was her best friend, Lauren.

"Did you pick up the juice, soft drinks, and ice?"

"What? Oh my goodness! The blood drive's tomorrow! I'll go right now. And Lauren? You've got to help me."

"Anything. Just name it."

⋐⋙⋐⋙

At seven, blood bank personnel, Women's Club members and Keynote facilitators overspread the bank's lower level. Stations quickly materialized in an elongated horseshoe, back dropped by white fabric screens. Volunteers took their places to direct traffic and deal with any problems. By nine, they were ready.

Dolly positioned coolers of extra juice behind her table near the exit. A blood bank professional, whose job was to pack bags for transport, set up beside her. "This spot by the exit, is ideal," the woman explained. "Some people freak out, seeing this much blood."

Lauren, one of several phlebotomists on blood-drawing

duty, caught Dolly's eye and waved encouragement. Elevators disgorged employees, many of whom were joined by their families. At two, Dolly spotted Frank stride in and observed with surreal detachment how he worked the room. He approached select people, gushed over them, and then cut to the head of the line. Had he always been such a performer? The marketing department courted the press. TV crews interviewed the presidents of the blood bank, the Women's Club, and Frank. In a booming voice, he took credit, three times, for volunteering Keynote's facilities.

Dolly felt sick. She watched as they prepped and drew Frank's blood into a labeled plastic bag and vacuum-sealed it. She hoped that it hurt. When his bag was deposited into the cooler beside her, she felt a wave of revulsion. That bastard. Sucking her blood all these years. What poor innocent person would he contaminate? They should have taken a few quarts from his jugular. Ruefully, she confronted herself. When did she become such a hateful person?

Frank walked toward the cordoning screen to join a pretty young woman who had motioned to him. Smiling, he took the girl's arm and steered her behind the screen. Later, as Dolly watched the girl move through the line, she succumbed to temptation and wandered nearby. She was lovely. Tiny. Big brown eyes and perfect features. Her name badge identified her as a teller named Juanita. Something clicked—the note she'd found in Frank's pocket. Dolly suddenly felt old, fat, and ugly, and retreated to the restroom to get a grip.

When the drive ended, the blood bank's president shouted for the workers to gather. "Congratulations! And thank you, on behalf of the premature babies who desperately need plasma, and those others whose lives you just saved."

Dolly scanned for Lauren, but she had remained near her

station. Dolly bent over the blood bags in the collection cooler and located Frank's.

Alone at home, Dolly searched Frank's pockets and, to her dismay and then anger, found more notes from Juanita, cryptic messages about discreet meetings. He walked in, surprising her, note in her hand. "You bastard! You thought I wouldn't find out what you do with your money. Well I know all about Juanita."

He impaled her with unblinking eyes. "Juanita? What are you talking about?"

"You know very well. The teller. You're having an affair!"

"You think I'm having an affair with Juanita?"

Dolly thrust the note in his face.

Glancing at it, he laughed. "You fool. You stupid, stupid fool! You couldn't get anything right if you tried."

Enraged and shaking, Dolly screamed at him. "It doesn't take brains to figure out what a snake you are! You lied to me! You've lied about everything!"

Amusement curled a smirk as he dismissed her with a flip of his hand. Catlike, she lunged, raking his cheek with sharp nails. Screeching he recoiled as blood oozed from parallel gashes. She jumped back, having shocked even herself.

"Get out of my sight," he roared as he retreated to the powder room to nurse his wounds.

Dolly bolted upstairs, shaking all over. Her cell phone, she realized, was still in the kitchen. Panicked, she cowered even long after Frank finished stalking and slamming doors.

Chapter 14

Kingsley, Barrie, and Margaret huddled in the restaurant's back corner booth. After summarizing her search for the missing blue-list files, Kingsley shared her conclusion. "Proving those loans are bogus involves getting my hands on those files and discreetly investigating each one." She smiled conspiratorially at the others. "I think I know where they are."

Barrie and Margaret leaned in. "Where?"

"That voice—I've heard it twice now. If the files aren't in Manning's office, they've got to be somewhere on Five."

"Unless that person took the files off the premises," Margaret said, shaking her head.

"That's doubtful. Those files have information that would be needed here at the bank. Think about it—loan payments must be made on time or a red flag goes up. No, they've got to be handy to keep it all straight. And there could be dozens more."

"How do you propose searching for them?" Barrie asked.

"The only time the building's completely deserted is Saturday night."

"If you're serious, you'd better do it immediately," Barrie said. "After the Tonya-Tree Trunk incident, a crash security upgrade is underway. Facilities and an industrial design firm are crawling all over the place. It's going to be huge—and immediate."

"What's that all about?" Kingsley asked.

Barrie rolled her eyes when Margaret looked just as perplexed. "You guys need a much better grapevine. A few days ago, some jerk barged off the elevator on Five where Tonya, the receptionist, sits. He was furious about something and demanded to see Warren. When Tonya refused, he threatened her with a metal pipe. She's supposed to guard the executive shrine, but not from lunatics with her life. If she hadn't dived under her desk, he'd have brained her. When everyone started screaming, the guy ran down the stairwell."

Margaret hit the table with her fist. "I've been telling them for years that our lack of security will bury us in lawsuits."

"That's exactly what Tonya's husband, Tree Trunk, threatened."

"Tree Trunk?"

"Mountain of a guy with no neck. He erupted off the elevator, also unchallenged, saw Tonya's desk awash in scattered papers and broken glass from their wedding photo. He marched straight back to Warren's office. According to the girls he yelled, 'You may not give a rat's ass about your own safety, but what about them? This bullshit about you being accessible to customers is crap! You're not accessible. They are. You suits can just duck out the back. What if he'd had a gun? What if there were several of them? I'm getting a lawyer and suing you and this whole damn place.' Or words to that effect."

"What happened next?"

"Warren went to her home to beg her forgiveness. Then he hired a top industrial design firm that's coming here from Columbus. He wants upgrades done yesterday."

"I heard that our keys will be replaced with swipe cards that identify the user and the time," Margaret said. "But I didn't know what prompted that decision."

"I'd better search Five right away."

"As in this Saturday," Barrie stated emphatically.

"I need a plan. Any suggestions?"

Margaret nodded in agreement. "We need a plan."

"The way I see it, we also need a lookout and an alibi," Barrie added.

"Why an alibi?"

"Suppose there's something highly sensitive in the executive area, like plans for a merger that someone else leaks. Or something valuable disappears, or new alarms have been installed that we know nothing about. We're not that experienced to go undetected. We must be able to prove we were elsewhere."

"Okay, but the most challenging part is the time it will take. If I'm caught, I could justify being in my own building, but ransacking Five? Finding, reading, and copying those files could take hours."

They put their heads together, ran different scenarios, and ended up laughing at their criminal minds. But in the end they had a plan that would begin Friday night.

෴

Todd's call Thursday evening caught Kingsley off guard. "Do you remember when we were at Hawk Mountain—I mentioned my search for an old stone farmhouse? A good possibility just came on the market and, well, they're all beginning to look alike. I could sure use a fresh set of eyes and a woman's perspective—that is, if I could talk you into a little field trip on Saturday."

Saturday? Not this Saturday. She had to focus on finding those files! But that would be evening.

While her mind raced, he continued. "Actually, this would be a two-part expedition. I also want to see the manor house at Hopewell Village. I understand it's faithfully restored. I'm particularly interested in the details—how they finished the floors, moldings and staircase, the windows, and fireplaces."

"I have a brochure here somewhere." She riffled through her desk drawer for Michel and Isaac's stash. "Hopewell Furnace: the forge dates to 1744 and the iron-making furnace to 1770. Says here it's a fine example of an early American iron-making community."

"That's it."

"I have a commitment for Saturday evening, but if we'd be back early, I guess I could go." She cringed, hoping that struck the perfect degree of nonchalance.

"I promise I'll have you back whenever you say."

She struggled to keep her voice casual and hoped he couldn't hear her grin through the phone. "Why not? It sounds like fun."

"One other thing. I've inherited a nonprofit fund-raiser from Frank Ziegler. Could I bounce a few ideas off you?"

"That's going to cost you."

He laughed. "I'll buy lunch."

"It's a deal."

They hung up.

Another Hawk Mountain-type day felt delicious from the safety of her own living room, yet a swipe of reality hit her. *Remember who he is. Be professional. Do not over react.*

It's a casual outing, not a lost weekend. Women—he could have whomever he wanted, and you don't want to be used. She grinned nevertheless.

∾∾∾

Friday at noon, Kingsley met Barrie, who came to the diner armed with a partial printout of the bank's employee directory. "I checked everybody on Five, eliminated the women, controller's staff, non-officers and anyone who missed the officers' meeting. That narrows it down to twenty-some people. Of those, we can eliminate Warren, Doug, Frank, and Todd."

"The voice had a trace of the local accent."

"That would be Pennsylvania Dutch. Let's see…" Barrie went through the list and crossed off several more. "What else can you remember?"

"He talked like his tongue was too big for his mouth."

Barrie frowned and shook her head.

"I had lunch with Warren and I'd know Todd's voice anywhere—" Kingsley stopped, annoyed at the way she had said it.

Barrie put down her pen and grinned. "Okay, Kingsley, give. I want the details. And don't try to tell me—"

"We're acquainted at best."

"That's not what I hear."

"Barrie! Listening to gossip is so junior high."

"Turn off that analytical brain for a while. You're still alive. Oh, kiddo, I'm so sorry. I didn't mean—"

Kingsley dropped her gaze and her voice. "I don't just miss Andy, but the whole business of being in love. Having someone who knows my flaws, but loved me anyway. But I'm not ready."

"But, hon, he's gone. And there's very nice guy, right in your path. Oh, god, I'm making it worse. Fine friend I'm turning out to be."

"You are a good friend. You say what you think. It's just that, well, I can't do affairs. I'd feel used when it's over. Afterward, I couldn't go back—settle in with my memories. What would Andy think?"

"You're trying to live up to some kind of standard as if he could see you? As if you'd be cheating? Don't do that to yourself."

Kingsley looked up and frowned. "Being reckless is self-destructive. I'd have to give up my job at the bank. I need peace of mind more than a man."

Barrie tapped the list with her pen. "Come on. Back to the task at hand."

❧❧❧

Friday evening, Kingsley and Barrie converted their plan into action. They chose a movie that ran three hours and parked around back. Hanging in the shadows until starting time, they avoided the snack bar and ushers then slipped into the theater and concentrated on the movie's content.

When it was over, Barrie concealed a cheap bracelet in the hardware that separated their seats. They left quickly by the rear exit, having seen no one they knew. Before separating, they reviewed their plan for the next evening and the equipment they'd need.

"Be at my place at seven," Barrie said. "Margaret will meet us here in the lot."

Chapter 15

A Canadian high swept in brilliantly cold. Todd, in plaid flannel, wool crewneck and cords, arrived promptly at eight. "Parking was tough. I'm way down the street," he said, helping her into her new leather jacket. "Nice jacket. Nothing like the feel of real leather."

"Present from my folks." She almost said birthday, but averted in time. *Too personal*, she thought. Could sound like she was fishing for something. They shuffled through leaves, many still clinging to yellows and reds that sparkled with frost.

"Mornings like this are simply..." She groped unsuccessfully for a superlative that equaled fall's tapestry.

His appreciative grin vanished when a navy sedan shot toward them from nowhere. Reacting instantaneously, Todd yanked Kingsley by her arm from its path. The car narrowly missed her and several parked cars.

"Idiot!" Todd yelled after the vanishing behemoth. He loosened his grip on her arm, gaping at the leather's twisted sleeve. "I'm sorry," he stammered. "Are you all right? Did I hurt you?"

Kingsley turned toward the commotion, absently righting

her jacket, but the sedan had already vanished. "I'm fine."

His face quickly softened. "Where were we? Oh, yes— looking at this perfect day. And it's been a great week."

"How do you do it?" she asked after they'd piled into his Explorer and headed cross-county. "So much responsibility, but you handle the pressure quite well."

"It's play when everything works. The bank surpassed third quarter's projections, and we're on track for a very good year. That took heroic effort on everyone's part." He smiled at her and looked back at the road, smile intact.

"But there's too many banks chasing too few deals. Aren't you afraid—"

"Wouldn't do it if I were. What would you undertake if you thought you could not possibly fail?" She had no answer. "My job's a prodigious challenge. I have a few guiding principles—don't rely on yesterday's knowledge, always plan and have a plan B, play honorably by the rules, but—" He smiled at her once again. "—I play to win."

"I'm surprised you have time for a restoration project. What got you interested?"

"I don't need much sleep, which drove my folks nuts. They bought me books to keep me occupied, and a library card to feed my habit. I fell in love with colonial history. But now, with the job under control, I have time on my hands."

"Is that because, compared to New York, life here is dull?"

"With apologies to Pandora, if I'd swung a cat by the tail in my Manhattan apartment, it would hit all four walls. I wanted room to spread out and earth to dig. Keeping a car was prohibitive in New York. Don't get me wrong: I love cities for their unlimited opportunity, the excitement, the arts and the theater. It was a magnet for young people jump-starting careers. Guess I outgrew it. From here, New York, Philadelphia, and even Baltimore are accessible, but look out your window—the fields, trees, fresh air, the birds." He cracked his window, admitting a bracing slice of fresh air.

"Do you have a particular house in mind?"

"Right here." He tapped his right temple. "A big old stone farmhouse with plenty of character. Ten-foot ceilings, an interesting staircase, working fireplaces in every room, plank floors, double-hung windows with hand-made glass. And land—at least ten acres. Can you reach the folder on the back seat?"

Opening it, she saw a number of photos stapled to check-lists.

"Each one I see helps me fine tune what's out there and hopefully remember what won't work. The one on the top's on the market."

She studied the realtor's black and white hulking structure. "It sounds like a wonderful dream."

"There's our turn." He pointed to a brown sign for Hopewell Furnace National Historic Site.

The rural two-lane bisected stands of skinny maples that fluttered a golden canopy. A dozen miles farther he turned at a split-railed pasture that enclosed a gnarled old orchard. Hopewell appeared beyond the next hill, its white buildings nestled in picturesque farmland.

"Let's see the mansion first," he said steering her down the curved walkway. "You be the scribe." He handed her the folder. He preceded to photograph and measure the exterior details—raised-panel shutters and wrought iron anchors, calling dimensions for her to jot down. "These walls are stucco on stone, which was easier and cheaper than repointing. I want exposed stone."

She made a note: tell realtor no stucco.

They stepped into a wallpapered foyer with very low chair rail. "This hallway's typical—runs front to back. Could you stand over there for perspective? I want to catch the height of the moldings."

She touched the trim and mugged for the camera.

He turned his attention to the staircase, which was narrow and hugged the right wall. "There should be a window upstairs on the landing, but this building has an addition. I wish we could go up, but the sign says alarms would go off." He leaned over the barricade and took a picture. "The staircase continues a half dozen steps on the opposite wall to accommodate the height of first-floor ceiling. The bedrooms should radiate from a center hallway, overhead. What do you think of it?"

"It's a grand entrance staircase."

"A what?"

"I see a Victorian lady in a beautiful gown descending to meet the love of her life. He's sitting over there, like the statue of Lincoln. When he sees her, he rises to meet her and walks, hand extended, in one fluid motion."

"You see all that?"

"They're going to influence fair-minded people to care for people society neglects. They have that power and they're going to use it."

"And I thought I was looking at risers and treads. You have quite an imagination."

"I think homes should be about people. Otherwise, they're just bricks and mortar." To his frown, she said, "You love books? Do you just see them on shelves? Or yourself reading by that working fireplace while a storm beats on the windows?"

"Yes! I see it. The room's filling with smoke and I'm struggling to open the window, which, of course, sticks.

Ugh! I get it open. Oh, no! It's five below with a wind-chill factor."

"That needs some work."

"The vision or the damper?"

"Both." He laughed and beckoned her toward the front parlor.

Kingsley leaned over the velvet rope. "Look at those windowsills—they've got to be two feet deep. You could have a year-round greenhouse, or candles with chimneys for short winter days."

"They're the depth of the exterior stone walls. Wish I could see what's under that carpet—probably pine. I'd want it exposed." He looked for a loose edge, but found none.

"Check out the tall clock, desks, and chairs in the opposite room."

"Picture this—you've been arrested after smuggling them into your SUV."

He focused close-ups of original mantles and took several more pictures. "Should they be stripped?" she asked.

"They used whatever wood was on hand and painted it." He shot more details before going outside to study the chimneys and the hardware that held the shutters in place. "Done," he concluded with satisfaction. "Now we can be tourists."

They ambled through Hopewell's blacksmith shop and store, tenant houses, and barn and checked out the furnace. Afterward Todd motored to a small country restaurant. While they finished club sandwiches and coffee, he added a few notes to his folder.

"So what do you think?" he asked.

"I'm afraid I'd go with my heart, overlooking the outhouse and no running water."

"I must have looked at a dozen by now, but there's

something wrong about each one. Take this old mill," he said, unearthing its photo. "Great structure, beautiful woods, lovely neat out-buildings and a stream, but the inside's a gutted cavernous space, which is not what I want to tackle. Besides, a neighbor told me that lovely stream turned into a raging river during Hurricane Agnes that came to their second story."

"There's something you can't put on your form. It's got to feel right." He smiled indulgently. She was surprised, all over again, by how handsome he was, eyes blue as his sweater. She eased elsewhere. "On the phone you mentioned Frank's fund-raiser?"

He shifted slightly, face turning somber. "Can we speak confidentially?"

"Of course."

"The bank's in for a major embarrassment if I don't act quickly. One of the community's nonprofit agencies is building a $2 million community center. Frank agreed to chair their capital campaign. I got a distress call from their board chair. Seems Frank attended just enough meetings to get his name on the campaign letterhead. I agreed to step in. They do have a professional fund-raiser, an active board and a volunteer steering committee, which I'd have to chair."

"Who's handling it now?"

"The board chair, but that's not her job. Frank was to plan a kickoff event for September. Instead he was merely going to have his staff write letters asking for corporate gifts."

"That won't get it done," she said. "They'd miss wealthy individuals and foundations. And it's so late. By the kickoff, all major gifts should be committed. The event should celebrate those totals and launch the public campaign for the remaining ten percent."

"My thoughts exactly. Sounds like you've done this before. Any ideas for a kickoff event?"

"How about a black tie dinner dance at the country club? Make it the social event to launch the fall season. Invite the community movers and shakers who are interested in family issues. Even if you charge the earth for the tickets, most will add personal donations. Ask the chef to plan something unique. Hire a band that showcases local talent."

"Sounds like a lot of work—" he started.

"The nonprofit should have history on committed individuals and where to borrow corporate talent. I'd be willing to help plan the event if you give me the name of the board chair. It will give me the opportunity to meet community leaders."

"And I would..."

"Conduct the steering committee meetings, and if you can't dance, you have ten months to learn."

"I was going to spend the weekend researching this mess, but you make it sound easy. Wait a minute—what's this going to cost me?"

"Your ticket, a personal contribution, the bank's corporate gift—"

"I can handle that."

"—a tux if you don't own one. And my fee."

"I should have known. What do you charge?"

"One dance of my choosing. Is it a deal?"

He grinned. "Best one I've made in ages."

She held out her hand and they shook. "Good," she said. "Make it a tango." His smile straightened out. "You've got ten months to learn."

"Look, Kingsley, I really didn't bring you here to offload an assignment."

"Of course you did, but I need to get involved in the

community. This presents an ideal opportunity to meet the shakers and movers. Besides, I have just the gown that's never been worn."

"I don't know what to say."

"Just remember my fee."

Their gaze connected and, after a brief lock, she looked away.

"What were you thinking?" he asked.

Thinking? Why couldn't you be someone from some other place? Or some other time? She pushed at the thought, afraid her fascination with his genuine warmth would reflect on her face. She smoothed the fringe on her placemat. "I was thinking that I envy you, knowing your goals. When I interviewed, they asked me where I envisioned myself in five years. I must have said something appropriate, but in truth, I was clueless. I'm a collection of fragments in search of cohesion. Maybe I'll find it in this community."

He nodded, his gaze focusing briefly beyond the window. "My ex-wife used to tell me my ideas, particularly the stone house, were asinine. In time I believed it." He patted her hand, but withdrew his quickly. "Thanks. Just for coming and letting me see through unjaded eyes." He glanced at his watch. "It's after two. If we're going to see the latest candidate, we'd better get going. It does, by the way, have indoor plumbing."

℮〜℮〜

A sign for Birdsboro grabbed Kingsley's attention. "Can you turn that way? I want to check out a client's property. It should be somewhere nearby." As they rode through the center of town, she craned her neck, reading road names. "Go slowly. Please."

"What are you looking for?"

She didn't answer, frowning in concentration. "It's got to be around her somewhere. There! Pull over in front of that bar." He looked surprised, but did as she asked. "Wait here: I'll just be a minute."

She jumped out and disappeared. Todd opened his door and followed slowly.

Three men in plaid shirts, jeans, and boots were drinking beer and watching NASCAR on the TV over the bar. They turned simultaneously. She felt out of place in suburban chic slacks, turtle neck and her designer leather jacket. They smiled appreciatively. Briskly, Kingsley pulled a map from her purse and drew lines with her finger.

"It's up there," one man pointed east. "About three streets."

"Can't be," another said. "Got to be five or six."

"You're counting the Wertz's driveway."

"And there's that school entrance."

"You say it was right or left?" she asked. "I don't know the area. It's a large business facility that should be some distance down a side road."

The men looked at her blankly then up at the tall man who had caught up.

"You oughtn't let her wander into bars by herself," one said to Todd, who shrugged helplessly. "It's that way, on the right, three, maybe six streets."

"Thank you," she smiled at the three. "You've been a big help." She walked out, Todd trailing, feeling their eyes.

"To be young again," one was saying.

"Speak for yourself, Jeb."

"That way." Kingsley pointed east. Finally she spotted a road with no sign. "Turn right, and stop." Leaving the Explorer, she crossed the road, looked into the dry, waist-high weeds. She cocked her head, smiling, and returned.

"Street sign's blown down. This is it." They rode past fields and a few small frame homes, all on the left, as she looked hard for mailboxes. "Sixty-seven, sixty-nine, seventy-one. There's no even numbers."

"Has to be on the right side. What's the number?"

"Seventy. Maybe we haven't come to it yet." A mile farther the woods swallowed them up. "Could you go back to the highway and retrace the route one more time only slower?"

Todd smiled indulgently. "Sure."

He crawled, motioning a lone car to pass while Kingsley hung out her window, studying the dense underbrush that finally yielded an overgrown lane. A metal stake, cemented into a rusted ten-gallon milk can, was half buried in the ground. On the stake was pasted the number seventy.

"There it is! Could you drive down that lane?"

"Yes'm." He inched the Explorer twenty-five feet until a fallen tree obstructed the path.

Kingsley got out and picked her way a hundred feet farther, shading her eyes against the western sun. Beyond an overgrown expanse stood the remains of a barn and a tiny frame house, both lacking roofs.

"There's nothing here," she whispered to the desolate scene.

She returned to the mailbox and, jerking its rusty door open, peered in and extracted an envelope with a Keynote National Bank return address. She pried at the seal.

"Mail tampering is a federal offense, lady," Todd called through the open passenger window.

Ignoring him, she held it up to the light and coaxed it until the glue separated. She withdrew and unfolded a Keynote National Bank statement that listed payments made and an outstanding balance of $425,000. She scrutinized it intently and then reinserted the sheet. After licking at traces of glue and pressing it hard, she put the envelope back and got into the car.

"Would you mind telling me what that was all about?"

"Oh, a customer has a loan on that property. I was just curious. Now—about that stone house…"

Todd looked skeptical but appeared to accept the quick change in subject.

They sped to the county's far-western border where Todd turned past a strip mall bordered by farmland and en- croaching development. He turned again onto at a dirt road that bisected the booming enterprise. He braked. Ahead stood an abandoned stone house displaying his realtor's sign.

"This is it," he said. "Watch your step—the yard is rid- dled with potholes and rocks."

Her eyes swept the imposing three-story structure, with an 1805 date stone under the eaves. It was once the farm- house for the surrounding land that now sprouted streets of cookie-cutter vinyl tract houses. Kingsley judged it to be just twenty feet off the highway. The last occupants had painted the huge shutters yellow, but now they were peeling. The solid, raised-panel oak door looked original.

"Come look in the windows," Todd called to her. Edging closer she could make out faded wallpaper and the top of a fireplace. "Hand-made glass panes. Aren't the ripples fan- tastic?" He counted. "Twenty-four panes—that's 'twelve over twelve.'"

Kingsley glanced at the highway. "Are you seriously considering it? But…"

Two barreling tractor-trailers smothered her voice.

He laughed. "You're thinking location, location, location? I'd move it into the country, excavate a new foundation, and position it to best advantage. I'd sell this lot for development. If I updated the plumbing and wiring and made one room and a bathroom livable, I could renovate leisurely. Wonder what shape the woodwork is in."

"We're too short to see, what with the hill."

"Here." He laced his fingers and boosted her by her boot. "Hang onto the sill."

Peering in, she could see dusty gray planks and faded green paint on generous wainscoting. She imagined burning logs and herself by the fire. But this wasn't her project, much less her future.

Motioning to be let down, she shook off the images. "It has a good feel. Just check the damper."

The setting sun jogged her to look at her watch. "I've lost track of time! I've got to get back." As he gave the house one last look, she bolted for the Explorer.

"I just might pursue it." He looked satisfied as they sped toward the city, but Kingsley's attention was leaping ahead. "I'll drop off my film for one-hour development," he called after her as she dashed up the walk toward her apartment.

She turned. "I am so sorry! Forgive me for being so rude. I lost track of time. Thanks for a fun day. Good luck with your project." She felt ridiculous, but hurried anyway.

"Go!" he called, laughing at her.

Todd dropped his film for one-hour development, killing time until it was processed. Snatching the prints, he riffled for the one by the staircase. There she was, trim little package, hamming it up. How different she was, away from the bank, professional and personal lives deftly cleaved.

He stuffed the package into his pocket and headed for Birdsboro and box number seventy. He reached into the mailbox but found it empty. He jerked, scanning the bleak vista dotted with trees. Straggly brown weeds, which had

looked untouched since summer's growth, had been trampled since their departure. Wind plucked at snapped twigs
and broken dead leaves rattled forlornly. He tried to shake
the scene's creepy aura, exacerbated by her lack of explanation. Slowly he retraced his steps, eyes sweeping the pe-
riphery. Whatever she'd found that made her gasp was now
gone.

Chapter 16

Saturday night, revelry and horrendous traffic ensnared Kingsley as she approached Barrie's condo community. She zigzagged impatiently without finding parking, narrowly missing a Hummer that cut her off. On the third pass, she spotted Barrie motioning to pull into her basement garage. The second she cut the engine, Barrie lowered the door.

"I moved my car to the alley," Barrie said. "Come upstairs." Barrie, in an outlandish pink, orange and red flowered shirt, black tights and a wide red belt, had teased her curls until she looked like a dandelion gone to seed. In heavy makeup, she appeared downright cheap.

"You look like a cat burglar," Barrie said. "If you want to be noticed, you need something flashy." She opened the closet and produced a suede jacket the color of green Play Doh. "Here. And earrings—you need bizarre." Kingsley exchanged her gold hoops for the bangles Barrie dug from an Asian lacquer box. "That's better. Now ramp up the lipstick. Pale pink's not going to get it." She pulled a godawful purple from her vanity. "Next stop, the movies."

After parking in the theater's rear lot, Barrie approached

the ticket counter. "I only have this hundred, and boy does it reek. Spilled a whole bottle of perfume in my purse. Smell it. I was holding onto it for an emergency, but I said to myself, 'Hey, you gotta have fun.' Besides, it smells gross!"

The clerk rolled her eyes at her co-worker as she counted out change but cut Barrie off curtly when she started to chatter again. Meanwhile, Kingsley ordered a large popcorn and backed up the line as she paid with small change. She dumped it all over the counter, the floor and the poor kid who complained he was only working to pay off his transmission, and this wasn't worth it.

They sat near the side aisle, and as the lights dimmed, slipped out the rear exit. Margaret was waiting out back. Barrie followed Margaret's car toward Keynote, exiting onto a secluded side street. Engine cut, they swapped their outerwear for black jackets and knit caps and hopped into Margaret's back seat.

Keynote's branch office, located left of the building's main doors, included a drive-up ATM on the side. Margaret swung wide, avoiding its cameras and, headlights killed, dropped the girls around back. They unlocked a rear entrance and slipped inside while Margaret circled away.

Margaret returned to the secondary road. She climbed the long driveway of the neighboring industrial complex. From her vantage point high on the hill, she could monitor the bank's front, side, and rear parking lots. Armed with a cell phone and high-power binoculars, she settled to watch and to wait.

Kingsley and Barrie, guided by penlights, took the stairs two at a time and crept into Human Resources on Three. "Over here," Kingsley hissed after scanning the long bank of personnel files. Her latex-gloved hands pulled Manning's file. "Got it!" Barrie flipped the copier switch from zero to

one, fidgeted while the contraption warmed up, then selected two-sided.

"Copy everything. We'll sort it later."

Barrie set the pages into the batch feed and fired, then
stuffed the copies into an interoffice envelope. After Kingsley refiled the originals and gave the room a cursory sweep,
she followed Barrie into the stairwell and tore up to Five. A
full moon splashed the executive area with eerie light and
ghoulish shadows that transformed objects to netherworld
creatures. They had laughed at how corny their excessive
planning had been, but now, in the dark, it was comforting.

"Got a break this afternoon," Kingsley whispered. "That
is, if we can find the file with a Birdsboro address." She circled the executive suite, comparing nameplates to their
culled personnel list.

Barrie disappeared into Warren Kramer's corner office
and, after scoping it out, reported back. "Great view of the
side and back lots, but Margaret's out of our range. We
should have brought binocs."

"Rats. That means we can't see if she runs into trouble."

"You start looking. I'll watch the lots till you need me."

"Got your phone?" Kingsley asked.

"Set it to vibrate."

Kingsley entered office number one on their prospects
list She wasted no time, checking anything unlocked and
opening boxes large enough to hold files. "Come here," she
hissed to Barrie. "Can you open these?" With expert preci-
sion, Barrie's gloved hands lock-picked the desk drawers
and relocked them when the search yielded nothing. Next,
she unlocked credenzas and file cabinets, leaving occasionally to scan parking lots.

Kingsley moved on to office number two, coordinating
her movements with Barrie's expertise. By office number

three, they'd perfected their routine, cutting the time by
several minutes. "This will take forever!"

"Don't think. Just do."

"Anyone we can eliminate?"

"Frank's office, I guess. Do it last if time permits."

Up on the hill, Margaret watched intently. A lone security light illuminated the ATM, fading its safety to black
within yards. Two customers used it, made U-turns, and departed. Gathering clouds passed over the moon with in-
creasing frequency, darkening the entire arena. Calm, she
thought. Just be calm.

Suddenly high beams flooded Margaret's dashboard and
glared in her mirrors. He'd come up so quietly and she'd
been so intent that she never saw him. Margaret took a deep
breath and rolled down her window. "Good evening, Officer.
How are you this evening," she lilted to the blinding flash-
light in her best choir voice.

"May I see your license and registration please ma'am?"
The voice sounded young.

"Of course you may. I'll bet I was speeding, right?" She
chuckled and handed him the papers with a motherly smile.

He returned to his car to run them, which felt like it took
twenty minutes although in reality it was more like five.
Margaret fervently scanned the bank's lots, but the officer's
headlights messed with her vision.

He returned and handed back her papers. "What are you
doing here? Unless you have a good reason, I'll have to ask
you to move along."

"I'm waiting for my grandson. Little Jimmy's daddy, my
son-in-law, is passing him off to me on his way to New Jer-
sey. This is the perfect spot. It's a public parking lot, isn't it?
I hope it is. If I move, they'll never find me. You see, young
man, my daughter and son-in-law live in York. I live way

on the other side of the county." She pointed over her shoulder, taking his eyes with her so she could steal a glimpse down below. "The turnpike entrance is right down there." She pointed south, same objective. "My son-in-law brings Jimmy this far and I take him home for a few days. When my son-in-law finishes his business, we do it in reverse. He's a little bit late this evening because Jimmy got carsick. Do you have any children? Let me show you my little Jimmy. He's such a doll." She produced a huge wad of photos. "Isn't he cute?" She flashed him a grandmother's grin. "The first twenty were taken at T-ball..."

She smiled at the photos and prayed this was getting old fast.

Back on Five, Kingsley groaned. "Zilch. The files aren't here, or they're very well hidden."

"If you're positive it was executive staff, we've overlooked something."

Kingsley glanced over her shoulder. "The copy room." They hurried in, not risking the overhead light until Barrie had wedged paper reams against the crack under the door. "The cabinets aren't labeled. Quick, just start at the opposite end." Barrie and Kingsley progressed toward each other.

The third cabinet was locked. "Over here."

Barrie had it open in seconds.

From inside Kingsley extracted an archive box and lifted the lid. File folders without labels held loan documents whose numbers she recognized immediately. "Hello!"

Barrie fired the photocopier, then searched the remaining cabinets. "There's several more archive boxes down here," she said to Kingsley who was absorbed, walking her fingers through folders.

"This is just old facilities stuff."

Barrie eased the file shut.

"Here it is—the Birdsboro file!" Kingsley leafed through the papers, studying what wasn't included in the bank's computerized summary. "Look at this!"

Barrie squatted beside her.

"It's a detailed description of the business's facility, its location and, most important, a schedule of draws being made to finance construction already in progress." Kingsley looked up at Barrie. "There's nothing there but two tumbled-down buildings!" Kingsley gestured impatiently toward the copy machine. "How long does it take that thing to warm up?"

"That one's prehistoric. Five minutes—we should have done that first."

Kingsley groaned. "Let's schlep the boxes downstairs."

"First, you've gotta check out these others. They look like more of the same."

Kingsley and Barrie exchanged triumphant looks. "They're all here!"

Up on the hill, the officer warmed to the mention of T-ball. Margaret stole a peek down below and thought she detected some movement, but the sky had grown very dark. Finally she stopped him from pulling his wallet, no doubt for his pictures. "You needn't keep me company any longer. I'll be fine, really. My son-in-law will be here any minute. And if anyone bothers me, I've got my phone. I can see for miles. Thanks again, young man. You can leave now."

With that, the young officer, whether out of respect or surprise, did as he was told.

The minute his lights disappeared, Margaret grabbed her binoculars. A car had parked in the shadows by the back door. Big. Dark. Black, maybe navy. Its lights were off and she couldn't see movement. However, a narrowing sliver of light that was escaping from the bank's back door meant someone had just stepped inside. Snatching her phone, she dialed Barrie's number.

Barrie sprang up, hissing to Kingsley. "We've got company. Quick! We've gotta get out of here!"

Kingsley checked the copier, still warming-up, momentarily torn.

"Now!"

Exasperated, Kingsley shoved several papers into her waistband, jammed the file into the box, and muscled it into the cabinet.

"Kill the copier!"

"We're trapped," Kingsley panted. "We can't use the stairs—"

Barrie's phone vibrated again. "She says, 'Use the south stairwell. Hurry!'"

They sprinted through the dark executive area, Barrie dominoing into Kingsley, who saw trouble first and froze— a slice of expanding light from the executive stairwell.

"Go! Go! Go!" Barrie pushed Kingsley's back and propelled her toward the controller's department where she knew every turn. Grabbing her wrist, Barrie drew Kingsley into the stairwell. Windowless and dimly lit, it echoed their sneakers as they sped downward.

"Did you lock everything?"

"Yeah, but that's the least of our worries." At ground level, Kingsley scrunched her eyes shut, grimaced, and eased open the crash bar, praying no alarm would go off. None did. Peeking left, she risked opening it farther and stuck out her head. "Come on!"

They hugged the building until Kingsley could scope out the deserted front lot. Headlights approached. They flattened themselves against the wall then peered out again.

It was Margaret, approaching the ATM. She got out and

walked in front of her car, making a tiny out-of-camera-range motion for them to stay back. Nonchalantly she made a withdrawal and wandered back, counting her cash. Car back in gear, she exited around their side of the building, cracking the passenger window. "Get in the back and stay down."

The girls dived for the mats. Margaret circled past the back door where the dark car still stood. She squinted at the mud-splattered Pennsylvania plate, fully prepared to floor it if necessary. Finding the car empty, she stopped and inspected its rear bumper before sliding past it uneventfully. Once it was safe she asked, "Did you find anything?"

"Yes, but we needed more time."

Back at the theater, when the back doors flung open, Kingsley and Barrie eased upstream through the exiting moviegoers. When everyone was gone, they found an usher. "You've got to help me," Barrie insisted. "I've lost my bracelet. I can't find it anywhere. It's got to be here. My boyfriend will kill me." Dutifully, he followed the girls. "Shine it around here," she said, letting him discover what she had hidden Friday evening. She thanked him profusely and gave him a five dollar tip.

Kingsley stopped at the concession stand and apologized again for the popcorn fiasco. His nod said, "It's cool. Just go."

She did.

"They'll remember us if we need them," Barrie said.

At Barrie's condo, Kingsley dealt the pages of Manning's life onto the carpet. Together, the three scrutinized its details. "How do we check out his background? I don't even know what we're looking for."

"Here's a home address on his Northwestern transcript. It's only ten in Chicago," Barrie said, dialing information.

She got lucky. "Hi. My name's Charlene Smith. I was a classmate of your son Manning's? Do I have the right Stoudt? I've lost track of him and thought…"

The room fell silent as Barrie listened intently, face drawn. Finally she spoke. "I'm terribly sorry. I hadn't heard. It's just such a shock. Please forgive me for disturbing you." She hung up.

"What?"

"That was Manning Stoudt's father. It seems Manning died ten years ago."

"Then who is this guy? And what have we stumbled into?"

They sat in stunned silence.

"Wait. Let's double check," Barrie said. "Ten years ago in Chicago—the newspaper's archive should have the obit." She connected with a bored second-shifter, only too happy to chat.

"I remember that one," he said. "A prominent family. Yep, here it is. Natural causes. Memorial fund, yeah, he must have had cancer."

She crosschecked the date of birth and other particulars, all of which matched.

The women returned to the documents. "Look at this," Margaret said. "Here's how our Manning got his job. He wrote directly to Frank Ziegler, alluding to his family's fortune in need of investing. Is that transparent or what! And there's a note to Jeffrey from Frank, simply saying 'Jeff. Hire him.'"

"And neither one checked!"

"Apparently not."

"The Birdsboro file—what did you find?"

Kingsley smoothed three rumpled papers. "According to this, Manning, or whoever the hell he really is, lent

$500,000 to construct a facility that doesn't exist."

"How could a scam like this happen?"

"The loan officer and the customer can be the only ones to physically inspect the property. In this case, the customer is nonexistent and the supporting documents are forged. The embezzler installs a mailbox on a rental property and uses it as the business address to receive bank statements and mail."

"Why not just rent a post office box?"

"That risks surveillance equipment and eye witnesses."

"So, how does he get the money? Loans must be repaid."

"To go undetected, the embezzler draws down funds to pay the premiums and interest until he's ready to abscond. At that point he transfers most of the remaining balance to a personal account—maybe offshore—which he'll clean out."

"And it goes undetected?"

"As long as he doesn't use his own name, miss payments, or trigger alarms."

"Like the Wire Products mix-up."

"Exactly. I'm betting that somewhere near Deer Lake there's a mailbox for Wireless, Inc."

"We have to report this, but how? 'We girls just happened to stumble across...'"

"Barrie! It's a little late to do this by the book," Margaret said. "According to procedure, Kingsley should have taken this to her supervisor when she first suspected something was wrong."

"Still a bad idea since Manning would know who fingered him. Who knows what else he or his accomplice is capable of?" Kingsley asked. "And we can't be certain that Nathaniel isn't involved."

"What about Warren?" Margaret said.

"No good," Barrie said. "He'd delegate it back through the executives."

Kingsley sighed. "We've got to trust someone. The loan scam precedes Todd's joining the bank. If I can just sound him out, hypothetically perhaps—"

"If he's the best choice, do it fast," Barrie said. "Margaret, if all those files are bogus, this scam could run into millions. What if executive's already on top of it? What if—"

"Stop," Margaret said with atypical impatience. "There's nothing more we can do tonight. We can have a post mortem after we sleep." She softened her voice. "Kingsley, what do you want to do with these documents?"

"I'll take them home, scan them into my computer, and hide the originals with the blue list. I'll back up my files and ask my neighbor Isaac to safeguard the disk. In his consulting business, he deals with confidential stuff all the time. I can trust him not to look at the contents."

They agreed to the plan and, at least for the moment, their comfort zones settled.

Chapter 17

Sleep eluded Kingsley until finally, at three, she got up and swallowed an Ambien. By Sunday afternoon, as she finished her laundry and polished surfaces that didn't need dusting, she began practicing her speech to Todd. Absently, she fluffed the silk flowers arranged in Grammy's blue pottery vase, angling it on the kitchen counter. Grammy used to tell her it was her favorite—that just looking at it made her happy. Summer mornings, Grammy would pull out dead stems and let Kingsley pick whatever she thought would look pretty.

How old had she been? Four? Five? She entered her study and patiently cleaned her computer's keyboard, all the while phrasing her version of events that led to their uncovering and verifying the loan scam. Their breaking into the executive area would require delicate explaining.

With the dusk came her dragons—that disconsolate pall of unshakable anxiety coupled with loneliness. *Change the scene. Find activity, lights and people,* she commanded herself. Quickly, as if to outrun her dragons, she swapped her work sweats for stretch slacks, an angora turtleneck, warm jacket and gloves.

Streetlights pulsed on as she drove toward the mall.

The minute she stepped into bookstore, the aroma of new books and fresh coffee revived her spirits. Sunk in an over-stuffed chair with a latté, she had time to replay the whole weekend's events. Hopewell was magic, and the Birdsboro detour outrageously productive, but she needed an entrée.

Her well-rehearsed speeches sounded contrived—which they were. And the way she'd ended their afternoon—so abruptly, so rudely. Had she even been listening to what he was saying?

An idea beckoned. She scanned book jackets, checking for old-house renovations. Her search yielded plans for decks, masonry and carpentry, volumes on lighthouses, barns and even outhouses, but no colonial restoration. She was close to abandoning the idea when a picture of old stone houses jumped from a sale table.

Turning the pages, she found beautiful shots of colonial homes, complete with fireplaces, banisters, glowing pine floors, and even a table spread with a Christmas buffet. What a find!

Impulsively, she inscribed a note while she waited in line. As she walked to the parking lot, her plan congealed. Why not take it to him right now? Just get it done. She knew his condo was close to the bank. Her car seemed to steer itself onto the bypass. She should call ahead but she'd left her cell phone at home. She exited south, scheming.

After presenting the book with her thanks for Saturday, she'd ease into the scam. Maybe get him to come to her place and take the papers tonight. Just play it by ear. She smiled, remembering his tactics—always have a Plan B. If Plan A doesn't feel right, just give him the book, go home, and get on his calendar for Monday.

The condos were clustered attractively, separated by narrow lanes with no communal entrances, decks, patios, or backyards. White pines, dogwood, Bartlett pears, and rhododendron rose from sculpted bark mounds. Glowing street lamps on redwood posts conjured images of the old lamplighter from long, long ago, who had been immortalized in a song.

She drove slowly, straining for names. Halfway through the development, she found his. She felt her resolve melt. *This is crazy,* she thought. *Turn around. Go home. Give him the book some other time.* Ignoring the voice, she rang his bell.

Although there were lights on inside, no one responded. She tapped the knocker, but feeling panicky, turned to escape. The door opened slightly, and as she turned back, she felt foolish. From the raised foyer, he towered over her and something about him seemed odd. "Kingsley," he said quietly as he opened it farther.

"I was at the bookstore and stumbled across this. Thought you might like it." This was coming out badly. "It was an impulse. A little thank you for yesterday. I'll leave it with you and catch you another time."

"Please. Come in." Even in the dim light, she was sure that something was wrong. Uncharacteristically disheveled, he had been drinking, and obviously a lot. She avoided eye contact, determined to leave as quickly and gracefully as possible. She groped for her speeches, but her mind had gone blank.

"I was thinking about that stone house you showed me and, I'll admit, was feeling a little rude for running off after you showed me such a nice day. Sorry if I've disturbed you. It's rather late and tomorrow's a workday. I'd better be going." She handed him the book and started to leave.

"That was thoughtful of you. Please, come in and sit

down." His attempt not to slur his words wasn't working. "Let me take your coat." He half lifted it off her shoulders before she could stop him, and then steered her across the tile foyer into a huge living room with a vaulted ceiling and miles of beige carpet. On the left wall, a tawny leather sofa and two matching chairs encircled a steamer trunk on which he set the book.

She sat stiffly on the edge of the deep sofa. While he bent to turn a few pages, she stole a look at the room. On the end wall, an Eames lounge chair and ottoman angled toward a fireplace that was flanked by bulging bookshelves.

Across the room, facing the couch, a sweep of draperies back-dropped a sturdy country table and chairs. Old eight-foot shelves held more books. She might have missed the stunning cherry tall-case clock beside the kitchen pass-through had it not chimed eight o'clock. The room lacked accessories, pictures, or personal mementos, save a few family photos. The only clutter was the Sunday New York Times, and a glass of melting ice.

Abruptly, he gave up the pretense of examining the book. "I usually don't drink very much. Had an unsettling call and didn't handle it well. It's true what they say about not drinking alone. I lost track."

While she was rummaging for the right thing to say, she heard herself ask rather bluntly, "What happened?"

To her surprise, he started to talk. "My best friend Randall called. Said Maureen, my ex-wife, has remarried, is pregnant. Telling mutual friends what a loser I was—that I'd been tested and couldn't have kids." He shook his head and reached for his glass, but stopped. "Even for her, that's an outrageous violation of my privacy."

"Do you still love her?"

"Hell, no! You asked me yesterday how I dealt with the

pressure. My job's a piece of cake compared to dealing with her viciousness." He leaned forward, forearms on his thighs, rubbing his hands slowly back and forth, eyes focused somewhere beyond the trunk. "When I confronted her about other men, she turned on me. Said it was my fault, that I didn't satisfy her, couldn't, never did." He continued to stare at the back of his mind. "She'd let me know that she pleasured herself. 'Why not? Everything you do is all wrong.' Do you have any idea how that makes a man feel?" He paused, as if dredging the sludge from the depths of his mind. "How's that for a come-on? Now you're supposed to say, 'No, I'll bet you're terrific. Here, let me prove it.'"

"How long has it been since the breakup?"

"Six, seven years, if you don't count the preceding five-year disaster."

Kingsley felt her eyebrows go up. "And she's still pushing your buttons? That's a long time. Surely you've met somebody—"

He shook his head. "Women are attracted to my position, my appearance. My brain and what I look like are accidents of genetics, not an accomplishment, but add it together and the expectations are phenomenal. And if I can't father children..." He looked up, avoiding her face. "Suppose I met someone special. At what point do I say 'oh, by the way, I'm good to be seen with, can buy you whatever you want, but don't count on a family?'"

"I think that you're selling yourself and real women short. There are no guarantees for anyone. And some women don't want children. Or already have all they can handle. If people love each other, they'll work it out. And what of the couples who have children, but the marriages fail miserably? I think, if the relationship's solid, the rest will fall into place."

She settled into the couch, forgetting her nervousness, and when one shoe dropped, tucked her foot beneath her. "She's done a real job on your mind. If she wasn't satisfied, why didn't she tell you what she wanted and needed?"

"I was supposed to know."

"How? Couples should communicate—tell each other what's fun and what's not, what feels good and doesn't."

"It wasn't about communication. It was about control, domination, and keeping me off balance. She had zero interest in getting it right. While we were still married, she ran with some pretty wild people. I had to be tested, scared to death of what she'd brought home. I went to an out-of-town clinic, imagining what the technicians must think about my screwing around indiscriminately. It was so degrading. She said the baby she aborted couldn't have been mine. That she's perfectly healthy, but I'm shooting blanks."

"Are you sure? If she lied about other things—"

He sighed.

"I'm sorry. It's none of my—"

"She claimed I'd known all along. During the divorce, when she couldn't tap into my trust fund, she sued me for misrepresentation and fraud. I had myself tested to prove otherwise. You don't need an MBA to understand zeroes. Randall, my lifelong friend, had seen I was drowning and had her followed. Turned over photos of important, camera-shy people to my attorney. Suddenly, there was a settlement and division of property for just those five years."

Kingsley realized she was barely breathing. By tomorrow, he'd regret this conversation.

"That tall-case clock was my great-great grandfather's. Granddad protected it for me until she was gone. And my books, she didn't want them. She didn't read. And she hated the Eames chair, although she tried to get it for spite. Fortunately, Dad still had the receipt from the sixties. It has the original Brazilian rosewood veneer and duck down. Because I'd always loved it, he gave it to me when I graduated from Harvard. When she deliberately scratched it with her car keys, I took it to Dad's for safe keeping."

"How is she still managing to get at you? And why would she want to after all this time? She must be feeding information to your friend, knowing he talks to you. You should shut that down."

"Yeah, I suppose. But that doesn't change things. I'll never understand why she hated me so much."

"Maybe not having you holds allure, or she gets sadistic pleasure tormenting you. Maybe she's jealous and wants to punish you for what you are and she's not. Or maybe she's sick. You may never know. What you need is distance."

"That's what my friend says." He looked up at her. "This call today—my guard was down. I'm sorry. I shouldn't be burdening you. I thought I'd jettisoned this baggage a long time ago."

"I wasn't invited, remember? I've intruded. I really don't have a clue how to help. I pry and chatter too much."

He smiled. "You have helped, believe me. A lot more than this," he said, pointing to his glass. "If I'd only known you were coming—" He sat back and faced her. "Could you stay awhile? Make some coffee while I clean up?"

"Sure. When was the last time you ate?"

He thought a minute. "Yesterday."

Todd disappeared down a hall. Shortly, Kingsley heard a shower running. The kitchen counter was bare except for the coffeepot, toaster, and a juicer. Colombian supreme she found in the freezer and filters in the cupboard. The pickings in the fridge were pretty sparse, but she found eggs, cheese, salsa, peppers, and onions for an omelet and a package of frozen hash browns. While the coffee dripped, she wondered—what if he'd been entertaining? Making mad passionate love on the living room floor? Had come to the door pulling himself together? She giggled at the image. No, he would have ignored the door.

"What's tickling you?" In black sweats and damp hair, he reminded her of the first time she'd ever seen him. She handed his plate and mug over the counter. "That's good coffee. You must teach me. I make black death."

Kingsley refilled his mug and one for herself. "Drink lots of water tonight. It's dehydration that causes hangovers." Returning to the living room, he opened the book and turned to the pages she'd bookmarked with small scraps of paper. "That house was photographed in Connecticut, but it's very similar to the one you showed me yesterday. Look at the little windowpanes. That's 'twelve over twelve,' right? See, I was paying attention."

He looked normal again as he studied interiors then set down the book. "I hope you don't think badly of me."

"Of course not. I know how hard it is to be tough, especially when someone blindsides me. We have to go forward. Todd?" He looked up at her. "You're every inch a man and don't ever let anybody tell you otherwise." He reached for her hand and, turning it over, rubbed it between his. "Now you're supposed to tell me I'd make a wonderful sister."

"That never crossed my mind. Why couldn't I have met you years ago?"

"Because I was in junior high."

Slightly unnerved by the mounting intimacy, she rose to leave. He helped her into her coat and reached for the doorknob, but turned back instead. Drawing her to him, with unguarded feelings, he asked, "Do you have any idea how special you are?" He kissed her with uncensored passion that melted her core then smiled at her as if in relief. "I've wanted to do that since the first time I saw you."

They separated, the brief moment passing.

"Guess I'm okay for a Sunday evening."

He laughed and bear-hugged her quickly. He stepped back. "You better go before I forget I'm a gentleman." His eyes swept her face. He kissed her forehead and held her for a brief moment. Finally he opened the door and accompanied her to her car. "It's very dark. Please be careful." He still blocked her path. "We'll talk. Soon. There's so much I've been wanting to say."

In her living room's void, she glanced at Andy's picture, feeling disloyal yet unable to ignore her myriad feelings for Todd. Forbidden comparisons demanded her attention. Even Todd, who had seemed on top of the world, had dragons too, but his road to healing seemed tougher than hers. She'd had the support of countless loved ones, her illusions intact. Death in its finality lent purity to the end of their story, but Todd's was an ongoing tragedy. Shedding her street clothes, she got ready for bed, longing for sleep to blunt her conflicted emotions.

Todd, in his own space, picked up her book, which opened itself to the page where she'd written:

T
Follow that dream.
It's a good one.
Thanks for Saturday.
K

He rubbed her imprint and recalled she had said that a few friends had once called her Lee, but K, just the initial, had come from her roommates The lack of a period meant there would be no end to their friendship. Pajama language, they called it—that which is shared only with intimates. Did that now include him?

Todd felt the cold splash of reality. "Oh, baby, what am I doing to you?"

He paced through the condo, gnawed by his conscience. Finally he left for the trails and ran to exhaustion.

Alone in her bed and dead to the world, Kingsley touched the bow of Todd's lip with her tongue, running her fingers through his soft hair. She savored his scent and released him enough to read searing passion in eyes that spoke volumes. She drew him closer, and closer. His strength semi-checked, the feel and smell, her hands running downward. The throb that her body built somewhere within her…

Kingsley awoke, gulping for air, not grasping immediately just what had happened. She dropped to her pillow to sort out the dream and the extent to which she'd been drawn to his force field. She tossed off damp sheets, padding out to the living room to drop on the couch. Shivering, she searched Andy's photo, anguished and torn. There it was. She'd fallen in love with a boy. Todd was a man.

Shaken, she went to the bathroom, turned on the shower and directed the steaming deluge down on her head to wash tears that, once started, she just couldn't stop. Her Victorian promise to live his life through her until she could join him now seemed ridiculous.

I just want to be normal, she quietly sobbed through the water. *Have someone to love, to care for, come home to, dream with, and make love to. Is that so wrong?* She exhausted herself and the water heater, then toweled herself with wrinkled fingers. She dropped back into bed and fell into a dreamless vortex.

At five, she awoke abruptly. Between swallows of coffee, she smoothed on fresh sheets, reassembling blankets, coverlet, pillows and shams. Slowly the caffeine swept out her brain. Tears, she had read, are cathartic, and she believed it. She gazed outside at predawn's velvet light and felt her spirit start to sing. She had survived one full year alone, and it was time to move on. Today, first thing, she'd unload the loan scam and savor what else he had on his mind.

Chapter 18

When Kingsley spotted Todd crossing the atrium, an uncontrollable grin took charge of her face. The clever greeting that she had rehearsed sounded lame.

"Forget the water," he said. "I need more aspirin. My head is splitting." He reached for her elbow and lowered his voice. "Did I completely blow my image last night?"

"Of course not."

He steered her away from the traffic, and turned grave eyes to meet hers.

She squeezed the arm he had turned to the wall. "At the risk of sounding like a corporate groupie, I think you're special too. I want to see you again. We could talk over something less lethal than scotch, like the relative merits of deregulation, or maybe something a whole lot more personal." She raised her eyebrows suggestively and ran her fingertip under his shirt cuff. "You could give me the grand tour of your place."

He paused entirely too long, casting unseeing eyes at the balcony, then down to the floor. "I am so sorry. I have misled you, which just wasn't right. I can't see you. I have too many problems that won't go away. You deserve something better." He paused, eyes to the balcony again, while Kingsley scrambled to arrange the right look on her face. "Oh, god," he said, avoiding her eyes. "That sounded awful. I'm no good at this sort of thing."

She pulled back her hand and struggled for composure. "I understand. I know about dragons—been bloodied myself. Sometimes they get the best of us. Well, if our ships ever cross again, toot." She swiveled her watch. "Gotta go." She turned to escape, but remembered her mission. "There is one thing—I need your help with a problem. Something wrong with our loans."

"I have time now."

"I don't feel safe talking here at the bank."

"Does it have anything to do with that Birdsboro property?"

"It does. I'll call your secretary to get the documents to you. They're at home. Sorry, I've gotta run."

"Wait a minute. Please—"

She darted into the elevator and sought the back corner behind its fast-closing door. *Count to three hundred by thirteens, the bricks in a wall.* She forced concentration, willing her face to hide his rejection, her eyes to halt the scratch of fresh tears.

Don't cry, don't cry, do not cry! Picture the veins in a leaf, the wisps of a cloud. By the time she reached Four, she could walk to her office, under control, and snap her door shut without losing it.

Marle rapped, said her name, and turned the knob simultaneously. With one look at her AA's compassionate face, Kingsley crumbled.

"Please, let me help. Anything, " Marle pleaded. She snatched a tissue. "Here."

"Nobody can. I've just got to work through something."

"Why don't I field your calls—keep people at bay? Buy you some time?"

Kingsley nodded. "I owe you."

Marle hurried out, colliding with Barrie, who closed the door in the time it took Kingsley to turn back from the window.

"Kingsley, what happened? You look awful, even for you. Give!"

"I made a terrible fool of myself. Yesterday evening I went to see Todd. We talked—and—" Kingsley struggled to steady her voice. "I misunderstood the situation badly. He isn't interested."

"He said that last night? Before or after y'all..."

"Nothing happened, but when I left, I thought—this morning he said—"

"That bastard! Kingsley, you misread nothing. The way he looks at you? Makes excuses to wander through lending? It's the talk of the bank. Tell you what—go home and pack, and I'll clear my calendar. We'll get some really good wine and some gourmet takeout. Have an old-fashioned male-bashing party. I have a repertoire you still haven't heard. I'll get you off to the Wards in plenty of time."

"Oh, Barrie, you're such a dear. I've got to stay and get this loan to committee." Kingsley tapped a fat folder on top of her desk. "And besides, I need to have Todd stop this evening—"

"Excuse me?"

"I'm still going to drop the whole loan scam on him. Don't worry. I won't mention you guys."

"And you think you can trust him?"

"He is a good man. I'm not wrong about that. He's just not interested in a relationship. I never should have let down my guard."

"Bet he has a wife and eight kids in Upstate New York."

"Nothing like that."

"I can come over this evening—"

"I'm thinking about calling it quits."

"You can't do that! You just got here. Look how you've turned your department around, to say nothing of salvaging all of us wastelings. Why, in just a few years you could have Nathaniel's job when he moves up. Who knows what else?"

"Barrie, unlike you and Todd, I can't make my job my whole life. I realize now that I need someone special, and that won't happen here."

"Promise me you won't do anything rash until we can talk. Men! Their power's obnoxious. Call me tonight as soon as you get rid of him."

"Please don't tell Margaret. She thinks so highly of Todd, and he's done nothing wrong."

"Sure," Barrie said with slit eyes. "What a prince." She hugged her and left.

Kingsley resumed looking unseeing out the window.

Marle returned. "Todd just got off the elevator."

Kingsley shot her a look of dismay and shook her head violently.

"Punch your conference line," Marle ordered. "It'll light up on my phone. I'll handle him."

Kingsley set the receiver down on her desk and scrambled for something compelling to do. Opening the file for Scarborough, Inc.'s loan application, she concentrated on the new venture that would mint gold for Keynote.

She reviewed the numbers and all the supporting documentation. After what felt like a reasonable time, she hung up the phone and responded automatically to somebody's knock.

Sunlight betrayed how tired and uncomfortable he felt.

"A minute?" Todd asked very quietly in a voice that she already missed.

"Of course," she said without offering him a seat. "You're going to love this deal." She swept the files with her hand. "Puts me over my fourth quarter goal one month ahead. That should ease your hangover."

"We need to talk about this Birdsboro business. You could be in danger. I have several meetings that can't be postponed. How much do you know?"

"I have written proof of fraud: that it's bogus. And that I'm in way over my head. I just didn't know who I could trust." Their eyes met. She ignored the force field, wanting to run until she dropped dead or got to St. Louis.

"I'm meeting out-of-town analysts at four. How about sometime between seven and eight?"

"Stop by my place. I'll give you the proof." She paused, choosing her words carefully. "If I'm wrong and found out, it could end my career. Perhaps get me sued or even arrested. If I'm right, it goes to the top. Can I trust you not to betray me? Say nothing to anyone?"

"Of course. I know how bitter betrayal tastes and wouldn't do that to anyone." He looked at his watch. "I'm late. Please," he said solemnly. "Leave it alone until we can talk."

"I think it's the tip of the iceberg. I'll fill you in later—take five, ten minutes max," she said with professional briskness. "Can't give it any more than that. I'm leaving for Philly. The Ward family's gathering for the anniversary of my husband's death. I may stay a few days if I'm needed."

"I'm sorry. This must be a rough time for you, and I've made it worse. About what I said earlier—"

She cut him off with a flick of her hand. "Just leave. Forget the whole silly thing. Already forgotten. I'm impulsive sometimes. Besides, I could never be serious about men who want to make my decisions for me."

"I just want to talk. Make you understand—"

She lowered her eyebrows. "If you want to see my dazzling deal show up at loan committee, you'll have to excuse me while I nail down the details. I only have a few hours. Nathaniel will present it while I'm away." She shot him a look, then added, "If you wouldn't mind closing my door on your way out? Thanks." She shuffled a few papers to avoid further eye contact and didn't look up until the door closed.

Knowing she'd taken a fork in the road to a place only God knew and He wasn't telling, Kingsley bulldozed her feelings aside. The Scarborough deal was so large that she'd need another bank to participate. Since the client hated big banks and loved Keynote, losing the deal wasn't likely. *This should have been an exquisite morning*, she thought, forcing herself not to think about the void he created.

She searched her files for other small-bank references and came up empty. She went to Nathaniel. "Call Fred Macmillan," Nathaniel said as he rummaged his Rolodex for Kingsley's predecessor's home number. "He was good and so honest."

"I never heard why he left. The lenders all think he was superb and the customers can't say enough about him. Do you know?"

"Jeffrey Johnston came to see me one Friday at four—told me that they—" He pointed toward the ceiling. "—were unhappy with him, that he was being terminated immediately. Being a newcomer, it wasn't my place to question Jeff or executive orders. I had to assume there was a very good reason. Now I'm not so sure."

Back in her office, Kingsley dialed Fred's number and, at his direction, quickly located the folder listing the banks that he recommended. "I put them in order with the best on the top. Good luck."

"You've made my job as a newcomer easy. Clearly, you did an excellent job. To say that you're missed would be a gross understatement."

Macmillan snorted but thanked her. "That's the first nice thing I've heard. I've wondered if staff thought I'd committed a crime."

When Kingsley hesitated, the man forged ahead.

"HR policy is very clear. If an employee is lacking, either personally or professionally, the supervisor is to talk with the employee and plan how to remediate the situation. If the employee doesn't improve, he's given a written warning. If that doesn't work, he's put on probation with a time frame. Then he's restored, demoted or fired. Of course, if he decks the boss or robs the bank, he's out. All my reviews were excellent. And there were no complaints that I knew of. It was such a shock."

Kingsley remembered that from the HR minutia she had initialed on her first day. "Did you ask for an explanation? Or a chance to defend yourself?"

"Jeffrey told me that Warren and Doug were 'uncomfortable with me.' The only thing I could think of was that I'd ticked someone off, that somebody had lied about me, that I'd witnessed something I shouldn't have, or some high-level person wanted my job for a friend or a relative. I didn't have a chance to defend myself."

"Did you consult an attorney?"

"A very good one who specializes in human resource law. Cost me a thousand bucks to learn that I couldn't win."

"Really!

"I didn't have a contract or a union. He said Pennsylvania is an at-will state; that they could fire me, or I could quit

without notice and without reason. He did say that what
happened to me was unethical and immoral, but that's not
illegal."

"So you decided not to sue?"

"I could have. The attorney was willing to take the case,
but he said my severance package and unemployment com-
pensation were probably more than a jury would award.
And even if I won, the bank could appeal. 'Bury me in
money' was the phrase that he used. 'Tie me up for years.
Maybe counter sue. Try to ruin my reputation and embarrass my family.' I had to sign within a very short time frame
or lose the package. I'd run out of time."

"Mr. Macmillan, may I ask you something in confidence?"

"Sure. And it's Fred."

"Okay, Fred. Did you notice anything suspicious in the
commercial loan portfolio?"

Macmillan paused. "I can't answer that kind of question
without violating the terms of my severance agreement. If I
divulge any details, or accuse the bank, any employee, or
director of wrongdoing, I'm in violation. Legally, they
could come after me."

"What can you tell me?"

"I did have a concern, but I handled it by the book. Took
it to Jeffrey Johnston, the head of HR. He said he would put
it through channels confidentially. I never heard how it
turned out because I left the bank before final resolution."

"Did you put your concerns in writing? And if so, do you
remember the date?"

"I emailed it to him on, let me think—it would have been
May thirty-first. I saved a copy of that email, but again, I
can't share it because it names an individual. I 'retired' Friday, June second."

"Could you at least tell me if you suspected fraud?"

"I can't answer that either."

"I'm on my private cell phone, so there's no way this call can be recorded. If you did not suspect fraud in the commercial loan portfolio, please stay on the line."

For all she suspected, the click and the sound of the line going dead stunned her. Her mind shot to Todd and, for the first time, she wondered if her choices were to walk or perhaps run away.

ᏝᎧᏝᎧ

The bank's fountain chimes sounded six times as she exited into a November evening as bleak as her mind. Raw wind gusted once colorful leaves, now depressingly brown, into spirals that nicked at her ankles. At home she was chagrined to see her parking space taken, forcing her to parallel park down the street. She trudged to her building.

Feed Pandora, she ticked from her mental list. *Pack, call home, and mentally buttress myself for the Ward's service for Andy.* Soul sick, she climbed the stairs slowly, reliving the moments one year ago. His poor wretched body closed in his casket. She prayed, *Dear God in Heaven, please grant me a few shreds of dignity to have that meeting with Todd, unload this loan scam, and send him away without losing it.*

Juggling her briefcase and purse at her door, she searched her pockets for keys and inserted the house key into the door lock. *Odd,* she thought, when it wouldn't turn. She tried it again, only harder. It still wouldn't budge. On a hunch, she tried turning it left and realized that the door was already unlocked.

Had she been that distracted at noon when she had

stopped home to back up her PC and give Isaac the disk to safeguard?

Pushing the heavy door with her hip, she eased forward. Street lamps provided the only illumination, the timer having failed to turn on her lamps. "Why not?" she grumbled into the darkness, pausing to let her eyes adjust to the gloom. "Pandora! Where are you, baby?"

She heard a faint noise somewhere nearby and froze, skin prickling. Some force drew her eyes left to the Chippendale mirror that faced her kitchen's entrance on her right. In the dim light her mind played a trick. Instead of a mirror she saw a framed portrait. She did not recognize the face and had no recollection of whom it might be. Before she had time to question the incongruity, the face in the portrait moved. A man. Big. Dark. Raising his arm. Instinctively she raised her hand to protect herself, but she was too slow. A horrible pain crashed through her head, turning everything black.

Chapter 19

D own!" Isaac admonished his Persian cat that had curled on his warm monitor, fluffy tail dangling in front of the screen. Concentration shot, Isaac updated his customer's billing report, stretched, and looked at the clock. Seven p.m. His partner, Michael, an EMT second-shifter, would be at lunch about now. He rose to make himself a sandwich and defrost meat for the walnut stuffed chicken breast they'd have at midnight.

As he wandered from window to window flexing cramped muscles, movement in the shrubbery next door caught his eye. When he knocked on the glass, a little creature looked up, white bib glowing against its black fur. How unusual, he thought. A kitten, so like Pandora. He watched for a minute as she licked her paw. Then he caught a glimpse of her turquoise collar. Startled, Isaac grabbed his coat and shrugged into it while dashing outside.

"How'd you get out? You don't have claws to defend yourself. You could be killed in this traffic." Approaching slowly, he kept up the monologue in soothing tones. Much to his relief, she stayed put. "Gotcha. Now, what's your story?"

He draped Pandora over his arm and stroked her fur from nose to tail tip. When his hand touched something rough, he stopped under Kingsley's porch light. Her feet were caked with something dark.

"Are you hurt?"

Gently, he turned her belly up and examined her carefully. It looked like blood, but he found no wounds. Something was terribly wrong.

Propelled by sheer panic he tore up her stairs. Kingsley's door stood ajar, the interior dark. A crumpled form lay just inside.

"Kingsley!" Isaac rushed in and felt for a pulse. She had one. He checked her breathing. She was. Phone. Yes, his cell phone was still in his pocket. He jabbed nine-one-one.

ควຽວ

Todd checked his watch. It was past eight and he was quite late. He jerked to attention as he approached Kingsley's block, which pulsed with red and blue lights. Double-parked, he dodged traffic and raced toward the commotion.

Police were keeping the curious at bay while EMTs wheeled a gurney toward a waiting ambulance. A thin blonde man hurried beside them, clutching a cat. Todd caught a glimpse of the victim's dark hair and then recognized Pandora.

"Kingsley!"

"You've got to stay back!"

Ignoring the cop, Todd wedged himself closer.

"Kingsley!" Her face, neck and clothes were covered with blood, her head wrapped in blood-soaked bandages. Her eyes were closed.

"She's dead," someone said.

"Did you know her?" someone else asked.

Bewildered, he nodded, unable to process the situation.

"Get some pressure on that," somebody barked as they halted momentarily.

"What happened?" Todd asked again, this time to the man holding her cat. Someone thumped the closed ambulance doors and it took off, siren wailing, while milling spectators compared information in hushed voices.

"Pandora got out. I was taking her home. I found her." Isaac started to cry. A policewoman approached him with questions. "I'll call her parents," he said and disappeared with Pandora.

Todd made his way through the crowd to her steps and was stopped at her door by police. "Who are you?"

Todd identified himself. "What happened?" he asked, staring in disbelief at the shambles within, as if a whirlwind had ripped through the place. Drawers and doors gaped, tables were overturned and items once arranged in neat little groups were strewn on rugs, some smashed on the hardwood. A large pool of blood congealed in the vestibule, and shards of blue pottery littered the floor. Kingsley's briefcase and purse lay to one side, both splattered with blood. A policewoman was checking Kingsley's wallet for ID. She touched Todd's arm gently.

"Sir, are you hurt?"

Stunned by the wreckage inside the apartment, he shook his head no.

"You're white as a sheet. You better sit down before you fall down."

He nodded numbly and sat on the stairs.

"It appears she surprised an intruder."

Todd transfixed on her blood.

"She was hit on the head and knocked out." She illustrated on her own head, running cupped fingers back and forth on her crown. "I'm no doctor, but I do know that head wounds can bleed profusely. I heard them say she was stable."

Isaac returned, still holding Pandora, and joined Todd on the stairs to compare information.

* හ*

As the Aldersons' vehicle surged west, the terrible consequences of head injuries raged in Sarah's mind. She looked at Henry, jaw set.

Returning her glance, he squeezed her hand. "She'll be all right."

She clutched at his confidence, although she knew he was scared. She thought of the early days of their marriage, happy and with a plan. They dreamed of a family, but after three miscarriages, they suspected they harbored a genetic abnormality. After much soul searching, tests and tears, she'd accepted it. They had each other, extended families and friends, meaningful work and rewarding activities.

Ten years evaporated before that special Christmas vacation. By February, Sarah knew she was pregnant, but this time she felt wonderful. In September she delivered a perfect little daughter, whom they named after her grandmother. Sarah remembered standing by Kingsley's cradle in tears, vowing she'd kill anyone who harmed her child.

Now, what if she had brain damage? That beautiful person. The one of whom everyone would say, why her? *Drive faster. No, don't.* Their car flew past myriad houses, whose windows blinked snatches of ordinary families, cocooned in their families' evening routines.

Henry swept into the ER after parking the car. "Where is she?" he asked Sarah.

"She's been admitted. They did a CAT scan and an EEG some time ago. The nurse said that's routine when a person's been out more than briefly and has vomited." Her lip quivered. "They need to make sure that her brain isn't swelling."

Henry passed her some tissues then steered her toward a bank of visitors' chairs.

A man in a gray business suit approached them. "Mr. and Mrs. Alderson? I'm Todd Henning from Kingsley's bank. I was on my way to meet with her when they were wheeling her out." Henry and Sarah jumped to their feet and approached the stranger. "Her neighbor Isaac asked me to tell you he'd meet you here shortly," Todd continued.

Sarah processed his grave face and quiet voice. His name rang a bell.

"This must be a terrible shock," he said. "Can I get you something to drink? There's a soda machine nearby."

Sarah nodded. "Some water would be nice. Thank you."

A nurse with a clipboard approached them. "I need to verify some information about your daughter. Does she have any medical conditions or allergies?"

Sarah rummaged in her purse for a card. "Call this doctor's office in Philadelphia for a list of drugs she can't take. She has a history of ulcers. Her husband spent days researching it, convinced it was bacterial, and he was right. He adored her, was so protective. This never would have happened if he hadn't—"

Henry put his arm around her as her eyes refilled with tears. "Sarah, we must get a grip before we see her."

"I'm sorry," she said to Todd, who was waiting at a discreet distance holding their drinks. "It's kind of you to take an interest. Many employers don't care. And it must be near midnight."

Isaac arrived with his companion Michael who, as an EMT, knew the hospital complex. He led them through the labyrinth of corridors and elevators to the ward, which was quiet and darkened. While the others waited, Michael spoke rapidly to the charge nurse who paged the doctor.

He materialized immediately and approached the huddled group, introducing himself. "Mr. and Mrs. Alderson, your daughter has a hard head," he said calmly. "Her skull isn't fractured and the CAT scan and EEG both look good. She has a concussion and lost a lot of blood, but we're expecting no complications. Lucky someone found her so quickly. We've sutured her scalp—a nasty gash, but the scar won't show through her hair. Broken bones in her left middle and ring fingers have been splinted. The fine cuts on her forehead are superficial. The bruises on her forehead—that's probably where she hit the floor. Her ribs are bruised. If they'd been broken that could have punctured a lung or her heart. She's going to be black and blue for a while."

"Can I see her now, Doctor?" Sarah asked.

"Of course, but keep it brief."

As soon as the Aldersons left, the doctor turned to Todd. "She was asking for Todd. Is that you? Let's talk privately."

They moved to the far corner of the visitors' lounge.

"What didn't you tell her parents?" Todd demanded.

"To say she was lucky trivializes what happened, but she was. This attack was brutal." He reached into his pocket. "They found this in her clothing—a chunk of pottery. The vase must have been cracked and given way, otherwise it would have crushed her skull like a nut. Had her head been positioned differently and a sturdier weapon been used, her neck could have broken. She said 'Grammy was watching over her,' whatever that means."

"Her briefcase—it's rigid with metal corners. Could she have struck that?"

The doctor leaned forward and lowered his voice. "I suspect that he kicked her. He must have worn sneakers or had lousy aim or poor footing. If he left footprints, that might help confirm an identification."

Todd raked his fingers through his hair. "Was she raped?"

"No."

"Is there anything else?"

"She put a tooth through her lip. That will be watched for infection. You'll have to be very careful with her for a while. For now, there's no such thing as a good position."

"Our relationship is—"

"I don't need to know. She was unconscious when they brought her in. As she was coming around in the ER, she mistook our bright lights for the ones in the tunnel—you know, the one people remember from near-death experiences. She was mumbling that she had to go back to 'tell Todd something.'"

"We had a misunderstanding this morning. Did she mention Andrew or Andy?"

"No. After a while she became more coherent and started fussing about not telling her parents." He smiled. "As if we could keep it a secret. She was insistent that we not worry them."

"Thank you, Doctor. Especially for your upbeat talk with her folks."

"I treat whole families."

"What can I do?"

"Can you protect her from the bastard who did this?" the

doctor asked rhetorically. He patted Todd's shoulder. "If she shrieks when you touch her, don't assume you've lost your charm."

His joke missed its mark. "If I ever find the bastard who did this, I'll kill him."

✧✦✧

Sarah gasped at the battered wisp lost in bandages and white sheets. Kingsley opened her eyes. "Done far worse skiing," she muttered, trying not to move her face when she spoke. "I heard—a noise. Saw a face in the mirror—" She closed her eyes, but shot them open, remembering.

They took turns holding her uninjured hand, talking soothingly.

In the hall, a nurse motioned to Todd. "Mr. Ward, they had to cut off your wife's ring. Her hand was swelling."

Before Todd could correct her, she'd darted away, leaving him staring at her butchered ring.

"Todd from the bank has been here for hours," Sarah remembered. "He's very upset—gave blood for you."

"Got to talk to him. It's important." Her parents exchanged skeptical glances. "Please. It's okay."

Promising to return in a few minutes, they beckoned to Todd.

The charge nurse, looking annoyed, began to march toward him, but the nurse who returned the ring intervened. "It's okay. He's the husband."

The charge nurse retreated.

Kingsley forced her eyes open, touched the bandage, and winced. She picked up her left hand and moaned. She tried her lip with the tip of her tongue, but found that both hurt. When she slit her eyes open, Todd had appeared, a study in concern. Tears trickled past her ears toward the pillow and she couldn't stop them. "Don't be sad," she whispered. "I'm fine."

"Yeah, right." Todd took her right hand and rubbed it aimlessly. "I am so sorry. I've let you down miserably. This day's been all wrong. If only my meeting hadn't run long. I'd have gotten there sooner—would have stopped him, killed him. What can I do? Anything."

"You faced the vampires for me. Do you feel okay?"

"Of course."

She reached for the sheet to blot her flushed face, which he gently touched.

"You're burning up." He found a washcloth, soaked it in cold water and returned to her bedside. Ever so carefully, he laid the cool cloth on her forehead.

"Oh, that feels good." She sighed and, taking the cool cloth, held it to her eyes until it warmed. "Again? Please?" He did and returned. "Please forgive me."

"Whatever for?"

"I didn't let you explain. Wanted to hurt you. I don't care about your dragons—just about you. I dreamed I saw Grammy and thought I had died, that I couldn't come back and say I was sorry."

He took her hand. "As soon as you're well, we're going to talk. And we're never going to let this happen again." He kissed her palm and then held it to his cheek.

"The papers. Please get the papers."

"What papers? Where?"

"Pandora's box." He looked as though she might be hallucinating. She tried again. "I hid a list: it's written in blue—account numbers. They're bogus. And papers about the Birdsboro loan. It's a scam. I have proof. And I found the files. Fred suspected as much—sent an email to Jeff, but then he got fired, and—"

"Slow down," he said. "I'll find the papers. Just rest."

Her face burned, head throbbed, and her stomach convulsed. When she reached for the pan, it clattered to the floor. He scrambled to get it, held it for her, and wiped her face with the washcloth.

She kept on trying, in spite of it all. "Manning's not Manning. Someone on Five is involved. It's huge. Get my backup disk from Isaac's house."

"I'll take care of everything. You just concentrate on healing, okay?"

She smiled weakly and stopped fighting. He emptied the pan and returned with water to rinse out her mouth.

"Guess I've blown my image big time."

"You're the bravest person I know."

She motioned him closer, and he leaned in. "Lobster. You owe me."

"I'll buy you the whole damned state of Maine."

She motioned to him again. "Don't make me laugh. Hurts my ribs. Get the papers, the disk."

"I will."

"I'm scared. What if he—"

"You'll be safe here, I promise. I'll see to it. And I will take care of everything."

Henry had started through his daughter's doorway and paused, but quietly withdrew.

"They'll throw me out shortly, but I'll be back," Todd said.

He passed Sarah, returning with Michael and Isaac, and located Henry slumped in a chair, his self-assurance gone once his wife turned the corner. Spotting Todd, Henry struggled to regain his composure.

Todd angled a chair to face him and sat.

Henry drooped. "I wish I could make her come home, close ranks and protect her. But we're years, years beyond that. How could anyone hurt a sweetheart like her? She's never done a mean thing in her life." Anguished, he hung his head. "These young women—they're so independent and don't understand how vulnerable they are. In many ways she's so strong, always there for everyone else. But up against such violence?" Henry looked up, as if finally noticing Todd. "Kingsley says her attacker knows that she saw him. He'll know from the news that she survived and can identify him. Do you think the police can protect her? Is hospital security enough?"

"I doubt that they have the manpower. She needs a bodyguard, and I know whom to call. I'll coordinate with hospital security and stay until the guard comes to make sure it's seamless. Sir, try not to worry. We'll know tomorrow just where things stand, but until that guy's caught, she will be protected." He gave Henry his card on which he had added home and cell numbers.

By the time the arrangements had been completed, the others had joined Henry in the lounge.

"You're coming home with us tonight," Isaac stated. "We're right next door and have a guest room." Reluctantly, Sarah and Henry said one more good night, and followed Isaac and Michael toward the exit.

Chapter 20

"W atch your step," the detective instructed as he admitted the Aldersons into Kingsley's apartment. Morning sun streamed through the elegant windows, incongruously splashing rainbows onto broken crystal and glass. After the crime scene technicians had processed the scene, a footpath had been cleared through the shards that had once included Grammy's blue pottery vase. "Mrs. Alderson, can you tell me what's missing?"

Sarah noticed the kitten's paw prints, inked in what must be her Kingsley's blood. She shuddered and squelched the involuntary urge to vomit. She swallowed hard and, taking a deep breath, picked her way through the rubble.

"Either the burglar was incredibly stupid or this wasn't a robbery," she said after a cursory inspection. "The vase in the china closet is Tiffany, and that painting is an original. Her sterling flatware is untouched—she has service for eighteen—and her jewelry seems to be here. That's a relief."

"Things can be replaced. People can't," the detective said curtly. "She's lucky to be alive. If he'd hit her harder— if the vase hadn't shattered—she would be dead. If he hadn't knocked her out, he'd have just kept on coming."

Infuriated, Sarah struck back. "That's cruel! Detective, in case you've forgotten, you asked us to tell you what was missing. She is our baby, our only child. Your condescension is unacceptable." She stalked from the room, colliding with Henry, who'd come from the study.

"Every file folder's been dumped, but none of her electronic devices were stolen. Here's something—her computer is on. She always turns it off. Always. The password's been breached and it's open to her business folder. The printer's on, too."

"He had to have been in the kitchen when she came in, and surprised her because she had few defensive wounds."

"Look at this place!" Henry said. "He spent a great deal of time looking for something. Maybe he thought he could sneak down the fire escape if she came up the stairs. And where is her car?"

"She must have parked on the street. Parking's at a premium in this neighborhood. Cars get towed all the time."

Sarah returned, sweeping the room with her eyes, and moaned sadly. Gingerly, she picked up the shattered frame that held Andy's picture.

Henry offered his handkerchief. "Don't cut yourself. Here, take the photo by its corners." Together, they dropped out the glass and carefully extracted the photo.

Sarah lifted sad eyes. "She always hated November. Something about the dying light."

"Ironic, isn't it? One year to the day since Andy's death."

"No, dear, that was yesterday. A year ago today she miscarried." They fell silent.

Todd, who had been observing silently from the door, joined them. "Kingsley asked me to retrieve some bank papers she thought were important." The detective pointed to her briefcase, but Todd shook his head. "This sounds really strange, but she said to look in Pandora's box."

"I wonder what she meant," Sarah said. "Pandora would have unearthed them. Cats dig in their litter. And they'd be a mess."

"Can we look? She was pretty insistent."

When the detective nodded consent, Todd lifted the litter box while the detective looked underneath. Affixed to the bottom with strapping tape was a Ziploc bag, which the detective unsealed with gloved hands. He extracted the pages with tweezers.

"May I see those?" Todd asked. As the detective unfolded them, Todd immediately recognized the Birdsboro address. The other sheet identified loan sequence numbers, handwritten in blue ink. On the reverse, he read a few scribbled words that made no sense. "Can we talk a minute?" he asked the detective and the men went into the living room. "I'd like to write down those numbers and take another look at the back."

"Mr. Henning, that's evidence. You must leave the investigation to us."

"Of course. I just need to assure myself that these papers pertain to a matter unrelated to Kingsley's attack—a bank matter concerning our loan department. I won't interfere with your work."

Todd made some notes, thanked the detective, and turned to her parents. "I need to get to the bank. Will you tell Kingsley I'll stop by later?"

"Of course. And thank you for all that you did."

&&&

"That's just plain mean. Look what he did!" Henry

looked into Kingsley's bedroom where Sarah was sorting a jumble of letters strewn on her rug. "He pulled all her letters and cards right out of their envelopes," she said. "Look, there are valentines, post cards, and notes Andy sent whenever he traveled."

"Do you think you should leave that for Kingsley?" he asked.

"Which is worse? Having her find this violation or fixing it? I don't have to read them."

"Here, this fancy pink one looks like it goes in that envelope."

Following his lead, Sarah assembled and sorted by postmark and date, and returned them to the flowered box that had somehow escaped being mangled.

Henry went to her study and began opening files in her business directory. "She said to look in the KNB folder for 'notes.doc.' It's here, but it isn't."

"Meaning?"

"He erased the contents by overwriting each document with an 'x', then saving his changes." Henry tried a few options, swearing under his breath. "Nope; they're gone. And he purged her trash icon." An idea struck him. "Hello! The idiot didn't delete the title from her index. According to this, the copy was last revised at six twenty-seven p.m. yesterday. That pinpoints the time he overwrote it, and I bet, when he heard her coming."

ᴄᴏᴄᴏ

"You look one hundred percent better than you did last night," Henry said as his wife kissed their daughter."

"I do feel less groggy and my stomach has settled. They gave me something for this killer headache, and my scalp's not as angry." She lifted her left hand with her right. "This will be a nuisance."

They brought her up to date on the morning's investigation, including Todd's retrieval of the papers she hid. "We took a stab at tidying your apartment," Henry said. "Think, Kingsley—did you turn off your computer the last time you used it?"

"Absolutely. I always shut down. It simply runs better next session if I reboot. It's ancient. I really should buy a new one."

"Good thing you didn't upgrade—your intruder left a trail."

Sarah squeezed Kingsley's uninjured hand. "Speaking of Todd, dear, he said he'll come visit this afternoon."

Kingsley sat bolt upright. "I must look a fright."

Her father grinned. "You are feeling better!"

"How am I going to wash my hair between this and that," she complained, gesturing to first her head then her hand. "I can't get them wet. And I've got nothing to wear."

"We ran by the mall. I couldn't resist this yellow lounge set—the fleece is very soft and you chill so easily. Look. Matching socks. Brought your favorite soap and body lotion, cosmetics, and contact lens stuff. Maybe a hot shower will make you feel better. As for your hand, we'll ask the nurse for a bag and tape it securely."

"Dad? Could Mom and I have a few minutes for girl talk?"

"Sure, hon. I'll go flirt with the nurses." He sauntered off.

"Did you find my birth control pills? I started taking them again for the pain."

"They're in your cosmetics bag. The new medication didn't help?"

"Horrible side-effects."

"There's always something new coming on the market. And if you ever have a baby, that may cure you."

"Mom, I've been meaning to bring that up but the timing never seemed right. We weren't having much luck and when we did, the miscarriage—my insides are kind of, well..." She trailed off. "Will you and Dad be terribly upset, I mean, well, not having grandchildren?"

"You're all that matters to us. But for your own peace of mind and future plans, I'd get a second opinion."

"I've already had two. I'm sorry to dump this on you. I just don't want you to be disappointed, if and when."

"Nothing you ever do could disappoint us. Besides, we're all adults here. If your father or I had a serious problem, you'd be there for us."

"You know that I would."

"The best part now is knowing you as an adult. Tell you what—why don't you get your shower while I'm still here, in case you need help?"

In fifteen minutes Kingsley returned, a towel wrapped around her hair, helped by a nurse. "I got some of the blood out, but it's pretty disgusting. The doctor will freak if I got my stitches too wet." She handed a towel to her mother, who carefully blotted the drips and eased a comb away from the sutures.

Henry returned from his prowling and whistled. "My, don't we look pretty. Well, Mom, we'd better get going or we'll hit rush hour traffic. Baby, are you sure you're all right?"

"I'll be fine."

"Give your old man a porcupine hug and a kiss—very carefully."

"We'll be back tomorrow to spring you," Sarah said. "Come, Dad, before Kingsley and I start to cry."

೧ಎ೧

"We couldn't let Kingsley face this alone, especially now," Barrie told Todd as she finished detailing their Saturday's escapade on Five.

At first Todd just stared at the women, an incredulous look on his face. "Just how did you get into that cabinet?"

Barrie made a circular motion with her hand. "I picked the locks."

He laughed. "But how did you know which cabinet?"

"We searched systematically."

"But how did you know to look there?"

Barrie stole a look at Margaret, who was getting impatient. Barrie sighed in resignation.

"We found nothing in any of the offices."

"You searched all our offices?"

"Only those whose voices might match. You can fire me if you want to, but Margaret never entered the building."

"I'm equally culpable," Margaret said. "I was the lookout. I did see something that might be important. I observed a dark sedan behaving peculiarly behind the building with its lights off. I couldn't tell if anyone was in it, but I got a good look—an older navy Buick LeSabre."

"Do you remember what time it was?"

Margaret dug in her purse for her ATM receipt. "This says nine fifty-eight p.m."

"Did you notice anything distinctive about the car? There could be lots of navy LeSabres."

"The license."

Todd's mouth twitched.

"I wrote it down." She gave him the slip of paper.

"How on earth—"

"Our fraud prevention training teaches us to note anything unusual that might be important. I didn't see any reason for a car to be hanging around. Employees would park in their assigned spaces, and, if anyone was carpooling, he'd leave it out front. Or at the mall, for that matter."

"You're very observant. I'll ask the police to run the plate."

"How much trouble are we in?"

"I think what you did was heroic. And it took guts to tell me. I just wish that you'd come to me sooner—let me handle it."

"Kingsley said we should have trusted you, although I don't know why," Barrie said with an edge.

Todd stood to signal the end of the meeting. "I'll have the head of security open the cabinet and give me the carton. To be honest, I'll need to research internal procedures. This is all new to me. But to answer your concern, I see no reason to tell anyone about Saturday. However, if there is a reward for uncovering fraud, it will be yours." As they were leaving, Todd said, "Barrie, could you stay a minute? Thank you Margaret." She exited, closing the door.

Barrie returned to her chair, as did he. For a moment they stared at each other. Finally he spoke. "I, um, realize she must have spoken to you. Did she tell you about Sunday evening? And our exchange Monday morning?"

"Only two thoughts—that she'd badly misinterpreted your intentions and, that because of something she couldn't repeat, she felt she could trust you about the loan scam." Barrie leveled him with a jaundiced eye. "Frankly, I think that's bullshit."

"You think I'm some kind of womanizer. That I'm taking advantage of her."

"What you do with your personal life is none of my business, but I don't want to see her get hurt. Who knows how much one person can stand? And she's had more than her share. It's like watching someone tear the wings off a bird. I don't want to see her resign, and she just might do it. I've said way too much. Now if you want to fire me for insubordination, go ahead."

Todd laughed. "You remind me of my friend Randall. Always did know when I needed my butt kicked. Believe me, I'd be afraid to cross either of you when I'm wrong." His face straightened. "Can we keep this conversation between us?"

Barrie looked at him, puzzled. "I can't figure you out."

"Me neither sometimes. Barrie, the last thing I wanted to do was hurt her. I should have let her choose the lesser of evils. We'll talk."

"Evil? She didn't call you evil. Fair warning—she won't tolerate your sympathy or guilt."

Todd nodded. "I know. It's not about either."

As Barrie was leaving, she nearly collided with the head of security, who marched into Todd's office. He snapped the door shut.

"This way," Todd said, a few moments later. He led the man through Five's expansive layout of executive offices. As they navigated the carpeted walkway that separated core functionaries from their high-ranking superiors, Todd felt the silence, sensing the eyes following him before pivoting to their work as the pair came abreast. The floor was so quiet it could have been midnight.

Todd led the security chief into the secure storage room then closed and relocked the door behind them. "In here." He pointed to a wall of locked cabinets and to one area in particular. "I need a witness in case security has been breached over some sensitive documents stored in this room."

"What did the box look like?" the security chief asked Todd as he unlocked the cabinets with master keys.

"A FastFiler archive box labeled 'Misc. Historical 1994-1999. Do Not Remove.'"

"It's not here," the security head said, stepping aside to let Todd look for himself. All that remained was a carton-size hole.

The pair exchanged glances. "Keep looking. It should be here."

Quickly they inspected all possible places of conceal-ment. The carton was nowhere.

"How do you want me to handle this?"

"Write a report with the details, including signature lines for both of us."

Chapter 21

At lunchtime, Margaret and Barrie popped in to see Kingsley, panting from tearing through hospital corridors. "You made the news," Barrie said, handing her the morning edition. "How are you feeling?"

"I'll live. They'd better question Manning, or whoever he is. Maybe he doesn't know he's been made. I know he's behind this. He probably helped ransack my place. He left the bank around noon on Monday and he knows that I always work past five, sometimes later."

Margaret and Barrie exchanged surreptitious glances.

"What?" Kingsley demanded.

They looked at each other again.

"What is it?"

"Manning's time is accounted for," Margaret said. "He couldn't have been near your place."

"Are you sure?"

They both nodded. "He was involved in something on the other side of the county."

Kingsley sized them up. "What else aren't you telling me?"

"We told Todd about Saturday night. You were right. He

said that he wouldn't rat us out. We made him promise. According to my executive grapevine, he and the head of security closed themselves in the file room. From the sounds, they were looking for something. Lots of cabinets and drawers opening and closing—quickly."

"And? When they exited, was one of them carrying the carton?"

"Nope. According to my source, they left empty handed. Got on the elevator and didn't come back. Hey, look at the time."

They got up to leave.

Barrie hung back, and whispered to her, "Trust me—you didn't misinterpret anything. I'll call you later."

∽∾∽

Shortly after they left, Kingsley heard footsteps approaching and slow at her door. "Good afternoon, Ms. Ward. Shouldn't you be at the office?"

She grinned at the man in immaculate navy and pale blue silk tie. "Oh, Todd, yellow roses are my favorite. And the vase—wherever did you find one like Grammy's?" She ran her finger over the delicate bouquet, its muted hues reminiscent of her vase's design.

"Well, you'd lost a few ornaments, and I know this antique dealer, and there was a mark on the bottom..." He set the vase on her bedside table.

"That was so thoughtful. I'll keep it forever."

"Come here. Let me thank you," she said, sliding to the edge of the bed. When he did, the bed's elevation enabled her to gingerly reach his shoulders and touch her cheek briefly to his. "I come from a family of huggers."

He scrutinized her face to look at her bruises. "Does it hurt very much?"

"If I wiggle my ears, raise my eyebrows, or yawn. My ribs are sore like I fell on the slopes. Everyone's been wonderful, calling and stopping. There are so many, right on this floor, in worse shape than I am. This afternoon they wheeled a gurney down the hall that was draped in an American flag. I was told that's how they honor deceased veterans. From time to time, I hear codes being called, running footsteps, and faint weeping. It's so very sad. I know this is a hospital, but I get to go home."

He smiled, patted her good hand, and nodded agreement. His face changed to his business expression. "I got your backup disk from Isaac. The detective has the papers you hid. You do realize you said they were *in* Pandora's box, not under it. What a mess. Don't worry: Pandora's potty meets her majesty's high expectations again."

"But about those numbers—"

"We've begun an internal investigation to determine if the loans on that list are legitimate or bogus."

"Will the list help?"

"Absolutely! We can't contact thousands of customers and ask if their loans are legitimate. And reviewing every loan on our books could take months. If the blue list contains bogus loans, we can look for the common denominator. If we're lucky, we'll learn the identity of the thief and pressure him to identify all of them. There could be many."

"Could fraud or loan review's people be involved?"

"That would surprise me. Those people are thoroughly screened, yet anything's possible."

"The handwriting on the back—whose is it? And is it important?"

"An ordinary to-do list. You know the type. 'Pick up dry cleaning, fill tank, call PC repairman,' and so on. The handwriting on both sides will be identified, but I'm guessing it was carelessness on Manning's part."

"I could have made dozens of copies. What was the point of ransacking my place?"

"To recover everything that you found. And, I hate to say it, to eliminate you as a witness. I'm sure the instigator wanted your blue list with its distinctive handwriting—perhaps fingerprints—that could identify the perpetrator."

"Why not simply ask Manning? He is the key. He wrote the loans."

Todd shook his head. "That won't be possible. You didn't hear? Barrie or Margaret didn't tell you? Manning was involved in a hit-and-run accident yesterday afternoon. Someone driving a dark sedan ran him off a rural road into a tree. The driver took off. Manning was airlifted to a trauma center, but he died en route."

Kingsley gasped. "He's dead? Was it deliberate?"

"According to an eye-witness account on the news, that's what it looked like. Interestingly, Margaret just gave me the license number of the car she spotted Saturday night at the bank. It's the same make and model, but the plates don't match."

"Then we've hit a dead end."

"Very. Kingsley, I've got to ask you: What could you possibly have been thinking?"

"Lobster. Winning our bet. And I can't resist a challenge I can get my teeth into, even if it's trouble. I couldn't let it go. I must have been a very good junk-yard dog in a previous life." She fingered the edge of her splint. "It was a game, an adventure in my otherwise drab life. It was fun and a challenge, playing detective. But I was foolish and deeply regret involving Margaret and Barrie. I put them in danger.

What will happen to them? Will they lose their jobs? That wouldn't be fair. It's all my fault."

He chuckled, shaking his head. "Nobody even knows you were there."

"Why would you cover for us? You could be risking your job. What if someone finds out?"

He chuckled. "You three going to tell?" His face sobered, his voice lowering to a confidential tone. "Last Saturday, I returned to Birdsboro to see what you found in that mailbox. Something had jolted you—that was obvious. You do not have a poker face. By the time I returned, the mailbox was empty, but the papers you hid under Pandora's box confirmed the discrepancy between the facility's description and what we both observed. There is no such business. I feel terrible that you couldn't trust me."

"It's not your fault. Even if I had shared my suspicions, I still would have been alone in my apartment Monday evening and surprised my assailant."

"I can't remember feeling this shaken. It's going to take weeks to rebuild my adrenaline." He picked up his coat and started to leave, but returned to give her forehead a peck. "No more Nancy Drew, you hear?"

She grinned until her stitches protested, but did not agree to his warning.

ເ⁊ɕⱭ

Kingsley overheard the detective presenting himself to the charge nurse and repeat the introduction to her grim-faced bodyguard. "Ms. Ward?" he called from the doorway, identifying himself as he knocked on the doorframe.

"Please come in," she said. He appeared startled by how she must look. *Just like the others,* she thought. First blinking then averting his gaze.

"Do you feel well enough to look at some pictures?" he asked.

More questions. "Sure. Please. Have a seat."

He remained standing until he had extracted a photo array from a manila envelope. He handed it to her and sat down. "Is the person who attacked you one of these men?"

She forced concentration, studying each face against the image locked in her brain. She studied the eyes as a separate element by covering their other features with her finger. Finally she admitted defeat.

"I'm sorry. I don't recognize him."

"Are you sure? I realize it was rather dark. The street lamps produced the only light. How about their features? Do any of them resemble what you saw?"

She repeated emphatically. "I'm positive. I'll see that face in my sleep." She swept her hand across the photo array. "He isn't one of these guys." She sagged into the pillow. She handed back the photos, flicking invisible dirt off her sheet. "Please, just catch the guy who did this to me. He must have left evidence. Maybe my neighbors saw him."

"We did interview a person of interest. Do you know a man named John Gatto?"

She reacted instantaneously. "That's a euphemism for suspect, isn't it? You won't let him go, will you? You'll keep him locked up—" She began hyperventilating.

"The person we questioned said he parked in your towaway zone, having not noticed the signs. Thought he should have been there less than an hour. Parking in that neighborhood is ridiculous, he said. Much later, when he thought it had been stolen, he called the police. That led him to retrieve his vehicle from our impound lot."

Kingsley unclenched the hem of the sheet she'd been scrunching until her fingers cramped. Instead, she couldn't help herself from picking at the tape on her splint. *Just stop it. Calm down,* she scolded herself.

"I can tell you what's common knowledge, thanks to the media," he said, "but some details are being withheld that might hinder the investigation or compromise prosecution. By the time the owner came to bail out his car, we'd run the plate. The numbers matched those that an eyewitness gave us for the navy LeSabre that hit Manning Stoudt's vehicle. The plate, however, did not match the car's VIN number, but a plate stolen from a car in the Philadelphia Airport's long-term parking lot. Mr. Gatto's plates had been swapped. He said he had no idea when that had happened. That the mismatch might not have been discovered until his next state inspection or if he'd been stopped for a moving violation."

"So you're letting this John Gatto go?"

"We have no reason to hold him, since you can't identify him. He's not denying he parked near your place. That, he said, was about one-thirty. He's a private detective who was supposed to meet a business prospect at a diner nearby, but gave up when that person didn't show."

"You mean someone stole Gatto's car, swapped out his plates, hit Manning's car, and abandoned it in my neighborhood, only to be towed by the police? That's ridiculous!"

"I agree, it sounds preposterous, but that's how it looks. Ms. Ward—let's focus on what happened to you. We received a tip that you stole sensitive documents from your employer. That a security firm, hired by the bank, was authorized to retrieve those documents from your apartment. An operative visited your apartment around three p.m. and, that finding your door unlocked, proceeded to your desk to retrieve the sensitive documents."

"That's a lie! I stole nothing. Even if I had, the bank

wouldn't handle it that way." She couldn't help it that her voice had risen to a squeak. "That's nowhere near protocol."

"Please, Ms. Ward. I'm not accusing you of anything. Your CEO, Warren Kramer, explained that your bank has no problem with you. And even if they did, they would never hire outsiders. That situations like this are handled internally—discreetly."

"I stopped home around noon and backed up the documents I'd scanned into my PC. A friend safeguarded the backup, which will show the date and the time that I last saved my changes. I had cleaned my keyboard on Sunday afternoon, so only my prints and the intruder's could be on it. Please. Can you do something with that?"

"And you're positive about the time you got home?"

"Absolutely. It was six-thirty. I was expecting a colleague around seven. I was focused on what I needed to do. How did this bogus 'security firm' find my apartment? I'm not in the book."

"The informer said his client, who claimed to be an executive at your bank—whom he refused to identify—gave him your address and your car's description. The client also approached him about following you."

"Do you mean this man Gatto followed me everywhere? Why didn't I see him?"

"That wasn't Gatto. He admitted that he'd been approached about a job that required 'extreme discretion.' Given the date, the time, where to park, and who to meet at the neighborhood café to learn details. Gatto kept the appointment, but he turned down the job because the potential client wouldn't give him a verifiable name. That it sounded suspicious. And the contact never showed up. So he left, only to find his car was missing. Had Gatto's car not been towed, we wouldn't have known these details."

"Do I have this right? Someone at my bank hired, say, a private investigator to break into my apartment to retrieve documents and slip away. But how does this man Gatto figure into it?

The detective shrugged. "Perhaps to provide a degree of separation?"

"But you're very sure that Gatto wasn't the guy who attacked me. Might my assailant have worn a disguise? Let me see those photos again." He handed her the photo array. She scrutinized each face to no avail.

Kingsley thought back. That day at the bank, when she'd found the blue list, the parking lot had been full, but when she left, it was nearly deserted. Her car would have been the only one whose owner had a connection to lending. Manning must have missed the blue list and contacted someone to retrieve it. Yet the voice that she'd overheard was someone from Five. Manning's office was on Three. Her mind felt fuzzy and her head started throbbing. She rubbed her temples, eyes closed and focused. That anyone from Five would trash her apartment was absurd.

Saturday—the expedition with Todd. When she left in his Explorer, which he'd parked out front, no one could have known about the detour through Birdsboro. Inspecting that property was a spur-of-the-moment impulse. A flash—Todd's exasperation at a car nearly sideswiping them when they were leaving for Hopewell Furnace. And that evening, the movies—out Barrie's back door in different clothes in a different car. Yet a similar car had shown up at the bank.

The detective was saying something. She refocused. "...we had hoped to find the shoes that left prints in your foyer," he said, "but the ones Gatto was wearing don't match."

"What happens now?"

"John Gatto had an alibi. And with Manning Stoudt dead, we can't question him. I'll leave you my card. If and when you feel up to working with a sketch artist, please call. And I hope your make a speedy recovery."

As the detective traversed the labyrinth of corridors, he considered the timing of Manning Stoudt's hit-and-run accident on Tuesday afternoon. The waitress he hit on remembered Gato, who claimed his LeSabre was stolen while he had a late lunch near Ms. Ward's apartment. If the evidence technicians linked his LeSabre to the car that hit Stoudt, corroborating the eye witnesses report of the license—

He stopped walking to think it through.

Can we place Gatto in the LeSabre after he said it was stolen? Was it enough that the car had been towed from Ms. Ward's block late-afternoon? Ms. Ward's identification, combined with Gatto's fingerprints, could have nailed him for her attack, but she hadn't recognized him from the photo, and no prints were found. Could they prove he was still in her neighborhood after five in the evening? If not, they couldn't detain him.

Chapter 22

Kingsley picked at her dinner, which seemed to stick in her throat. Tray table pushed aside, she slumped into the pillows and tried to find a comfortable position. Everything ached. She was flipping through channels when she heard Todd speak to the guard. She scrambled to sit up and couldn't help feeling her expression must look eager. He knocked on her doorframe and grinned when she motioned him in.

"A daffodil in November! I hope you feel as good as you look."

She grinned stupidly. He was still dressed for business, and she was struck once again by his height and professional presence. It could have been eight in the morning. He set his topcoat on the foot of her bed and drew up a chair.

"Was Margaret's information useful?" she asked after he settled.

"I gave it to the police and they ran the plate through the DMV. It was stolen."

"If they can't learn who's responsible, it won't be safe to go home." Quickly, she gave him a detailed summary of what she had learned—and not learned—from the detective.

"Until they catch him, that guard's on the job, and no arguments, please. Now—would a little bank gossip cheer you up?"

She grinned. "Tell me."

"Warren insisted that the security upgrades be made at warp speed. Typically, all new wiring would be installed before the old ones would be disconnected. That would be done on a Sunday when the bank is closed. However, given the circumstances, they were trying to do it simultaneously. And get this—at the same time tech staff was installing the new mainframe. The power interruptions were driving everyone crazy. By mid-afternoon our employees were downright hostile, as were the customers. Warren responded by closing the bank at four thirty and sending everyone home."

"I should be there. My department is very short handed. Speaking of which, I'd like to know why they let Fred Macmillan go. Something's not right. Could you make a discreet inquiry?"

"I'll try, but personnel issues are confidential."

"You can trust me."

He laughed. "Touché. What I meant was, they won't tell me. But you mustn't worry about your department. It'll still be there when you get back. Take all the time that you need."

"I just wish my head would stop hurting."

"'Drink lots of water: it's dehydration that causes a hangover.'"

She tried lobbing a pillow at him, but when her ribs protested, her throw missed its mark.

"I called the Community Center's board chairman about a kick-off event for the fundraiser," Kingsley said. "She loved your idea of a dinner dance. I said I'd chair the committee, and I volunteered you to be the emcee and make the dinner speech. Is that okay?"

"When did you call her?"

"This afternoon. She said she'd book the club immediately. That without a venue there would be no event. She called back. It's a done deal."

"I don't know what to say, except thank you."

"Oh, Todd, everyone I know has been calling or stopping. Some even traveled great distances. It was wonderful to get away from myself. I remembered what you said about our bank needing to be involved in the community to help others. But don't forget—you owe me a tango, and I'm holding you to it."

"I did promise, didn't I?" He looked at his watch. "I have a dinner meeting at six. I'd better get to it." He started to leave, but hesitated, not seeming to know how to exit.

"Hug?" she asked.

Grinning, he came over and gently did so, then quickly departed.

By nine, visiting hours ended and stragglers departed. The dimly lit ward became very quiet except for the nurses who focused on critical patients. Kingsley went into the bathroom and swallowed two extra-strength Tylenol she'd dug from her purse. She tested the angry bruises that covered her forehead and winced. The path of black stitches that resembled a baseball's didn't worry her nearly as much as the adjacent bald area. She'd think about camouflage later. Bent at the bowl, she splashed cool water on her face. She rose slowly so her head wouldn't throb and raised her arms to relieve her bruised ribs. Thank God for small mercies—they could have been broken, collapsed a lung or punctured her heart, and taken painful weeks to heal. Already she itched to escape.

She returned to her bed, surfed through the channels, but clicked it off. Darkness outside crept into her being, and tentacles of loneliness threatened her core. A rise in her heart rate that pounded in her ears signaled an impending panic attack. She shivered. *One more day, just get through it.* Then what? Would she ever feel safe?

She tried once again to find some distraction and paged unseeing through several magazines. Finally she got up and paced laps, back and forth, from the door to the window in an effort to curb excessive adrenalin. But she could not extinguish the questions that raged in her head.

What is it you want? She stared outside at the blackness, seeing nothing but memories. She remembered sitting at Andy's desk after all its contents had been archived, and thinking, *My mind is as blank as the top of this desk, my whole world blown away. I simply cannot risk that again. It's not about death, but about being left.* There. She'd given it words. Abandoned, no matter how or the reason. First Grammy, then Andy. An incongruous thought made her smile. Pandora. Spending the rest of her life with a cat.

The bank—she acknowledged—wasn't just a job. It represented all that she'd salvaged, separate from her family, their contacts, and her former life. And Andy. Yes Andy. He'd never been there.

I thought I could do this. Start over, be tougher, but look what a mess I've created. Get a grip, she scolded herself. *You're stronger than that. What would Grammy say?*

She remembered her five-year-old self in Grammy's cozy home, trying to read a book that was beyond her ability. "Put 'can't' behind the door and try," Grammy would gently say, reinforcing that it was all right to fail if she tried again. She stared at the nothingness beyond her window, assaulted by sleet from a fast-moving front. Todd slipped in so quietly she scarcely heard him but, aware of a presence, looked up.

"Like a little company?"

"You came back. It's terribly late. Who let you in?"

"There was a little mix-up about my identity. They'll cut me some slack since this room is private."

She noticed he'd changed into jeans, a navy V-neck and sneakers, just a regular guy. He laid his jacket on its usual spot. "I'm so glad you're here," she said, sitting on the edge of the bed. He produced a small paper bag and gave it to her with a conspiratorial smile. "What's this?"

"A little bird told me that you weren't eating, so—Dr. Henning's cure. Whole-wheat bread, natural peanut butter, the kind I took hiking, remember? And orange juice, fresh squeezed. Institutional food is quite dreadful. And, to show you I'm not a fanatic…" He pulled out a small cellophane package.

"Chocolate Tastykakes! What a memory you have."

"You can't have them first. Unless I miss my guess, your blood sugar's dragging and you're feeling depressed."

"My mouth is so dry—"

He adjusted the bedside table, and poured some juice into a cup. "Start with the juice. One of my little indulgences. A bagful of blood oranges sacrificed themselves, so you'd better drink it."

"This is incredibly good!"

He smiled with satisfaction. While she sipped and worked on the sandwich, he talked of his meeting, repeating the jokes and tales about people she might find amusing. When she had finished, he asked, "How are you doing, really? None of this 'fine, fine, fine' stuff."

She sighed. "I'm so grateful for the guard and all that you've done. They're springing me in the morning. I'm desperate for life to feel normal again." She studied his face, paused, and debated. "You don't have to look after me. I'll be fine. Really."

He fidgeted with the cuff of his sweater, face becoming somber. "If I could, I would erase everything I said that evening."

"I'm glad you told me about your ex and your situation. It was important and needed saying. Now it's out of the way." A peaceful silence settled around them.

"I can't remember ever being this comfortable with a woman. And there's so much we should talk about, but it's so late. Do you think you can sleep?"

She rubbed her arms, shivering, even though the room was quite warm. "When I doze, I get flashbacks. And there's the nightmare. I know there's a bodyguard, but I can't relax."

He pulled his chair closer and patted his lap. "Come here." She hesitated, but when he insisted, she slid off the bed. He eased her onto his lap and settled her head into his chest. "The nightmare—tell me about it."

"It started when I was a child. I'm drawn into a tunnel that gets darker and darker but there's no light at the end. It's a void, complete darkness—no sound, no feel, no smell, no temperature, no moving air. I wake up gasping, as if I've tried to swim a long distance under black water. As a child, I thought I was dead and couldn't find God. No people, no souls, nothingness. Everyone, everything gone."

"Your personal dragon."

She nodded. "It's not like dreaming or being unconscious. It's total sensory deprivation. I'm aware of being trapped in a hell that isn't about devils. It's an incredible void. When I was little, I imagined that death was like that."

"I have a thought. Whenever you have the dream and wake up, try to remember what you've eaten and how long ago. Maybe an attack of low blood sugar is exacerbated by whatever's upsetting you."

She sighed and rested her head on his chest. "Couldn't hurt, I suppose."

"I'll stave off the dragon if you'll try to relax. Think of nothing at all, or a place you've been totally happy."

She thought of Hawk Mountain. "There was one special day—"

"You're like an Olympic skater who's fallen and hops up quickly, hoping nobody noticed, and keeps right on smiling and skating. You've had a terrible shock and been carrying too big a load by yourself. It scares me to think how close I came to losing you and missing what might have been." He rocked, ever so slightly. "You really are very special."

He realized she'd fallen asleep. Time eased away in the dimly lit room. Gently he set her back on her bed and covered her up.

"Sir, you'd better go. We've looked the other way as long as we can."

He bent briefly to kiss her forehead and then whispered his thanks to the nurse.

გადა

Todd exited the building, took a deep breath, and let it out slowly. Millions of stars were breaking the canopy of lingering cloud-wisps racing away, leaving a crispness that cut with sheer beauty. The vastness urged perspective on him, a speck. She could be dead and that impersonal institution for which they both worked would send an offer to some lesser person, all traces of her reduced to the paperwork that still bore her name. The part about losing her— he'd thought it and said it, a fluid revelation to himself. He wondered whether she'd heard him and, if so, what then?

As he unlocked his door, the grandfather clock chimed midnight. He'd only planned on cheering her up, but the experience had broken him down to essentials. His eyes fell on her book and he thought of her listening. Empathizing. Underscoring values he thought were important but that Maureen had scorned. Suddenly the condo felt terribly empty. Wired, he picked up a novel and read until three. When he finally gave up and pulled off his sweater, he noticed her fragrance and smiled.

Chapter 23

Dolly Ziegler paced when she wasn't wiping the counter or just wringing her hands. Finally, she heard a vehicle crunch on the long driveway that circled around back to their garage. Pushing away panic, she thrust her shaking hands deep into her pockets.

"Adam's Locksmith Service, ma'am?"

Dolly opened the kitchen door wider and studied the young man in gray overalls with Lew scripted in red on a white patch.

"My instructions say you have a key broken off in your basement lock and you've lost your desk keys."

"That's right. Thanks for coming on such very short notice. I hope you have plenty of time. Someone stole my purse, so I also need the locks changed."

"No problem, ma'am. 'Adam's Your Answer.'"

Dolly directed him first toward the cellar where he shined a beam into the old-fashioned keyhole and nodded knowingly. "First the diagnosis, then the cure."

His good-natured merriment made Dolly relax enough to lead him into Frank's study. Until that very moment, she was terrified that she'd lose her nerve. "My husband misplaced his keys to this desk. I lost mine years ago. Now there's only one set, and he has spent hours ransacking the house. I've searched everywhere but it's hopeless. He'll be upset if he gets home and can't open his drawers."

"Piece of cake, ma'am. I'll get what I need from the van."

Dolly panicked. "You won't have to change the desk locks themselves, will you? We just need spare keys."

"Not a problem." Lew disappeared and reappeared quickly with a large metal toolbox.

"I'll be in the kitchen if you need me." She escaped and returned to her lookout, even though Frank wasn't due until late. New door locks—that part was easy because she was always home before him. Now, if she left, she just wouldn't lock up.

Two hours later, Lew set his bill on the kitchen table where Dolly completed check 101 from her new bank account. After thanking him for the twentieth time, she hustled him out. What would Frank do when he found that he'd lost control of her trust? And the house? The media was filled with accounts of violence that resulted from lesser problems. She hadn't the courage to confront him, but at least she had locks. Now the study—that must be searched. She phoned her best friend.

"I'll come right now," Lauren said. "Just give me a minute to throw the clothes into the dryer." Ten minutes later, she let herself in the back door.

"Here's your new house key," Dolly said, pressing a copy into her hand. "The others will be in my pink chenille bathrobe pocket in the guest room closet."

"Dolly, you're shaking. If you don't want me to see what's in those files, I can stand guard while you look."

"No, please! You've got to stay with me."

"Okay, but I want my cell phone handy in case he catches us and gets violent."

Together, they searched systematically, quickly eliminating the belly drawer, as well as the top and bottom side drawers. A large middle drawer on the right suspended dozens of legal-size Pendaflex folders. She walked her fingers through their contents, dismissing banking material, business letters, and reports. She closed it and opened the left center drawer.

"The trust papers are here!" Dolly said. She pulled out a folder and opened it carefully on the desk's surface. "These copies have his notations. We have to be extremely careful. Frank has a special way of filing. He's so disturbed if one paper is longer than another that he draws a pencil line with a metal rule and trims it. New goes on top. He bonks the papers, bottom first, followed by the left side, to stack the contents precisely. He centers the pile in the folder. If it's not perfect, he'll notice."

"He's obsessive-compulsive," Lauren muttered. Together they examined each record, but Dolly replaced the folders herself. "Dolly, what are you thinking?"

"The early days. We were happy, weren't we? I thought I was. The babies were such a miracle. Our relationship crept into decline when I wasn't looking, like mildew that grows on the cellar walls. The night of Doug's party—our situation's irreversible, isn't it?"

"And potentially deadly. If I were you, I'd start proceedings."

"I would have given him anything." Dolly looked sadly around the study that had once been her father's. "I feel like yesterday's garbage."

"Come on, Dolly. We've got to keep going. Unlock the file cabinet."

Quickly they dismissed myriad banking material. By the time Dolly got to the bottom drawer, Lauren could tell she was no longer digesting the contents.

"You sit and I'll hand you a folder if I find anything interesting." Lauren scrutinized papers from other banks that she found in the bottom drawer. Why would Frank have a drawer full of statements from other peoples' accounts? "Dolly, do you recognize any of these names? Quincy Tyler..." She read several more, but Dolly shook her head no to each one. The customers' addresses ranged over five counties and all showed loan balances over $400,000 with recent payments for principal and interest.

Opening the last folder, Lauren found a sheet with handwritten nine-digit numbers, dates and amounts. Behind that were several passports. *That's strange,* she thought. She'd just seen Frank's in his desk drawer. Could these be old ones? Dolly's or even the kids? Opening it, she saw Frank's picture. It was his all right, but then it hit her—the name wasn't. She checked a second and a third passport, again bearing Frank's photo. When she checked the name against the bank statements, she verified that Frank had passport that corresponded to each loan customer's na Inside the folder, she found other legal documen' Frank's photo smiled back from every one. "W hell—Dolly?"

Seeing her friend crying soundlessly, Lau how fragile she was. "Hey, kiddo. Let's lea' tomorrow." Lauren refiled the material her' the kitchen to scout something strong. P goblets of sherry, she sat beside Dol' bank stuff. My guys have gone hunti in peace at my house. Why don't can deal with the rest in the morr.

Dolly looked up, finally seeing. "I've got to be here when Frank comes home. The locks…"

Lauren frowned and studied her friend. "Well, okay, as long as you keep your cell phone with you. If he gets nasty, call nine-one-one. He'll do anything to protect his precious reputation." Leaving the lamps lit, the old friends headed for Lauren's. As they drove the short distance, Lauren did mental math. Those accounts totaled millions. Had she done the right thing to cut short their scrutiny? How much danger was Dolly in? Lauren needed time to think and figure out whom she could trust.

∽✄✄

Sunday, Frank holed up in his office, oblivious to his wife's activities. Restlessly he rehashed that last meeting with Juanita. How badly he had misread her and the depths to which she could sink her tentacles! She had to be stopped. Late into the evening, he prowled, straightening pictures and centering lamps. Finally he went to his desk and began tidying its orderly contents.

He opened the drawers and, looking into his files, was immediately disturbed. A corner here and a misaligned paper there screamed violation. Could he possibly have left it unlocked? He passed a jaundiced eye over each file, but nothing was missing. An ounce of prevention was definitely in order. He measured a few twelve-inch lengths of black thread and draped them strategically over the files. He closed and locked each drawer. If anyone snooped, he would know.

Next, he called his secretary's voice-mailbox and left a message: he would be taking off Monday and Tuesday for personal business. He could be reached on his cell phone,

but only, only if absolutely necessary. And cancel his meet-ings—no, make that reschedule them for the following week. Replacing the phone, he sank into his chair to consider his options.

ↄ৶ↄ৶

Tuesday dawned as gray as Dolly's spirit. Her Monday resolve to finish the files was dashed by the cleaning crew's untimely arrival. If only Lauren wasn't at work! She had said, just search—you can do this! Dolly checked once more for his car then entered his study. Resisting the urge to rummage, she forced her mind to Polaroid the contents.

Most of the credenza she needn't touch—books, journals and logo gift items. She bypassed folders with names that meant nothing, like Quincy Tyler, Adam Arnold, and others. Under a stack of charity plaques, she spotted a manila enve-lope and carefully extracted it. One tiny letter—J—labeled it. Inside she found receipts for an apartment, a car lease, and bank withdrawal slips, the smallest of which was $5,000. Her shaking hands dropped and spilled the contents.

She was his lover! Siphoning her money and squander-ing his on that girl! She seethed to her core, anger and hurt, suppressed for so long, boiling white-hot. She threw on her coat, yanked on her gloves, and stormed from the house to show Lauren.

ↄ৶ↄ৶

Early Wednesday morning, Shirley Granger moved de-spondently through the passageway that connected branch administration's back offices, the vault, and safe deposit area with the main branch. The previous week Todd had listened intently about her work history and her ideas, saying he was looking forward to working with her, a valuable resource. Late Tuesday, however, Warren had appeared at her office with his decision that branch administration would remain under Frank even after a second EVP was recruited. The deal sounded done.

Shirley's executive headhunter had delivered blow number two just that morning. She had, once again, failed to nail a comparable position at a Cleveland bank. He had showered her with encouragement, pumped up her ego, lauded her many fine qualities, but in the end it came down to her lack of a college degree. She had protested that she had the experience, but so did the other candidates. Frank would be tougher than ever to please. She was stuck and dead-ended.

As she passed the safe deposit area's privacy booths, she noticed a small shiny object on the carpet in front of the vault where the tellers safeguard their cash overnight. Bending to retrieve the offensive object, she glanced around for a wastepaper basket. Finding none, she dropped it into her pocket.

Connie, the branch manager, met Shirley halfway down the passageway. "Margie's coming unglued," she said of the assistant branch manager. "One of our larger customers has become even more obscene with the tellers."

"Your people don't have to tolerate that. I'll talk with her now." Shirley pushed through the heavy glass door and entered the branch.

Connie looked at her watch. At exactly eight, the timer would release the vault door for the tellers to pull their cash drawers and supplies. She glanced at the wall clock and groaned. It said seven-thirty, slow from yet one more power interruption. She had climbed to reset it several times yesterday and would have to do it again. Hopefully that rewiring nonsense for security upgrades was done. When the tumblers finally clicked, Connie pulled on its handle and the foot-thick, two-ton door glided on its well-oiled hinges.

Meanwhile, Shirley found Margie, who graphically replayed the latest lesson in creative obscenities. "None of our training techniques are working," Margie fretted.

"Let's get staff together. You all have my permission to—"

Screams halted the conversation as Connie's shrieks reverberated throughout the branch. Shirley raced toward the vault. Connie, wide-eyed and terrified, was pointing inside. Shirley saw it immediately and grabbed Connie's shoulders as the branch manager began to slide down the wall.

Inside the vault, the body of a small woman with dark curly hair was slumped over the contents of one of the cash drawers. Her eyes were half-open and vacant. A horrid stench floated into the corridor.

"Don't look," Shirley said, helping Connie into her office and easing her into a chair. "Somebody bring her some water."

Connie lowered her head between her knees and sucked air.

Satisfied that Connie wouldn't pass out, Shirley tore through the branch. "Margie—call nine-one-one. Tell the operator we need police and an ambulance immediately." She motioned to the teller closest to the door. "Post signs on both doors and the drive-up window saying we're closed temporarily." The she turned to a ten-year employee. "Call Mr. Kramer's secretary. Tell her we need him immediately. Get him out of a meeting if she has to. I'll explain when he gets here."

Beckoning her staff to gather, Shirley reiterated relevant

emergency procedures. "Lock and guard the atrium and exterior doors, and don't let anyone in except executive staff and emergency personnel. That goes double for reporters." She returned to the vault, leaving gaping staff to share whispered details.

Local police arrived, sent for the coroner, followed by two detectives and evidence technicians. Juanita Rodriguez had been dead for twelve to eighteen hours, apparently stabbed with the Keynote letter opener that lay nearby, covered with blood. Strobes fired as the technician processed the scene. An incongruous scrap of bloodstained cloth fabric, lying on the victim's sleeve, was gathered with tweezers, dropped and sealed into an evidence bag.

"Looks like blood under her nails, someone said. "Bag her hands."

It was done.

Warren, Shirley, and Connie sat with the detectives in Connie's office after the coroner took charge of the body.

Connie took small sips of water. "The vault door is on a mechanical timer, Detective. No one, including the manufacturer, can open it from the outside once the door is shut until the timer triggers the mechanism to unlock it. I checked the timer myself around three. The door stays wide open, against the wall, until closing time. Everyone knows, from their first day of training, not to touch it until we're through for the day."

"And you were here when it opened this morning?"

"At eight, yes."

"Do you know when it was closed last evening?"

"Let's see…" Connie closed her eyes and reflected. "We closed both the branch and the drive-up window at four-thirty because of work being done on the electrical system. I looked at my watch at five-ten. The exterior doors were already locked, and Juanita was on the phone. I left her while I ran an errand upstairs." She started to cry. "She was alone and unprotected in what should have been the safest of places."

"When did you return?"

She reached for a tissue. "It was five thirty-five. I remember looking at my watch. The branch was empty, so I assumed Juanita had left. I checked the vault door, which was closed, collected my things, and went home. We should have been open until six, and the drive-up window until seven. Juanita had been so excited to get two hours off with pay."

"You saw her at five-ten in the branch?"

"Yes."

"And the vault door was locked by five thirty-five?"

She nodded.

"And nobody can get into the vault when it's closed?"

"If we want access at a different time, I must reset the timer before the door closes. Once, someone shut it at three o'clock by mistake. We had to get a security guard to protect the teller's cash drawers overnight because we couldn't get into the vault to put them away."

"Suppose somebody gets locked in?"

"There's an emergency handle inside, which everyone knows how to use. Even if that malfunctions, there's ventilation and an emergency light. I suppose someone could have been shut in and exited later, but how could they see if the coast was clear? The vault has no window or monitor. The timer would also have to be reset, and only two of us have that information."

"What about the cash drawers? Is anything missing?"

"Apparently not, at least they appear untouched. But we'll check the cash against last evening's inventory. One more thing, Detective—every employee at Keynote has at least one of those letter openers. They're a popular item that's been in our logo shop since the name change years ago. They're identical, and in my opinion, unnecessarily sharp."

The detective put his notepad away and walked toward the vault. "Ms. Granger, what about the security cameras?"

"That may be useless because the power was off, but you're welcome to view any footage we have at security. They can pinpoint the length of the power interruption and whether anyone entered or exited. Can I send my staff home?"

"I'd like to ask them some questions first. Maybe they saw something." He did and nobody had.

It was quite late when Shirley stumbled into her home and poured a double Scotch antidote. She'd been decisive, dealt with, and calmed the staff, most of whom opted to stay. Finally, they had reopened the drive-up.

She drew a full tub and laced it with oils. Drink poised on the rim, she slid into the water. Even candles and soft music did little to soothe her frayed nerves. Had she forgotten anything? She had directed all media calls to the police, and issued a stiff warning to personnel bank wide not to talk to the press. The reporters—they'd shown up in droves, trying to nab staff for comment, but to no avail. She gulped at the scotch. Juanita—that poor lovely creature. And the perpetrator. Why commit such a heinous crime and then not take the cash?

She reran the details. The bank began emptying as early as four, eliminating just about every employee. Five workmen had been together in the basement the entire time, struggling with archaic wires and chalking up overtime. Building keys—how many were out there?

If only they'd done something sooner.

Drink drained, she crawled from the tub, toweled, and pulled on a nightgown and robe. Wearily she started to hang up her suit. When she checked pockets, her hand touched something hard and she pulled out the forgotten metal scrap that she'd picked up outside the vault. She looked at it under a lamp. The crushed object shined like real gold. A decoration from a desk set? A charm? A jeweler would know its worth. She dropped it into her purse to investigate later. Exhausted, she crawled into bed.

Just before dawn, she dreamed she was going to Doug's retirement party, but kept getting diverted. She arrived at a racetrack where Keynote bankers were gathered in formal dress and Derby hats. Jockeys paraded their steeds, and someone was pointing to a particular horse that wore a white satin blanket with a gold shamrock, studded with green. The guests were shouting, "He's lucky! He's lucky!"

"Ticket, please," a strange little man who looked like Warren was saying. All Shirley found in her suit pocket was a crushed piece of gold metal. "That's lucky," he said. "I'll take it instead of a ticket."

The alarm jolted Shirley. Had she only imagined that she'd never slept? She groaned, her head splitting, but forced herself up for the ongoing challenge.

Chapter 24

B y six Wednesday evening, the Aldersons were ready to leave Kingsley's apartment. Sarah bustled with fake efficiency, gathering coolers in which she had brought enough food for a Thanksgiving dinner. "Are you sure you'll be safe? We could stay."

"I won't be alone. Todd's coming later."

"He seems very nice, dear. Solid. Responsible. Dad was impressed and relieved that he knew what to do. I'm not going to lecture, but it's high time you went out and had fun. Now—about your weight—"

"Mom, I know. I get that you're worried, but don't. I intend to eat like a ditch digger or I'll have to buy all new clothes." A familiar voice came from the stairway. "That would be Isaac returning Pandora. My attack cat will protect me, and the guys are next door."

Reluctantly, the Aldersons headed home.

Todd arrived later, toting bottles of wine, crackers, and cheese. "Got the cure," he said as he hung his jacket on the nearest doorknob. "You allowed to have spirits? If not, we won't tell."

She giggled and peered at the bottles.

"This is Chianti from a Tuscany vineyard. My buddy liberated it, and since it's not bottled for commercial export, it isn't defiled with sulfites. You can drink all you want and not get a headache. That should have a certain appeal."

"That rates real crystal."

"Sit. I'll find them. This shouldn't be chilled. If you'll just try a really good red at room temperature, you'll be converted." He opened her china cabinet and frowned. "How many got broken?"

"Most of them."

"Are they Waterford?" he asked, hefting one survivor. She nodded. "Next time Randall flies to Ireland, we'll send him shopping." He poured two mismatched glasses, then scrounged some napkins. "First look—see the deep red color? That means it's aged. Now swirl the glass and see how it coats. Notice the 'legs.' Next you're supposed to sniff it like this." He stuck his nose deep into the glass and made a disgusting noise that made them both laugh. "Now slurp a little past the back of your tongue without swallowing to get equal amounts of air and wine on your pallet. There. Now you try it."

She did, nearly choking and grabbed at her ribs when she laughed.

He removed a new philodendron from the coffee table and together, they stretched out stocking feet, but when she leaned against the edge of the cushion, she yelped.

"It's okay," she said quickly, easing herself to a new position. "Just a twinge."

"Just how bad is it. Are you in pain?"

"This will help a lot," she said of the wine and took another taste. "I'll get an old tee shirt and mark it with Xs so everyone will know where not to bump." He studied her eyes and feeling that he could read hers, she shrugged. She brushed off a tear with a laugh. "You should have seen the groundhog I nailed when I fell skiing. Talk about bruises—both him and me."

"Show me," he said very quietly.

"I can't—"

"Please. I need to know what he did."

She hesitated and, turning her back, lifted her sweater.

His breath caught. He gently touched the bruises on lumps that ran an angry spectrum of colors. "I'll kill him. I swear. If he ever comes near you, I'll kill him. What can I do? Anything?"

"Pour?" She sighed. "If I wanted to be mysterious or alluring, I've blown it."

"Enough about that. Let's get on with the cure." He refilled their glasses and arranged her cushions. "How about some music?"

"The stereo's broken."

He got up to check it. "Here's your problem. Your speaker wires are detached. There, that should do it," he said, inserting the wires into their respective terminals. He opened the changer to read the labels and punched forty. Enya's silky voice hushed into the room. He settled beside her. They listened awhile in comfortable silence.

"You've been so kind. I slept well last night."

"I didn't plan it."

"Sometimes the best things happen that way. I had a wonderful dream. I was in the back yard of a very old house, surrounded by fields. Friends were picnicking under large trees. There was a rose garden like my grandmother used to cultivate, only this one had a fountain." She slid a little lower into the couch and smoothed the nap on his cords with her toe. "I've had time to think and have faced some realities. Moving here was a step in the right direction, but I need to go farther. Make a real break—maybe study abroad or at Duke for a year. I'd intended to pursue my doctorate, but that didn't mesh with my marriage to Andy. Oh, don't look so alarmed. My lease has eight months to run so there's plenty of time to plan for transition."

"If you're trying to get a reaction from me, you're succeeding. I think that's a terrible idea."

"Why?"

"Your problems will just tag along. Face it, Kingsley. You're a people person: a family person. You've had what matters most torn away, and you can't replace that with intellectual pursuits. Believe me. I tried it." He set down his glass and turned to face her. "I want you to stay. I know I'm responsible for some of your turmoil. I've led you on, and not too subtly, then turned off abruptly."

"What really happened?" she asked.

"I guess it's inevitable that we have this conversation." He studied the coating on his wineglass. "You need someone who can give you what I can't. I needed to get out of your way before things went any further, but I waited too long. Like the kid who has to be home by six, but stays at the park for one more ride and one more and one more. For years I avoided involvement, feeling no connection with anyone I met. A few dates and sooner or later, I'd see shades of Maureen. Fortunately, there were never enough hours to pursue all the things I enjoy. The years slipped away.

"And then I met you. I was fascinated by your complexity, and how you just kept on trying, unspoiled and unjaded, caring and making things happen for others, in spite of your loss. It was such fun, just being around you, hearing your thoughts, catching your enthusiasm, seeing how you loved so many things. I found ways to put myself in your path.

Sunday evening, I knew just how real it was. I could feel it and knew you could too. I was up all night, confronting myself with this single most selfish thing I could do. I remember the first time I saw you at the gym, terrified that I was about to attack you, prepared to defend yourself with your keys, but then grappling to put me at ease.

"Monday morning I had no idea what to say. I wanted to save you from whatever I would subtract from your life. I saw your reaction—you scrambling to make it all right, no matter how hurt you felt. I did not know how to fix it."

"Oh, Todd—if only we'd talked. You can't do my thinking for me—make my decisions. Nobody can."

He sighed and shifted his gaze to the distance.

She took his hand and smoothed the tips of his fingers, studying them as she spoke. "What I learned Sunday doesn't matter to me. But maybe, just maybe, your life is what you want. I've seen you at work, on top of the world, and that makes you happy while emotional upheaval makes you miserable. People say 'let's be friends' when they really want is to escape. Your friendship's a treasure I don't want to lose. We should find a way to keep things from getting awkward and distant."

"You're doing it again, do you realize that? I don't want to be let off the hook. I do want to see you. How I feel hasn't changed. But if you are more comfortable being friends, just say so now, and we'll make it happen."

"I was hurt and angry, even though I realized later that you couldn't know what happened to me." She settled into the couch. "When Andy died, I was pregnant and subsequently miscarried. Six months later, a letter for Andy was forwarded to me, to thank him for participating in clinical trials for a male birth control pill."

"I never heard of it."

"That's because the trials stopped abruptly when preliminary results showed poor results. Among the twenty percent that conceived, there were many miscarriages."

"Do you think that's what happened to you?"

"I suspect as much. He told his father he planned to participate, but didn't tell me. He knew I'd pitch a fit because I—we—supposedly were trying to get pregnant. And besides, I don't believe in experimenting with drugs. If I'd known the danger, I'd have stayed on the pill."

"You should be furious. He took chances with your health. At the very least you should have been included in that decision."

"I suppose. But Andy was a kind, caring person who would have died before hurting others. The research results weren't publicized until after his death, so he was unaware of the danger. I have two choices—let it fester or just let it go."

"Is there any permanent damage to you? I'm sorry. That's too personal."

"I...well, it appears so. I gave my parents a heads up about having grand critters instead. My point is that I'm downright hostile about other people making decisions for me. If I make bad choices, at least they'll be mine. And, I guess, you could say we're in the same boat."

"Could we rewind to the place where we simply had fun? I do want to see you."

"I'd miss this the most. There isn't anyone I can talk to so openly."

"Come here," he said, gently snuggling her against him. "What you're describing is real intimacy, which isn't about sex. It's a matter of trust—to share what's core deep without fear of betrayal, ridicule, or rejection." He ran his thumb gently down her arm. "Tell you what—let's take our time. Get to know each other outside of a crisis."

"I'd love that."

"First, there's that lobster."

"I really did lose the bet. There was no such business."

"We could argue that technicality for hours or pick a Saturday when you're up for adventure. I have something special in mind."

"What about the bank?"

"I've been unable to find a written policy prohibiting us from having a personal relationship. Besides, we're both professionals. Tell me, has the cloud lifted?"

"I feel a great peace."

"That's the wine."

Chapter 25

W hat part of 'not here for anyone' don't you understand?" Frank's tirade fizzled abruptly as two men with badges and determined faces appeared by his secretary's side.

"Mr. Ziegler, we'd like you to come with us, please. We have some questions we'd like to ask you."

"If it's about that teller thing, I can't help you." He flipped a hand in dismissal as he reached for a file on his desk. "I haven't been near the bank for days."

"Please, Mr. Ziegler, I'm sure you'd rather not make a scene in front of your staff."

Alarmed, Frank backed off the attitude and put on his best schmoozy smile. "Detectives, I really don't have any information for you, but we can talk. Have a seat and I'll close the door." They held their ground. Looking from one to the other, Frank saw his options evaporate. "Arlene, I'll be back shortly."

❧❧❧

The police interrogation room was hardly a typical venue

for a man of Frank Ziegler's stature. He cast wary eyes at the nauseous green walls, ancient tile floors, and opaque window. No decoration broke the austerity except that huge mirror. They sat at a large metal table on chairs that creaked when he squirmed.

"Before we question you, we must advise you of your rights. Do you wish to have your attorney present?"

"What for? I've done nothing wrong."

"Tell us about your relationship with Juanita Rodriguez."

"I had nothing to do with her death. Our acquaintance was strictly professional."

"You have your ties custom made, is that right?"

Frank looked down and stopped fidgeting mid-stroke.

"Let's see the label."

Frank turned it over. It was brand new and he hadn't yet clipped it. He showed them.

"Can you explain what one of these labels was doing on Juanita's body?"

"I have no idea! Because I'm so tall, the little tail of my tie can't be anchored in the label, so I cut it off. The label, not the tail. Anyway, I work in that building. A label could have fallen anywhere and gotten tracked into the vault."

"There was only a twenty-five minute time frame in which the murder could have taken place. I doubt if there was very much tracking. There's blood on it and it's not hers. I bet the label came off when you killed her. Did she scratch you? Is that what happened to your face?"

Alarmed, Frank's hand flew to his cheek. "That's nonsense! Why would I kill her?"

The detective ignored the question. "Can you explain the meaning of the note we found in her pocket? It says, 'Meet me after closing. F.' Your initial is very distinctive."

"I sent that days ago."

"Look at the date."

"She was working on a special project for our private banking customers. I had to meet with her often. Make that occasionally." Frank studied their hard, cold faces, feeling his anger turn to panic.

"According to your bank records, large sums of cash were withdrawn in amounts equal to the cash we found in her apartment. Can you explain that?"

"I can't and I don't need to." Heat rose in his face. "It's a coincidence."

"And the blood under her nails isn't her type. Any idea how it got there?"

"No! And it couldn't be mine. I never touched her."

"Then you wouldn't mind giving us a sample of your blood for a DNA comparison."

Frank's seething glance swept from one to the other.

"Look, Mr. Ziegler, you can clear this up quickly. If you comply willingly, we won't have to get a court order, which of course would be granted."

"Am I under arrest?"

"Not at the moment."

"Then I demand to be taken back to my office. I'm not saying another word without my attorney."

Hours after he'd left with the detectives, Frank exited the bank's elevator into the executive area and barked at Arlene as he stormed past her desk. "Cancel my appointments. Make any excuse that sounds reasonable."

She followed him into his office. "You already rescheduled some from Monday and Tuesday, remember?"

"Let me see the calendar." He glanced at it, scowling. "Keep these and move those," he said digging pencil lines into the list. Now leave me alone. Arlene?" he called after her. "I'm sorry. I'm just not myself."

Arlene shrugged and kept walking. Alone in his sanctuary, Frank closed the door and buried his face in his hands. Pulling out the telephone directory, he scanned the attorneys until he found the most famous one. Luckily, the great man could see him.

At eleven the next morning, Frank faced R. Samuel Roth at a small conference table in his city office. After retaining his services without quibbling about the $10,000 retainer, Frank blurted out his predicament.

Sam took copious notes without comment, and finally spoke. "Frank, you must be completely honest with me. Anything you say is privileged, but if I'm going to help you, hold nothing back. I can't be blindsided later. But," he advised, "if you confess to me, I can't let you lie on the stand. That would be suborning perjury. Now—do you know anything about the death of Juanita Rodriguez?"

"Absolutely not."

"There are any number of approaches we can take should that not be true, from self defense to accidental to diminished capacity. I must know."

"I did not kill her! I did not kill her! I didn't!"

"Okay. Let's move on. Is there any way your blood could have gotten onto that label or under her nails?"

"The label, I doubt it. I don't remember cutting myself. But her nails, that's impossible."

"How did you get the scratches on your right cheek?"

"The wife found a note in my jacket pocket and thought I was having an affair with Juanita. She was furious and clawed me. Luckily, she missed my eyes. I think it surprised both of us. She's such a mouse."

"What day was that?"

"Saturday."

"The murder took place the following Tuesday. Those scratches look pretty fresh."

"I keep nicking them shaving."

"Juanita was left handed—"

"So is my wife. Look, Sam, I couldn't possibly have killed her. I was in Philadelphia at the time of the murder."

"Can you prove that?"

"I don't know."

"Look, Frank, if you're positive that there's no way your blood could have gotten under her nails, then you should cooperate with the police. They're going to get a court order anyway."

"What if somebody else matches my DNA?"

"That's impossible, unless you have an identical twin."

"If the test will get me off the hook before this gets into the papers, that would save my reputation. Will you go with me?"

Sam checked his calendar. "Sure. We can go now if you're ready. When the DNA doesn't match, they'll have no reason to suspect you."

ↀↈↀↈ

Friday morning's headlines blared in seventy-two-point type:

BANK EXECUTIVE ARRESTED IN VAULT MURDER
EVP Franklin P. Ziegler Implicated
Police late Thursday arrested Franklin P. Ziegler, executive vice president of Keynote National Bank, in connection with the murder of Carol Drexler, also know as Juanita Rodriguez, formerly of Chicago.

Ziegler was arraigned on second and third degree murder and related charges according to the district attorney's office.

Although police aren't revealing the evidence linking Ziegler to the Drexler homicide, sources close to the investigation say that blood evidence found at the scene has been identified as belonging to Ziegler.

Drexler had been employed as a teller under the name Juanita Rodriguez at Keynote National Bank since June.

Fingerprint analysis and investigation by police revealed that the victim had assumed the identity of Chicago physician Juanita Rodriguez prior to moving to Pennsylvania.

Drexler previously had been convicted in Ohio for conspiracy and fraud in connection with a loan scam at a Columbus bank.

Branch manager Connie Davis discovered the body in the vault Tuesday morning when she opened the vault door at eight a.m.

R. Samuel Roth, Esquire, Ziegler's attorney, entered a not guilty plea and requested that the community leader be released on his own recognizance. He was released on $250,000 bail.

The article recapped previously published details of the murder, a rundown of Frank's career, and various quotes of disbelief and support from long-time friends and customers. That Frank had garnered respect in the community wasn't lost on Kingsley. She tried to puzzle through how it was all connected, but couldn't.

ぐぅぐぅ

Frank paced, entreating Sam to believe him. "That's impossible! The blood couldn't be mine! I never touched the girl!"

"Look, Frank, the odds of the blood belonging to someone else are nil. Are you sure you didn't have an argument with her some other time? I need something to go on. Think!"

Frank tugged at his tie. "The closest I came to any bloodshed was when my wife scratched me and I kept nicking it. And I donated blood recently."

Sam dismissed that with a shake of his head. "You're in a real jam. If you have an explanation, tell me now. You said you were in Philadelphia at the time of the murder. Can you prove it?"

"I'd rather avoid—"

"The murder took place during a twenty-five minute time frame. You couldn't be two places at once."

"Maybe the bank's video cameras picked me up."

"At the vault? I understand they weren't functioning."

"At a Philadelphia bank branch. I was there at the time of the murder."

"Why in God's name didn't you tell me that sooner?"

"I didn't want my personal business made public. Besides, I thought the blood test would squelch this whole mess."

"Tell me the specifics and my private detective will verify your alibi."

"But the blood—"

"If you can prove that you had an alibi, I'll find a way to get that excluded. Break in the chain of evidence. Sloppy work at the lab. Overzealous police. Are you sure you have no idea how it got there?"

Frank shook his head.

Later that day, Frank and his attorney met with the assistant DA and detectives. "The blood under Ms. Drexler's nails cannot have come directly from him. He was elsewhere at the time of the crime, and he says you already know that. He was as surprised as anyone at the alleged match. Somebody dropped the ball at your lab or framed him." Sam smiled benignly at the detectives who exchanged hooded glances. "Go ahead, Mr. Ziegler. Tell them."

"You said she was killed between five-ten and five thirty-five? I was in Philadelphia, and I can prove it."

The assistant DA did not blink. "This had better be good," she said.

"The circumstantial evidence is very strong against you," the first detective said. "Not just the blood evidence, but bank records and this phony private banking story. We can think of several reasons that you would be angry enough to kill Ms. Drexler. A love affair gone sour. Blackmail, especially if you knew who she really was."

Frank interrupted him. "Just before closing that Tuesday afternoon I was in a First Union branch conducting personal business. My employer doesn't have to know everything about my financial affairs. I do keep accounts elsewhere." He scribbled an address. "Go to this branch and ask for the teller who was on the left end of the teller line. She's tall, African-American, and wore a gray suit with a red blouse, a black necklace, and matching earrings. She'll remember me. Hell, I bet my picture is on their security tape. I was wearing gray slacks, a navy wind breaker, a blue and white pin striped shirt, and a navy golf cap with a Mt. Top St. Thomas logo."

"What kind of business did you say you had there?"

"Personal. It was personal business."

"We'll check out your story." As Frank looked from one

hostile face to another, one bead of sweat trickled beneath his hairline. He made no motion to wipe it away.

※※※

The technical expert delivered the bad news after pouring over the First Union tapes. "You're not going to like this. He's telling the truth. Look at the time. The security camera mounted directly behind the teller clearly captured Ziegler's face. Oh, he did have the visor pulled over his forehead, but look here." He blew up a section of face. "See the eyes? And the scratches? It's him all right."

"Damn!" The detective punched his palm with his fist at the second setback. The teller had recognized the competing executive and thought it was odd that he banked there.

"How do we explain the blood under her nails? And on the label?" They looked at each other blankly. "Why didn't he tell us this sooner? You'd think he'd have bawled 'alibi' at once. This doesn't feel right."

Before sundown Friday, R. Samuel Roth had all charges withdrawn. Thoroughly shaken, Frank returned home, only to find that his key didn't fit. He pounded and cursed her to no avail, but finally gave up, slinking into the comfort of his Mercedes.

A hotel suite, room service, a stiff drink, and a filet—that kind of rock to sit on and think held enormous appeal. The time had come to execute his plan.

If only he'd shredded the papers in his study, but maybe no one would ever find them, and Dolly was too stupid to grasp their meaning.

※※※

"Suppose Ziegler reset the timer?" the detective hypoth-esized in between bites of his Philly cheese steak and gulps of hot coffee. "I know the man's guilty, and he's not that smart. We just have to prove how he managed the illusion."

His partner watched midday traffic stream past the diner that sat beside the highway. "Perhaps he had help."

"Then explain the blood evidence—it's Ziegler's, all right."

The two munched for a few moments.

"Wait a minute. Try this. Ziegler was once a branch manager, right? That vault's an antique that they show off on tours—came from their original building. He must know how to reset the timer."

"But Shirley Granger said once the door's closed—"

"That's not where I'm going. If I heard correctly, the timer was set sometime earlier in the day. The last person working simply closes the door. Slam. Click. Now suppose you were Frank and you wanted to set up an alibi. That vault's in a corridor that's fairly remote. You simply reset the timer to reopen at eight p.m. instead of a.m., convenient-ly place yourself at a distant camera, chat up the teller, and return to meet with Juanita. The time of death could be off by as much as two hours. Don't forget, they didn't find her until eight the next morning. He'd have had to arrange to meet her." He rubbed his forehead, and looked off in thought. "Let's check his email and phone records, both home and at work for any communication that day. And the time that the workmen knocked off. And who arranged to have the electricity turned off and staff sent home early. And how visible is the vault's timer, anyway?

"Would the manager have easily noticed the change? And the vault's temperature—by how much could the time of death vary? Did Juanita have a bank key?"

"All tellers did."

The first detective shook his head. "Why did they even bother with locks!"

"The security cameras were only off a very short time and he's not on the tape near that time. Wait—let's check all the way back to that morning and forward to midnight."

The waitress circled with coffee and menus. "Dessert, gentlemen? Everything's homemade—apple, cherry, lemon meringue, shoofly, Boston cream, chocolate cake."

The men grinned at her.

"Wife's got me on a diet of bananas and birdseed," one said. "I'll take the cherry with two scoops of vanilla."

Chapter 26

Margaret, the head of real estate lending, beckoned the young management trainee into her office. "You look perplexed, Bruce. What can I do for you?"

"This refinancing application is for an employee." He handed it to her. "Should I have access to the personal information I'd need?"

"Nice catch. You're a quick study, Bruce. Why don't you leave it with me and I'll take care of it myself? And thanks." Margaret frowned at the documents for Jeffrey Johnston and his wife Suzanne's primary residence. She'd known Suzanne for many years. An economics professor, Suzanne had definite ideas about financial planning and this application didn't jibe.

Suzanne was on a mission to pay off the house, while focusing current income on her children's education. Margaret pulled the account up on the screen and became even more puzzled. If the mortgage was due to be paid off in eight months, what prompted an eighty percent refinancing now?

She studied the application carefully. It was completed in broad-point blue fountain pen, which also was used for Jeffrey's signature. Suzanne's, neat and fine-pointed, was in black. She studied her friend's signatures with a magnifying glass. They were perfectly straight, but one was slightly tipped on the line. Flipping pages, she located two other signatures and superimposed them using her windowpane. The three disappeared into one. That meant all three signatures had been dropped in electronically.

If the refinancing was approved, a check for $180,000 would be deposited into their joint account that read *or*, not *and*. Either Jeffrey or Suzanne could withdraw funds.

Knowing what she did about Jeffrey, Margaret felt she had no choice but to call. "Hey, Suzanne, great solo at church last Sunday. Your voice gave me the shivers. Listen—I have an investment idea that might interest you. If you have a few minutes, I'd like to stop by. You done for the day? Great. I'll swing by."

At four, Margaret pulled into her friend's two-story colonial, a three thousand square foot jewel surrounded by an immaculate half-acre lawn. Suzanne had just arrived, the garage door still open, when Margaret knocked.

"How's Jeff?" she started, taking the offered kitchen chair while her friend poured water into the Krupp's reservoir. Margaret watched Suzanne's face surreptitiously for tells.

"He's away—one of those guy trips. Golf and fishing. You know the kind."

"We usually ride the elevator together. I realized I hadn't seen him for a while. I was afraid he might have the flu."

Suzanne busied herself with artificial efficiency, setting the table with placemats, silverware, creamer and sugar, dainty china cups, saucers, and plates. She arranged shortbread cookies on a matching plate and retrieved the coffeemaker's carafe. She sat. Poured. Waited.

"What's up?" she said finally.

"Listen, Suzanne, I remembered your financing plans for college and thought we might have a better plan than refinancing your home. So, before putting through your application, I thought we could chat."

"You're mistaken. We're not refinancing. We don't need to. My commissions will pay for college with money left over. And we've been saving since they were born."

"There must be some miscommunication between you and Jeff. He turned in this app." Margaret extracted the application from her briefcase and slid it across the table.

"Let me see that!" Suzanne took the papers from Margaret and scanned them quickly. "What the hell?" She erupted from her chair. "I did not sign this. What's going on?"

"Maybe he has a tax advantage in mind?"

Suzanne paced, mumbling figures. Finally she thumped back into her chair. "Margaret, please don't tell anybody. Jeff disappeared a couple weeks back. I have no idea where he went, except that he took his warm weather clothes and some personal possessions. He's left me."

"I am so sorry." Margaret paused for a beat, digesting what she'd already suspected, before addressing the problem at hand. "The check was to be direct-deposited to your joint checking account."

"Please tell me that hasn't been done yet!"

"No, that's why I'm here."

"All our accounts are joint. What if he's cleaned them out?"

"Let's go to the branch and check your accounts. Then you can decide the best course of action—perhaps close your joint accounts and reopen others in your name. That goes for the kids' accounts, too. But Suzanne, don't panic. There may be a perfectly reasonable explanation."

"Like hell, Margaret. Nobody forges my name to a $180,000 loan application by mistake."

❧❧❧

Late Sunday afternoon, Kingsley looked through her peephole in response to impatient knocking. A large plush teal creature with satin bat wings and matching scaled tail flapped its forked tongue at her. Laughing, she flung open the door to greet Todd and the puppet attached to his arm. "Who's your friend?"

"His name is Fearless and he's come to protect you from all of his ilk and change your perception of dragons." He removed the puppet and worked it onto her arm.

"He's wonderful. Thank you."

"Do I get a hug too?"

"Come here, mister." She wrapped her arms, Fearless and all, around his neck. "Come on in and sit down."

"I can't stay—the bank's in an uproar about Frank's arrest and the vault murder. You were right about Manning not being Manning. According to Warren, he and the woman we know as Juanita were implicated in an attempted bank scam in Ohio. At that bank in Columbus, she used the name Maria Domingues. The charges were dropped against her in exchange for implicating the mastermind and the forfeiture of her accounts. They didn't have any evidence against Manning. Just suspicions by association."

"And they came to Keynote together?"

"Within a few months of each other. Having learned how to perpetuate a scam, Manning needed someone in the branch to open fake client checking accounts after he wrote bogus loans. He recommended her to Jeffrey via Frank, who was trying to fill minority slots."

"Does that mean their deaths are related?"

"Possibly. The police questioned Warren, Doug, and me about a special program Frank was supposed to be offering private banking customers with Juanita's help, and whether they had a personal relationship. We knew nothing of either. The police have learned that Manning Stoudt's real name was Mark Young."

Kingsley gasped and he grinned at her reaction. "The owner of Wireless Inc. at Deer Lake!"

"Only on paper. We figure he thought he could make a big score, using his lending authority and access to bank records, and then split.

"How did he do it?

"First, he filled out the paperwork and approved a construction loan for $200,000 for a nonexistent company he called Wireless, Inc. Since his lending authority is $500,000, such a relatively small loan would not raise suspicion. Next he told a teller—guess which one—that the customer, Mark Young, was unable to come in personally to open Wireless's business checking account. He, Manning, would get the customer's signature and bring it back to the branch. Manning picked up the checkbook, presumably to deliver to Mark Young. Of course he kept the checkbook and ATM card himself.

"Using his real name, Mark Young, he rented a spot at Deer Lake and put up a mailbox to use as Wireless's business address to receive bank correspondence. He also opened a checking account in the name Manning Stoudt at an offshore bank. He drew down $20,000 from Wireless's line of credit and attempted to transfer it to Wireless's business checking account to make monthly payments. He could also, if he wished, transfer funds to his account for his personal use.

"In short, he could write himself checks from a bogus account or do ATM transfers to himself. After the first $20,000 draw, he still had $180,000 to pay down the principal and interest. That was set up to draw automatically. No one would be suspicious as long as the payments were made. I guess his plan was to clean it out at some point and disappear. Most embezzlers get into trouble by skipping the intermediate step and sending funds directly to themselves."

"But it didn't work."

"It might have gone undetected for years had he not confused the account number with Wire Products. Paul Yokum caught it, and you pounced."

"That was smoothed over."

"Not entirely. Nathaniel mentioned your run-in with Manning to Jeffrey Johnston. Jeff lives near Deer Lake and, knowing the territory, was immediately suspicious. He ran a background check on Manning. According to information found in Jeff's personal files, he used a private detective named John Miller to run his fingerprints. Jeff should have turned Manning over to fraud, at which time Manning would have been fired and brought up on charges. Instead, he passed the information to someone in executive who blackmailed Manning into writing much bigger bogus loans, including your Birdsboro one."

"That would explain the statements I found in the mailbox as well as the conversation I overheard the day I took the blue list from Manning's office, getting trapped in the copy room. Why didn't loan review spot it?"

"The paperwork from the loan application process goes in two different directions—the computerized loan files and the branch's system, but there's no cross referencing. In time, loan review would have picked up on it, but that could have taken years. We need to address that problem immediately."

"Will Jeff be indicted?"

"If they can find him. He hasn't been seen since Manning and Juanita were killed."

"Suddenly this sounds so much bigger."

"I'm wondering if we should keep your bodyguard for a while."

"What for? There's no need. With Manning dead, there's no one left with a motive to hurt me."

"Except for the bastard who bludgeoned you."

Kingsley shook her head. "If he was hired to toss my apartment and I caught him off guard, that train has left the station. He'd have no reason to come after me now. Common sense says he'd make damned sure that I'd never see his face again. It's a big country. Besides, the newspapers said I couldn't identify 'a person of interest.'"

"Well, if you change your mind, feel unsafe, or the circumstances change..." He looked at his watch. "I'd better get to my meeting with Warren. If you're up for it, he would like you to be present as well."

"Give me a minute to change?" She yanked on wool slacks, a turtleneck sweater, boots, and a parka. Gingerly, she adjusted a ski cap to cover her stitches. A quick glance in the mirror confirmed that her face looked just awful, but she didn't have time to experiment with makeup.

"Your life must be chaos," she said. "I'll understand if you have to work next weekend."

"We have a date with a lobster. Remember? And that's chiseled in stone."

೧೩೬೩

"Ladies, Todd, come in," Warren urged. After everyone

was seated, he closed the door. "Margaret and Barrie, you know everyone. Kingsley, I'd like to introduce Fred Macmillan."

"Of course!" As they shook hands, sparks of mutual delight crossed between them. "We've met on the phone. Fred gave me valuable information without breaking his severance agreement."

Warren nodded. "My heartfelt thanks for everything you did to uncover the fraud. Fred McMillan was the first to try to report it. Doug and I have been successful in luring him out of retirement. We'll be announcing today that Nathaniel is being promoted to the new EVP slot and Fred will rejoin us as head of the lending division." He turned to Kingsley. "What I'm going to say now can't leave this room. With the bogus loan account numbers you identified, we hope to trace the entire operation. You will receive a percentage of the total from the bonding company as well as a reward from our fraud prevention program. You'll also get my personal letter of congratulations, a copy of which will go in your permanent record."

"What happens next?" Kingsley asked.

Warren leveled them with a look. "I am trusting you with insider information. Not one word. All of us keep very quiet. We wait and we watch. When somebody accesses those bogus accounts, our special lending officers will follow the money. Only the people in this room, the police, and those who absolutely need to know are aware that a trap has been laid. Even executive staff is out of the loop. When the perpetrator shows himself, the FBI will arrest him. I must impress upon you that complete confidentially is essential. I'll need a list of anyone with whom you've discussed this."

"I told no one except Todd—and that wasn't until Monday," Kingsley said, "the police, and my parents. That's it."

The others concurred.

"If you learn anything else, say nothing to anyone except Todd or myself."

☙❧☙

Special lending watched and waited, poised to follow wherever the bogus transactions might lead. Suddenly all the flagged accounts were drawn down electronically to minimum balances, the funds being transferred to other accounts in various five-county banks. The focus expanded as other jurisdictions came into play. The following Saturday, the balances were transferred to yet one more account. The individual was identified when he showed up to collect a certified check.

Early Sunday, Frank Ziegler left a rental car in Philadelphia International Airport's long-term parking lot. He entered the terminal, passed a leather duffel bag through security, and planted himself at US Airways departure gate. With his right hand in his pocket, he traced the outline of the security wallet suspended inside his pants. Hyper-alert, he remained vigilant and would until he could safely execute Plan A or Plan B. Shortly, he would know which one.

His original plan, so brilliantly conceived, would have been seamless, had it not been for two stupid women—greedy Juanita and Dolly. He had been forced to regroup too quickly, but now he had an excellent contingency plan.

When the time had come for execution, he punched the editor's number on his cell phone. "This is Franklin P. Ziegler." He looked at his watch. One forty. "I'm calling a press conference early this evening to make a major announcement. I have personally uncovered a crime at our bank. I'll verify the exact time and place later. This is so big that the wire service will pick up on it. Be at the press conference if you don't want to be scooped by the big city papers and look ridiculous and back-water slow." He disconnected without giving the editor time to respond.

Relaxed, he watched planes taxi beneath the huge windows while others mounted skyward into cumulous clouds. He flicked his wrist—five more minutes. He would decide which identity and corresponding boarding pass to use at the very last minute. Fools. He'd show them all up. He couldn't lose. He'd either be the quintessential hero, solving a loan scam and claiming the reward, or retiring to an obscure island with no extradition treaty to enjoy all that money for himself. Perhaps he should build his own golf course. Tieless, he stroked himself anyway. *Sly fox—you are a genius.*

Mesmerized by his Rolex's sweep second hand, Frank followed the countdown. "Final boarding call. Would passenger Quincy Tyler please report to the departure desk." He slipped the winning passport and boarding pass from his pocket in case they asked for a photo ID. He had neglected to ask if he'd need that to board. *The island wins*, he thought. He rose, never seeing the approaching contingency.

"Franklin Ziegler?"

He jumped.

"Come with us, please. We have a warrant for your arrest for embezzlement, fraud, and conspiracy."

They read him his rights.

"Now just a damn minute. You've got it all wrong." Frank swiveled his glance from the suits to the waiting gate. His heart rate took off, his face instantly hot, and he started to sweat. In the process of cuffing him, an agent loosened his passport and boarding pass from his sweaty fingers.

"Quincy Tyler?" The detective looked Frank square in

the face while holding his fake passport open to the picture. He flicked his gaze back and forth—passport, Frank, passport, Frank. "What's the story here, Frank? You got a twin from whom you were separated at birth?"

This couldn't be happening! How did they know? What had gone wrong? Speechless, he was led away in handcuffs. The police secured him in the patrol car, and, unlike crime shows he'd seen on TV, took an inordinately long time conversing among themselves. That worked to Frank's advantage as his heart rate settled and he regained a modicum of composure.

He'd play the hero/crime-solver card. That would entitle him to the reward. His excellent attorney could even get forgiveness for the necessity of his having forged credentials. A little smile overtook his face. A ghostwriter could spin his hero/banker book tale that would be a best seller, followed by an action movie for which he'd consult— maybe star. Talk shows, guest spots, book tours. National— no make that worldwide—speaking engagements. He couldn't make what Bill Clinton did for such gigs, but he still could count on big bucks. He grinned until his face hurt as he pictured himself dripping in the proceeds that extreme wealth would bring. And he wouldn't even have to leave his own country, except for mind-blowing vacations.

Chapter 27

As Kingsley spritzed on a haunting new fragrance, she tried to remember being so excited. She couldn't. Todd's only hint was "an historic venue with legal seafood," meaning fresh caught. She slipped a new dress over the French curls that camouflaged her healing wounds. The sales woman swore that the dress matched her eyes and that very few women should wear slinky knits. After dabbing special makeup over her bruises, she guided hoop earrings one-handedly. Stepping back, she grinned at her happy reflection. A knock—it was time.

When Kingsley opened the door, Pandora took one look at the man in immaculate navy and fled, no doubt remembering him as the clumsy pet groomer.

"You are so beautiful," he said admiringly. "Let me help you on with your coat." He checked the security pad, tested the door, and steered her down the steps to a waiting black Continental and chauffeur. "The women in my family say 'never make a lady dressed for the evening climb into that Explorer.'" He smoothed her coat away from the car door and circled to his.

At the regional airport they crossed the tarmac to a private jet. Upon spotting them, an exuberant redheaded man hurried toward them, arms extended. "You're right. She is gorgeous!" Todd's best friend Randall Shannon did his best to embarrass Todd with his inane chatter. Finally he lowered his voice. "You're going to lose that bet, buddy."

Randall bounded up to the cockpit door, motioning for them to follow. "What bet?" she asked.

"Maybe I'll tell you some day."

"If you need anything, you'll have to come forward," Randall called, as he and his copilot began preparations. "We can't hear a word from up here."

They settled for what Todd described as a short flight. "Randall and I grew up together. After the Academy, he stayed in the air force for a number of years. Now he runs a charter service for businesses and wealthy individuals. He's meeting friends for the evening, and then he'll fly us back."

Kingsley finally had a chance to relax and gaze at her escort. Class hung as comfortably as his well-tailored suit. He reached for her hand across the small aisle. "Are you going to tell me?" she asked.

"That you're the most beautiful woman I've ever seen? Yes." She smiled and asked about their destination. "Boston. The lady requested fresh lobster, so we'll go to the source."

"And to think it all started with a chance meeting at Hawk Mountain and that insane bet." The jet roared into a navy blue sky, as December twilight blanketed the farmlands and ancient Appalachians.

"I have a confession. It wasn't a chance meeting. The previous Friday you were talking with Barrie when a group of touring board members passed your office door. I was with them, and just as I passed, I heard you invite Barrie to hike at Hawk Mountain. She couldn't go. That Saturday, I was there when they opened, feeling every inch like a stalker. It's a good thing you came early, or I would have lost my nerve."

"You did all that? It was a wonderful day. We could have talked forever. There were no dead spots."

"I wanted to see you, but didn't know how. Our working at the same bank made things awkward. I couldn't just ask you out."

"I was sure I'd made terrible impressions when you found my gloves at the gym. Didn't you recognize me at the luncheon with Warren?"

"You bet I did."

"But you didn't let on."

"I about died when I saw your ring while we were hiking. Hitting on married women is against my code. It's funny, though—I had a sense you were really alone. And I did win the bet. My goal was to see you again. If I'd had any inkling I'd put you in danger..."

"What will happen to Frank?"

"A two-prong investigation is underway, not only into the extent of the loan scam but to analyze our procedures. As for Frank, there's a preponderance of evidence against him, especially since he was nailed with the funds. Still, I can't underestimate him. An attorney like Samuel Roth wouldn't let him plead innocent without a good strategy. If only Frank had used his brain better, or realized his limitations. Enough about Frank and the bank. Tonight they don't exist. You and I do."

He leaned across the small aisle and kissed her. The plane banked, tipping the skyline of Boston before straightening for the approach to Logan. After they deplaned, he hailed a cab, which navigated Sumner Tunnel, passing signs for Quincy Market, Faneuil Hall, and Blackstone Street. Turning onto North and then Union, it stopped at Forty-First.

"We're here," Todd announced. "The Union Oyster House, Boston's oldest restaurant, and the oldest in continuous service in our country since 1826."

Taking his hand, she stepped from the cab and passed into its charm. They climbed stairs to the second floor and were shown to a high-backed booth where they settled into its cozy privacy. Todd ordered drinks to accompany their appetizers.

As they sampled grilled oysters, baked stuffed cherrystone clams, clams casino, oysters Rockefeller and shrimp scampi, small talk took on a velvety quality.

The mellow sounds of happy tourists blended with New England accents. Kingsley realized that if she blinked, her beautiful evening would pass into memory. She wished she could freeze it forever.

"Does your lobster meet expectations?"

"Mm—excellent! Especially with their seafood stuffing. I've never tasted anything like it. I wonder what other bets we can make."

"That we will do this again." He set down his coffee. "Every time we've had a real chance to talk, I've felt a special connection, especially during those quiet evenings we spent at your place."

She smiled. "Me too."

"You've touched something I thought was long dead or that I was incapable of feeling. When you were attacked, I was beside myself—panicked that you might slip away before we could pursue it. I railed at the injustice and my stupidity." The darkness that had crept into his eyes quickly passed. "Kingsley, I love you. I have from the start. Do you think you could ever feel that way about me?"

Her heart hammered so hard she was sure he could hear it, and she knew she would remember his words forever.

She reached for his hand. "I do love you and that scares me. I can never take anything for granted again."

He grinned. "There are so many things I want to tell you, share with you, do for you. At Doug's party, I'd wished you were there. I had more fun with you and Pandora, even though that event marked a milestone for me. I zoned out on the speeches, thinking about you, wearing that cute little black thing, all over kitty litter. Will you be comfortable having people know that we're seeing each other?"

"It could get awkward, especially, well, if it doesn't go well."

Todd held her gaze. "I had given up hope of ever finding someone like you. Didn't think you existed, or if you did, that I couldn't compete. My feeling won't change, but if yours do as you get to know all my bad habits, I promise I'll never do anything to hurt you. I have always been loyal to my friends and to those whom I love. Just ask Randall."

Kingsley struggled to check her emotions. Her whole life was changing, a free fall from safety, perhaps to a far better place. "What I've been feeling—it's such a long story."

"Start with 'I was born at a very young age' and don't leave anything out."

 caca

Randall followed Todd into his condo, chattering non-stop about a recent golf tournament. "...A par three, 100 yards, gale howling right in my face, so I took my eight iron and stung that ball at the precise moment the wind chose to die. Man, that ball must have sailed a hundred-fifty yards." He laughed, shaking his head.

"We'll need to settle up—"

"I was flying anyway."

"Not till I called, you weren't."

"Look, Todd, I built my business on your referrals. It's the least I can do."

"But if you hadn't followed through, given great customer service, that wouldn't have mattered."

"I—ah—brought my ledgers if you wouldn't mind taking a peek. Help me pull out the weeds."

"Got special waders. You must computerize and, this time, no arguments. And the way you're growing, you need a manager."

"I'm waiting for you to partner with me."

"No thanks, Randall. Your flamboyant lifestyle doesn't fit me. I'm perfectly happy flying a desk." Todd disappeared into his room.

"Okay, let's have it," Randall called, tossing his coat onto a chair. "I have a key, don't need a babysitter, know where you keep your booze and your coffee. Why the hell are you here and not there?" Todd returned from his bedroom, minus his jacket, tie and shoes.

"Fix you a drink?"

"Bourbon. I'll get it." Randall concocted and Todd fixed his own, then they flopped on the couch. "I could've let myself in—"

"It's, well, complicated."

"Complicated my ass! From what I saw, it couldn't be simpler. There's a force field between you that could have short-circuited my instruments. She is fantastic and, more to the point, she's hot for you. And look at you—you're a mess!"

Todd laughed. After taking a swallow, he attempted an explanation which, to someone like fast-flying Randall, would take some doing. "From what little I've learned, her marriage was just about perfect. She's having a rough time letting go. And now that she knows he was murdered, she won't have closure without learning why. I suspect at some level she feels like she's cheating. I can't compete with a dead man, and I don't want to be the bridge between the guy who was and the one who will be, whether he's the next or the tenth. And there's an element of taking advantage. She's just so vulnerable. I feel like I've known her forever, but in reality it's less than three months. I think she needs time."

"This isn't tenth grade. She's a real woman. You could be making a huge mistake, letting her think she does nothing for you. You could end up being the brother-friend-cousin-uncle-you name it person because, at some level, you make her feel undesirable."

Todd shook his head. "She's a real lady, an old-fashioned girl. Men gape at her and she counters by being aloof. She's built walls of protection around herself." He took another swallow and looked at his friend. "I don't want a transitional rebound. I want something better."

"Don't wait too long. Bet you could slip in your competitors' drool. I don't want to be around when you screw it all up." He savored his bad choice of words. "Know what I think?"

"That you're going to tell me—"

"You're too smart for your own good. Stop thinking. Give in to your primal instincts—a lost weekend, rain on the roof, a fireplace, fine wine, old bearskin rug, just let it happen. Since you asked."

Todd laughed and changed the subject. "How was the lady you met this evening?"

"Let's just say that she was no lady and leave it at that. Just another 'hustle,' looking for a guy she thinks might have money. Thinks? She came right out and asked me about my net worth." He shook his head. "At least it was fun seeing my friends, but I wish they'd stop fixing me up."

"You still miss Janie."

Randall let out his breath and looked down. "Janie had class. Got a Christmas card—twin daughters, baby boy, buttoned-down banker-type husband, no offense. Nine years of my life and gone. Now, don't you blow it. We have a bet, and I want my baseball card back."

They were quiet a minute. Randall chose one more tack. "Thanksgiving's coming. Turkey for two, lots of fun while it cooks—"

"She's going home for the holiday."

"Maybe you'll be invited."

"I hit it off with her parents, but once they learn about my disastrous first marriage, they'll want something far better for their daughter, especially after marrying a Ward."

ҽ⌇ҽ⌇

Randall stumbled from Todd's guestroom and groped for the phone. "What! Oh! Kingsley, I'm sorry. Gees, what time is it?" The clock obligingly chimed ten. "It's the middle of the night." He laughed. "Not in his room. Bed's made, the obnoxious old neatnick. Ah, he's coming in now—been to the gym, looks like, probably working out his frustrations. I don't know why you bother with him. Now me—Hey!"

Todd grabbed the phone. "It is a good morning now," he said quietly, turning toward his study and closing the door.

Randall pulled out a carton of orange juice, stopped mid-lift to his face, and took a swig anyway. Shortly Todd returned smiling.

"Got an invitation for Thanksgiving and—" He paused, enjoying the moment. "—she's riding with me, returning the same day. Something about a backlog of work. And, I've been invited to meet the Wards."

Randall laughed, motioning him away with his hand. "I would not trade places with you for the world." Yawning, he ambled back toward the guestroom.

"I'm going to the bank for a few hours," Todd called after him. "We'll grab some dinner later and then look at those books."

Randall mumbled agreement, but Todd's thoughts had already moved on.

Chapter 28

Not recognizing the name on the caller ID, Kingsley ignored it. Ordinarily automated telemarketers didn't leave a message. This time she heard a male voice.

"Ms. Ward? The police may have told you about me. I was a witness—"

She lunged for the handset. "Hello? I'm here. Who are you? What do you want?"

"Ms. Ward, my name isn't important. I witnessed your husband's accident, although I'm positive it was no accident. It was deliberate. I have failed miserably to get the police's attention. I gave my information to them—maybe because I waited too long and I have a record—they aren't taking me seriously, especially since, from what I've read, the fuel oil company settled for 'an undisclosed amount.'" He sounded as if he'd been running.

"Why are you calling me now?"

"Let me back up a little. I'm a salesman with a multi-state territory, including Pennsylvania. My company manufactures a line of hunting and fishing clothes and accessories. Shirts, vests, shell bags, gloves, recoil pads, tote bags.

Lots more. We also specialize in left-handed styles and market to smaller retail stores known for high quality at affordable prices."

Great, Kingsley thought. A new telemarketing angle. What horrible taste. She started to hang up.

As the handset nearly touched its base, she heard, "I saw your husband's killer again."

She clamped the phone back to her ear. "Repeat that?"

"While I was swinging through Tioga County—that's prime hunting country—I stopped for lunch at a small town and saw that same guy again. I hung around long enough to see what he was driving. This time it was a Ford F150. I followed him until he went into another store. I got the license and the ID number on his state inspection sticker. A friend, who swore he'd kill me if I revealed his name, accessed Penn DOT's motor vehicle records, got the VIN number that corresponds to the inspection sticker and learned that the license number I gave him did not match the car's registration.

"So he ran that plate number to get that driver's information. He learned that the owner was an old woman, probably just updating the registration and her license, whether she drove anymore or not. Turns out the plate on her car had to be stolen. Guess she hadn't noticed the difference—how many old gals can recite their license number?

"Anyway, on the night of the accident, I was sure I recognized the vehicle that hit your husband's Subaru. That car was parked at the next exit's truck stop. I couldn't get the license number, but I did sneak a picture of the driver." A long pause followed. "Hello? Are you still there?"

"Yes. If what you're saying is true, I can't get my mind around it."

"I understand if you think I'm a crank. I'm just trying to do the right thing."

"Where did you say you saw this guy again?"

"North of Wellsboro, Pennsylvania. That's in Tioga County."

"Did you share this with the police department?"

"I tried. They were polite, listened, looked at the picture I shot the night of the accident. Which I might add wasn't exactly professional quality. I gave them a copy anyway. In the end. they said that the reconstruction team confirmed accidental, and that they did not have the evidence or man-power to pursue an alternate theory, especially outside their jurisdiction."

"You've gone to a lot of trouble for a stranger. Thanks, anyway."

"I have one more idea—and it's a long shot. May I send you copies of the two pictures I took? The night of the acci-dent and in Tioga County? Maybe you'll recognize this guy. Put it together."

No way I'm giving this guy my address, she thought. "All right. If you wouldn't mind sending it, in care of my name, to a local bank's branch." After giving him the address of the bank, she hung up—trembling. Her life was spinning out of control all over again.

In the coming days, when she heard nothing further, she returned to work and a mountain of unfinished business that immediately dominated her existence.

ᒉᕋᒉᕋ

After all the hoopla her returning to work had created, Kingsley relished another week's passing in which she was no longer the center of attention. Her pain had subsided, her stitches removed, and the bruises were fading. With makeup, she looked almost normal. Commercial lending, like the rest of the bank, hummed with excitement about fourth quarter's numbers. And the bank was poised to surpass the year-end's projections. Dreams of promotions, bonuses, stock options, and extra vacation days brightened the atmosphere. Kingsley, however, was content to cocoon in her normal routine.

"It's marked personal," Marle said as she handed Kingsley a plain white number ten envelope.

Kingsley stared at its hand-written address, her name misspelled and having no postmark or return address. "Did you see who delivered it?"

"Nope. Someone dropped it off at the branch. One of the tellers brought it upstairs."

Kingsley took the mysterious envelope into her office and set it aside. After finishing the report that required her undivided attention, she handed the documents to Marle for execution. Only then did she remember the envelope. She slit it open, expecting to find a sheet of business or personal stationery. Instead, she extracted a blank piece of bi-folded duplicator paper. Two small photocopied pictures were tucked inside. She gasped, unable to stop the pictures from slipping through her fingers onto her desk. Looking at her was her assailant—the man in her mirror—times two.

Kingsley bolted from her office, shot up the stairwell two steps at a time, and dodged through the controller's departmental cubes into Barrie's private office. Barrie jumped from her chair, abandoning the spreadsheet she had been scrutinizing. "What's wrong? You're white as a sheet."

"Look! Look at these pictures. It's him! The guy in my mirror! The guy who assaulted me. The police showed me a grainy picture from a surveillance camera at a truck stop the night of the accident. I couldn't identify him. This guy who claims to have witnessed Andy's accident took both these pictures." She dropped them onto Barrie's desk.

"Slow down, girl."

"He says he took one the night of the accident at the truck stop when he recognized the guy approaching the car that might have hit Andy. Recently, he spotted that same guy in Tioga County and shot him again. It's him! The guy in my mirror. This cannot be an a coincidence."

"Where did you get them?"

"From the witness himself! He swears Andy's death was deliberate. He called several days ago and delivered these to the branch." Between hyperventilated gasps, she repeated the caller's account and how the police had rebuffed him.

"Sit down. Let me get you some water. Take slow, deep breaths."

"What's going on here? Why would anybody kill Andy and then try to kill me? My attack was supposed to be about the blue list. But now? What did we do? And to whom? The police—they aren't interested in the witness's story. And I can't get my mind around a connection. It's like a dream that disintegrates to vapor and evaporates the harder I think. Should I hire a private investigator? Ask for my dad to ramp up some pressure?" Kingsley got up and started to pace. "Bad idea. He'd just want me to come home. He'd dig a mote around the house and fill it with alligators." She paced faster and realized she was laughing and crying at the same time.

Barrie took Kingsley by her shoulders, shook her gently, and pierced her with a look that meant business. "Sit. Chill. Calm down."

Kingsley thumped back into the chair.

"I can only imagine how threatened you feel. And how angry and how frustrated by this horrible crime."

"I thought it was over. I'm such a wimp to need someone to fight my battles."

"Kingsley, you're stronger than you think. You can solve your own problems. Look how far you've come, just in one year."

"But nobody's listening to me. My image is some naïve little lady."

"Blunt that. Rely on yourself."

"That's easy for you to say. You're tough."

"I wasn't always. Battled with brothers for my father's approval. With a mother who was embarrassed that her sweet little daughter paid for flying lessons by washing airplanes."

"You did that?"

"As a child, I hated that artsy-fartsy little girl stuff. Spent hours under my brothers' junkers, passing them wrenches. Never wanted to be a boy—just to do guy things. Competing was easy—just had to be twice as good. I never let them see me cry when I fell short. I'd dust myself off, plan better, and make sure I succeeded next time."

Distracted by Barrie's inane chatter, Kingsley calmed. Gulping another swallow of water, she shrank deeper into the guest chair. "I don't know where to begin. He's still out there."

"At the beginning. Consider the humble potato sack."

"What?"

"It's a metaphor for solving life's knotty problems. Visualize this: the sack is sewn shut with a chain stitch. To open the sack you must determine which thread, if pulled, will unravel the stitches. Each sack has two end-threads. Pull the wrong one, and you'll have to unfasten the chain backward, one knot at a time. Pull the right one, and the entire length unravels at once. Problems are like that—find which event came first and exploit it."

"Andy's accident—"

"What preceded that? Which, in turn, brought you here to the bank? Where you started digging into problems in the lending portfolio. Did the two of you own property that someone wanted? Did you both witness a crime which, at the time, had no meaning? Go through the media archives, interfacing your whereabouts with major crimes or who wasn't supposed to be with whom—a senator with a hooker? You could be an eye witness."

Kingsley shook her head. "That's pretty far fetched."

"Your turn—you brainstorm. Who would be threatened by a situation that still exists after a year? Or what person might have it in for you both or your families? Like revenge?"

"Those two have no common denominator. Unless he thought I was in Andy's car too. No, a survivor would have been big news. That isn't it."

"Oh, but there is a common denominator." Barrie tapped the photos with her index finger. "This guy. Try to remember if you've ever seen him some other place." She snapped her fingers. "Or, if a photo can be aged, can it be regressed? Make him look younger?"

"Potato sack."

"Yeah. You got it. Give it some thought, then form a plan."

Kingsley laughed, in spite of herself. "Flashbulb! I'll just find him and ask him! Now there's a plan. Thanks."

Grinning, Barrie shook her head and nodded at her spreadsheet. "My fee—go book some loans to feed our bottom line. Seriously, K? Think long and hard before you're tempted to go after this guy."

Kingsley nodded agreement and her thanks to Barrie and exited through the controller's cubicles, thankful that no one was staring at her. Evidently numbers types found budgets and financial reports far more interesting than her histrionics. She took the stairs down to Four, pausing on the landing to catch her breath. She needed answers, no matter how long it took or how dangerous.

When Marle had no crises pending that needed her immediate attention, Kingsley went to the copy room and approached the machine that produced the crispest details. From the black and white menu she selected the finest resolution, set the man's images face down on the glass, closed the lid, and hit print. In two seconds flat, the machine spit out her copy. After scrutinizing it, she revisited the menu and adjusted the scale to print lighter. She hit start again. Two more attempts produced museum-etching quality that looked even better than the originals. Pleased, she hit "five," collected her copies, and returned the machine to its default settings. The rejects, she shredded.

Back in her office, she looked apologetically at the folders piled on her credenza. As badly as she wanted to bolt, she looked at each client's file, tackling those that needed minimal attention, or that could be dealt with quickly by Marle. Clipping notes to her AA, she handed off the latter, letting her know that Monday was quite soon enough. Kingsley glanced at the clock—four-thirty. Friday. She packaged the more complicated files into a satchel, promising her invisible clients that by Monday they would get excellent service. She headed for her car to head home.

After a light supper of reheated quiche and fresh fruit, Kingsley settled in the corner of her couch, a chenille throw warming her legs and feet. Pandora slept, wedged between her and the cushions. Kingsley pursued the first client's loan application for the third time, realizing she hadn't digested its essence. She set it aside, along with the other two that waited on her coffee table. She smoothed Pandora's glossy coat from ears to tail tip and felt her little motor ratchet up. She slipped farther under the throw and gave reality a rest.

The phone jerked her so completely that Pandora jumped to her feet and hopped off the couch. Kingsley peered at the caller ID that looked vaguely familiar.

"Did you get the pictures?" a male voice asked without any preamble.

"Yes, I did. Thank you."

"The reason I'm calling—and I won't bother you again—is that I forgot to tell you that I gave the same photos to the police. You know, in case you want to persuade them to reopen the case." Before she could question or thank him, the man hung up.

Should she get in touch with that detective again? She looked at Andy's picture, now in a new frame sitting on her dresser. As if she needed a reminder of exactly how he had looked. The light in his eyes. The shy smile. He had been a beautiful person, every feature model perfect, yet so unconcerned about such superficialities. How unfair, his loss! She had an epiphany. All this time, she and so many others had been mourning his loss to them. But what about him? His time stopped one year and one month ago. What had he missed in that time, and would continue to miss in the life that was stolen from him?

Suddenly she was furious. She snatched up the photocopies of the evil man who had extinguished Andy. She'd claw out his eyes, given half the chance. If she had a gun she would shoot him. Stab him with Grammy's butcher knife. Throw lye in his face. *Calm down*, she cautioned her impulsive self. *Make a plan, not from anger but from logic.*

She took one of the few remaining Waterford wine glasses from her credenza. In the kitchen, she uncorked and filled it with room-temperature chardonnay and added ice cubes—connoisseurs be damned. Find him herself? That wasn't what Barrie had suggested at all, but that was exactly what she intended. Locate. Identify. Ask the burning question: Why? She'd have to improvise what to do next. If only she had a gun and could shoot it.

From Grammy's antique writing desk, she pulled several sheets of her personal stationery, *Kingsley Alderson Ward* embossed in black on cream velum beneath a ragged edge. She dare not make her words to her parents, the police, or even to Todd sound like a suicide note. If her plan went badly, however, she needed them to know who was responsible and why she had decided to pursue matters herself. She found it unnecessary to draft several versions as words flowed onto the sheets. She trimmed each pair of photos, tucked them into her folded notes, and addressed the envelopes. She would leave them beside her computer where her father would look first. If her plan succeeded, she could destroy them when she got home.

Chapter 29

Shortly before daylight, Kingsley rang Barrie's doorbell and hollered again. "Please! Let me in."

Barrie disengaged three locks and cracked the door. She scowled at her friend, finger-combing her hair from her eyes. "You could have just called."

By the looks of Barrie's halo of tousled blonde curls, her rumpled oversized tee and flannel shorts, Kingsley realized she had awakened the night owl and possibly scared her.

"I've had an epiphany and need to borrow your lock pick. Now. Today."

"Whatever do you need it for? What are you up to?"

"Something I've got to investigate myself. And I can't involve anyone else. Please! Didn't you tell me to solve my own problems?"

Barrie rolled her eyes. "What I meant was 'don't count on a man.'"

Kingsley extended her hand, palm up, and waited for the next volley.

"All right. But you'll need my crash course, steady hands, great ears, and serious concentration. What kind of lock is it?"

"Whatever would be used to secure a cottage or a hunting cabin—a padlock? A deadbolt? Something you'd use in wooded obscurity—use your imagination."

"Can you at least describe the locks? Type and brand?"

"Won't know till I get there."

"Kingsley, I don't like the sound of this. What's this about? And how soon are you going?"

She glanced at her watch. "As soon as I'm armed and trained with the pick."

Shaking her head in defeat, Barrie motioned Kingsley into her kitchen. From an old-fashioned cookie jar she withdrew a small leather bag and selected two metal pieces.

"This," she said holding one up, "is a tension wrench. The other one is a rake. Don't mix them up. Inside, a lock has five pins. The object is to drop the pins, one at a time, in the correct order. That order is random and differs from lock to lock. And it changes each time you try. Slip the tension wrench into the lock. While the tension wrench keeps a little tension on the five pins, insert the rake. Use the rake to push each pin down, one at a time. Listen carefully. You'll hear a ping when it falls. Each time the lock doesn't open, you must start over. When you hit the right combination by chance and move all the pins in the right order, the lock will open."

"Let me practice on something."

"Over here—the basement door." Barrie opened it wide, engaged the deadbolt, and extracted the key. "Let me throw on some clothes while you practice. If you're not a quick study, I'm going with you."

"That won't work. Not for the scenario I've got planned."

"Which is…"

Kingsley shook her head. "I can't tell anyone, even people I trust. Got a string that needs pulling."

"At least let me hang out nearby, phone at the ready."

"Nope. I can't risk involving you in a felony."

"A felony?" Barrie sighed. "Oh, all right. But at least give me a timeframe and general destination so I can call in the troops if you need them."

"Can I absolutely trust you?"

"Duh."

"I'll scribble my plan and seal it in an envelope which you will not open until five p.m. And I'll phone you a status report around three. After that you can call reinforcements."

"Deal."

꿈꿈꿈

An hour later, Kingsley pulled into her neighborhood Enterprise's parking lot, studied the likely candidates, and chose a black SUV. Paperwork completed, she parked her rental around back near the Lexus and transferred the bag she'd packed for the trip. That included a camo-jacket, pants, and fisherman's hat with insect netting, her wellies, and LL Bean day walkers.

At a McDonald's drive through window, she ordered a number six, too distracted to notice what that included. She pulled into a parking place and, in between downing hot fries, plugged in her Garmin and entered the address for the Tioga County Sheriff's Department on the small town's main street. That journey, Ms. Garmin reported, would take a minimum of three hours. The Garmin dutifully noted the locations of nearby fast food chains, where Kingsley would change clothes. If she pushed, she could be there by eleven.

Leaving Wellsboro in her rearview, she sped north, deeper into Tiago County until she arrived at the small dot on the map. She had no trouble locating the police department, municipal building, and library, located in a huddle on Main Street.

Inside the sheriff's office, Kingsley approached the first friendly face she spotted and asked to speak to someone with local roots. The kind, older man who responded looked like someone who wouldn't mind chatting.

"I hope you can help me. For years I've been trying to locate my biological father without any luck. My only clue had been that he came from somewhere in north central Pennsylvania. My grandparents forbade any mention of his name—my mother was a teenager when I was born—but evidently my mother located him before she died. I found this picture in a box of mementoes—no name, just a note on the back that said, 'K's father.' I do not want to intrude on this man's life. It's possible he never knew about me. My birth certificate indicates 'father unknown.'"

She passed the picture to him, watching his face for a tell. There was none. He walked to the window, tilting the photo in his hands to maximize the light.

Slowly he shook his head. "Either he's not from around here, or he's very reclusive. And thousands of hunters and tourists visit the area. Doubt that he's ever been in trouble with us. If you'd had a name that would be helpful."

"Thanks all the same," she said, reaching for the picture, which he didn't relinquish.

"You going to be in town for a while? I can make a copy and pass it around. Maybe someone else knows who he is."

"That would be fine. But could you impress upon them that discretion is extremely important? Bombshells like this could ruin lives."

"Of course." He disappeared with the picture.

Given a moment to consider her options, Kingsley pulled a small notepad from her pocket and wrote down her name and home telephone number on a blank page. Good idea? Bad? What the hell. She tore the page from the notebook and swapped it for the picture when he returned.

"Should you happen to see him, I'd appreciate a call. I have to go home in a few hours."

He read what she'd written, and slipped it into his pocket. "Good luck," he called as she exited onto Main Street.

Hardware store. Every backwoodsman needed one—or so she, a city girl, had been led to believe. Driving a lazy loop around town, she searched for a possible candidate. A thought—the background in the witness's picture showed a slice of a building. Why hadn't she thought of that before? She studied the building's architectural details and began driving a methodical grid. And there it was.

"I hope you can help me. For years I've been trying to locate my biological father without any luck…"

The older man in a cobbler's apron smiled kindly. Immediately, she felt guilty for her blatant lie, but she continued her tale of woe nevertheless.

"Sure. I'll take a look." He had no more than glanced at the picture than a broad smile overtook his face. "I know this fellow. Doesn't come in but three, four times a year, but has been around for some time. Big fellow. Doesn't talk much."

"Do you know his name?"

"Nope. And before you ask, we wouldn't have any credit card receipts. Always pays cash."

Kingsley sighed. "I'm so disappointed. You see, I'm from out of town on a day trip. Must get back to work. To hang out for even a few days isn't possible."

"I get what you mean about not wanting to spring yourself on him, but maybe if you went to his cabin, spoke to him, sounded him out..."

"You know where he lives?"

"Well, sure. He rents from a friend, who I might add is darned glad to have a cash tenant who takes good care of the place. Never a call to fix this or that—must do repairs himself, judging from the hardware he buys."

"Would you be willing to give me directions?"

On a notepad that bore the store's logo, the man drew a map, complete with approximate mileage and markers. "When you get to the V, leave the macadam and take the dirt road on the right. At the next V, bear left onto a dirt lane. You may have to hike the last half mile or so, unless you're driving an ATV. If you're afraid someone will bother your car, you can leave it behind the old lean-to. It's the only one you'll come across."

"How far is it? Altogether?"

"Twenty...twenty-five miles. I'd say you can't miss it, but that's the kiss of death."

Kingsley appreciated her choice of wheels a dozen times over, as the SUV easily navigated the dirt road. And topping off the tank had been brilliant. An hour later, she located what her directions referred to as a lane and rechristened it the Ho Chi Minh trail. She stopped and cinched her shoulder belt tighter then continued her adventure through muddy ruts that were impossible to circumnavigate. Her shoulder and ribs ached from the unforgiving shoulder belt, and the healing gash in her head began to throb.

Turning around, she realized, wasn't an option as the trail that was bordered with hundred-foot tree trunks eliminated the possibility of three-point turns. She was nearly despondent when she spotted the lean-to. Hard packed mud that abutted the lean-to provided what must serve as a turn-around. Veering right, and circling tightly against its back side, she positioned the SUV perpendicular to the path from which she could easily complete the circle. And quickly, if that became necessary.

She grabbed her duffel from the back seat, changed clothes, and pulled on her Wellies. Hiking shoes would be sucked into the mud, and perhaps herself with them. Stepping onto the path, she paused. This truly was God's country. As she stood quietly, birds that had become silent when she opened the door began singing again, their songs echoing beneath the lofty branches. Moss and lacey ferns, dried yellow by fall's progression, proliferated beneath virgin oaks, birches and tulip poplars. How easy it would have been to forget her mission.

She studied the narrow path that had been recently rutted by humungous tires. Forcing concentration, she listened for human sounds. There were none. A quarter-mile down the path a cabin emerged, sheltered beneath massive oaks. Behind it, where the tire tracks led and vegetation was trampled, squatted an oversized rustic garage. Ducking into dense twelve-foot thickets to obscure her intrusion, she edged toward the cabin.

Tangled undergrowth that rose to the trees' lowest branches extended to within a few feet of the cabin's rear door. Heart pounding, she crept toward the door. She peeked in. Deserted, she realized. Or could that be wishful thinking?

Crash!

She jumped back, flattening herself against the log exterior. When no further sound came from the cabin, she risked another peek. On an old-fashioned draining board stood a one-eyed cat. Only then did she notice the doggie door. None had barked. Gently, she touched the doorknob, her

imagination screaming about an alarm, but none materialized. The knob wouldn't budge. She grasped it harder. The
knob protested from infrequent use, but relented and opened
on raspy hinges. The cat glared with a feral eye, hissed, and
darted past her, escaping into the woods.

The gloom, the dampness and oppressive aura of ancient
fires reinforced that she was alone in an unoccupied cabin.
Whipping out her penlight, she began to systematically
search every cupboard, drawer, and possibility of conceal-
ment. She found nothing that would suggest a link to herself,
to Andy, or their families. The place was devoid of human
habitation. As an afterthought, she examined the floor-
boards. The cabin, built on planks supported by concrete
blocks, had no cellar. And the floors had no rugs. Glancing
up, she saw foot-wide pine boards, draped with cobwebs
that defined the top of the cabin without including as much
as a gallery.

The garage. Before stepping out back, she circled the interior and peered through grimy windows. Still alone. The
garage dwarfed the cabin by several fold. A massive wood-
en bar latched two doors together that were big enough to
admit multiple trucks. Around the left corner was a personal
door, secured by a padlock and deadbolt. She had guessed
right. *God bless you, Barrie.*

Holding the penlight in her teeth, she teased at the deadbolt until it relented. Barrie had been emphatic to remember
which way it engaged should she need to do it again. Pain
shot through her healing lips when the penlight shifted, but
she ignored it, concentrating on the stubborn padlock. When
she couldn't stand the pain any longer and tasted blood, she
abandoned the penlight and forced her eyes and ears to the
task. Finally she convinced the padlock to comply.

Kingsley eased the door open on well-oiled hinges, almost forgetting the penlight until the gloom hit her. Retrieving it, she entered the cavernous space. Rough-hewn walls held all manner of tools and a variety of in- and out-of-state license plates. On closer inspection, she noticed the plates bore current registration stickers. Two parked cars left room for a third and a large working area.

By the far wall stood a navy Buick LeSabre. That was it! The very tank that had shoved her Andy to his death. Transfixed, she edged closer. Circling to the front bumper, her penlight revealed recent repairs which, given the age of the vehicle, were believable. She couldn't stop herself from reaching, but then jerking her hand back from the bumper.

Search, she commanded her roiling stomach and hammering heart. Find evidence, proof. She wrenched herself back to her task. With so many drawers and doors, she hardly knew where to begin. And just what had she expected to find? She imagined it would take a skilled CSI team days to process the scene. She searched, jumping from one area to another, realizing she didn't understand what the documents meant. The guy used some kind of code.

But one cabinet held file folders smudged with black fingerprints that were hung in no discernable order. Each was labeled with more cryptic code. Or was it? She squinted and chose one at random: BRE: AFD.

Papers inside the folder referenced Bradley R. Ebert and Albert F. Downing. Ebert's paperwork appeared to contain a report: dates, a project's description in code, another code and a date. Downing's held billing information, including tax records, describing mundane construction projects including a code. Ah ha! The IRS could not catch this guy for tax evasion.

Nearly crippled by an anxiety attack, she finger-walked through the files. AW: SP Andrew Ward! And—Sidney

Paul? Snatching the papers, unable to read them, she folded them in four and stuffed and buttoned them into her right-thigh cargo pant pocket.

She noticed a long-legged stool pulled to a surface that must serve as a desk. Underneath was a wooden box that resembled a shoeshine kit. She pulled it into the light, lifted the lid and looked inside. In the depth were a half-dozen flip phones.

Taped to the lid was a list of what must be their pass-words. Grabbing her notepad and pen, she scribbled the numbered passwords and stowed the pad in her shirt pocket. Noticing each phone had a corresponding number, she picked one phone at random.

Entering the password, she fired up the phone. No surprise, no bars. Of course. Determined, she stepped outside and tried again, which produced a weak signal. From the main menu she touched the phone icon and chose recents on the appropriate screen. A list of numbers unrolled. Thumbing through them she stopped at a number whose area code and first three digits were familiar. She tapped redial and nearly dropped the phone when she recognized the voice.

"You have reached the mailbox of Jeffrey Johnston..."

She scrolled, hoping she'd find a link to Sid or Thomas Paul, the latter being the runner-up to Andy's trust award. But no names appeared. If the numbers were for cell phones, they could have been purchased anywhere in the country. She picked up a second and a third phone, but their area codes were unfamiliar.

Why she hadn't heard it sooner, she didn't know, but a vehicle was approaching. Not wanting to lose the precious phone with Johnston's message, she lifted her jacket tail, stuffed it into her right hip pocket and one that she hadn't tried into the left. She buttoned the flaps. Her own phone was in the SUV, but she doubted she could get reception anyway.

As quickly and quietly as possible, she crept out the personal door, clicked the padlock closed but left the deadbolt unlocked. Perhaps he'd think he'd overlooked it. Flattened against the exterior wall, she inched toward the back corner. Her plan: when bad guy entered by the front garage doors, she'd escaped through the wood's dense cover. As she risked peeking around back, what she saw was a denim wall and a huge hand grabbing at her. She screamed as he closed his grip around her neck and shook her like a rag doll.

"Just couldn't leave it alone, could you?" His uttered growl struck her dead-on as belonging to a monster.

Chapter 30

Her captor half lifted, half dragged her back into the garage, and tossed her effortlessly onto the floor where she landed in a heap. She stole a look—a mountain of a man whose identity was instantly recognizable. Without further words, he began opening drawers, cursing and muttering, as if oblivious to her presence. She rubbed her throat where he'd nearly strangled her. A lump was rising on the knee that had struck the floor first, and her elbow throbbed. She prayed that she could still run, given the chance.

As if reading her mind, he whipped around. "Don't even think about leaving." He returned to his searching. "You're done."

"What did you have against Andy? And me? What did we ever do to you?" Her voice came out as a scared little rasp.

He turned, sneering. "Absolutely nothing."

"Then why?"

He grinned. "Nothing personal. Just a business transaction."

"What business? Banking? Medicine?" she stammered.

"My husband is dead, and you nearly killed me. I've got a right to know why. Tell me. Just what is your business?"

He grinned. "I fix problems—for a price."

"What? Who? Who hired you?"

"Guess it doesn't matter now, since you won't live long enough to tell anyone. You rich society people make lots of enemies. Draw lots of jealousy. Step to the head of the line without a thought of the people you've trampled."

"My family never hurt anyone. I didn't. He didn't. We earned—"

He whipped around, angry face blazing, fists clenched at his sides. "Earned? Everything all by yourselves? No big money to buy the best schools? The top jobs? Exclusive memberships? People hate you enough to even the score."

"Tell me the truth! Who targeted Andy? And me?"

"I told you the why. And the two jobs weren't even related. You figure out who. Or you could if you had time. Me? I'm impartial. I really don't care as long as I'm paid. That's what I do. Then I disappear, letting my clients pursue—whatever."

"You can't get away with it. People know where I am. Know I was looking for you. And what you look like."

He shook his head. "Young lady, nobody will find you." He snapped a drawer shut. "Time to go." He chose a Virginia license plate from the far wall, and with a power screwdriver, affixed it to an old brown Impala. He pulled the keys from the ignition, opened the trunk, and closed on her with a half dozen strides. She shrieked when he wrenched her to her feet, pain coursing through her leg. He dragged her toward the trunk. Furious and scared, she screamed curses that reverberated off the log walls. She punched, clawed, and kicked with a year's pent up anger, but she was no match for the big man. Effortlessly, and unperturbed by her assaults, he folded her up and tossed her into the trunk. He slammed the lid. She beat on it until she was sure she had re-fractured her fingers.

She knew instinctively by the loud scraping noise that the man had pushed open the huge garage doors. After he slammed the car door and fired the engine, she commanded herself to listen. Memorize the route he was taking. The driver's side door opened, the huge garage doors scraped shut and the car door slammed shut. By the car's motion she could tell he'd turned left, back down the path she had followed. Her head hit the lid with each pothole and rut. Suddenly, she remembered his cell phone. Could there possibly be reception out here? She dug into her right pant's pocket, extracted it, and fired it up. What was that password? Of course—it was password. Two bars! Thank God for towers in His country. She tried nine-one-one, but the bouncing car caused her to miss. Gripping it tighter, she tried again.

"Nine-one-one. What is your emergency?"

Her frantic pleas and impossible directions must have made her sound crazy or like a kid playing a prank.

Kingsley heard—could it be? Motorcycles! From inside the trunk it sounded like a road rally. The car stopped. Male voices. With a sinking heart she heard what sounded like good old boy chatter, her yelling and pounding being drowned out by the revving of motorcycles' engines. She kept yelling until her voice failed and the engines' noise faded into the distance. The car began moving again.

Try nine-one-one again. Horrified, she realized she hadn't ended the call, and the battery indicated four percent. She hit end, powered up and redialed nine-one-one, but the backlight went dark. She thumbed end. Perhaps if she gave it a little rest...

Another idea—maybe if she kicked out a taillight that

would get someone's attention. That she realized must be a
TV myth because no light fixture was visible. Could he
have taped them under? Wriggling around her confines, she
fingered the trunk's interior. That yielded nothing. An electrical wire? She felt where the taillights must be, and
touched circles around the adjacent surfaces. Nothing.

Once more, the car stopped. She could hear traffic.
Someone nearby called to somebody else. *Yell!* If she could
hear them, they could hear her. But no sound came from her
wrecked vocal cords. They sat, engine idling. She wondered
if he had left the car to buy—what? A shovel? She strained
to listen. Finally, she heard what sounded like footsteps approaching both sides of the car. If only she'd worn the steel-
toed construction boots she used to spade her gardens. Rubber wellies didn't make much noise, but she kicked anyway.

"Drive!" The second voice barking the order was male
and unfamiliar.

"Jeep in position?" Her captor's voice.

In response: "If you got the money." Silence.

Kingsley tried to position herself in ways that didn't hurt.
The trunk was void of anything soft—an old army blanket,
burlap, or mats. Rust—that's what it smelled like. And
damp earth. She sniffed, hoping to capture a clue about their
location, if only she had a chance to escape. The driver
braked hard, cursed, and floored the vehicle, ricocheting her
backward and forward against the trunk's walls. Skunk
permeated the enclosure, so strong it smelled sweet. She
gagged and willed herself not to throw up.

Kingsley tried to account for how long they had driven.
Her captor must have returned to town to pick up his buddy
and whatever else. That stop had taken about fifteen
minutes. Add another fifteen. She had an idea. As a child,
she'd memorized Lincoln's Gettysburg Address to recite in

a play. Her cadence had been timed to take X-many minutes. If she recited it to now, and counted the number of times until they stopped, and guessed at their average speed. But in time, she lost concentration and count.

The car bumped to a stop. The driver's door opened and slammed. Click—the trunk flew open. The monster stood over her, assessing her with dead eyes. Ripping a length of tape from a roll, he encircled her legs. She kicked to no avail.

"Help! Somebody help me!"

He tore a short length, and as she opened her mouth to scream again, he slapped the tape on her face. Grabbing both wrists with one hand, he looped long lengths around her wrists and hands. Without a word, he shoved her backward and slammed the trunk lid. The driver-side door opened, the car sagged left, and the engine fired simultaneously with the door's slam.

By the time her captors stopped again and opened the trunk, it was dark. Leaves crunched as they seemed to be walking toward the dense woods, the tops of hundred-foot trees being her only orientation. The branches loomed against the moonlit sky like haunted specters. She tried lifting her head and craning her neck to see what they were doing, but her vision was obstructed by the trunk's depth. Were they going to kill her? Leave her for wild animals?

The big guy returned to the car, hauled her out, and tossed her over his shoulder like a sack of grain. He took twenty paces, and stopping abruptly, spun toward the car and paused stalk-still.

"Company," he hissed to his cohort.

From her vantage point over his shoulder, all she could see was the ground until she arched her neck backward and lifted her head. She spotted the other man poised with a shovel by a wide gash in the earth. Was the plan to kill her or bury her, dead or alive? He was right—they'd never find her, at least not in time. Outraged by the thought of her devastated parents, she clubbed at his back with bound fists.

Without explanation, the big guy bolted for the car, her head bouncing against his back, her injured ribs screaming in protest. He dumped her into the trunk, slammed the lid and, with his buddy, jumped into the car and sped through ruts, rocks, and waylaying branches. The car finally eased into what smelled like a stand of pungent pine or hemlocks. Two doors opened then crashed shut. An interminable pause. From somewhere nearby, a different engine fired and, from the sounds, continued off-road, its engine's thrum decreasing like a train in the night. Then silence. Complete.

As she had struggled to scream when he'd slapped on the tape, her mouth had been open. How wide was the tape? Gingerly she pushed her tongue beneath the tape and her upper lip, widening the gap. She tried likewise to loosen the tape from her lower lip, sliding her tongue toward her nose. Slobbering, grimacing, and contorting her mouth, she worked circles under the tape, but it stayed affixed. Exhausted and scared, she rested awhile.

She must have been dozing, as a dog barking startled her so severely that she jolted, bouncing her head off the lid. Drool covered her chin, the moisture having loosened the tape. As she scraped her bound hands against the wet tape, the corner came loose. Working through the pain of her lacerated lip, she rubbed until it hung loose. With her forearm, she brushed until it came off. Teeth! She bit, pulled and gnawed at the tape that imprisoned her hands inside her jacket until they were free. With a few swift motions she unfettered her ankles.

"Yes!" she exalted, momentarily victorious until she remembered those bastards would return whenever they'd finished their dinner. Or hatched a new plan to dispose of her, the stupid witness. Maybe the panel that separated the trunk from the back seat could be breached. Wiggling into position she felt for screws, nuts and bolts, buttons, levers, handles, whatever...

Nothing.

Wrist smacking her forehead, she remembered the phones and extracted them from her pants' pockets. No service. No surprise. She rested a minute, thinking, remembering. Three minutes without oxygen, three days without water, three weeks without food. Or maybe she'd die of exposure. If this nondescript car was not missed, she could die, alone in wooded obscurity. That gave fresh meaning to God's Country. If Barrie got nervous, she'd call the police. They'd find her abandoned SUV with no trace of where she had gone. And they'd driven hours into the woods. Bone weary, she huddled in a corner and fell asleep.

Warmth awakened her. Disoriented, she tried to stretch and jammed her feet on the trunk's interior. Feeling around, she realized that it must be morning. The trunk lid felt warm. She sniffed—the aroma of warm pine was unmistakable. And rubber. She smelled warm rubber. Another escape route popped into her mind. Rubber strips between the trunk and the car's body, kept out the elements. If she could find a loose end and pull it—Barrie's potato sack theory! This Chevy was quite old. Concentrating, she identified the edge of the lid and explored its closure with sensitive fingers.

Alarmed, it became obvious that the trunk's interior must have been customized to imprison victims. Even this vintage model should have safety features, such as interior latches, access to brake lights, airflow and child-safety escape mechanisms. At least she could yell, kick, and pound.

If I get out of this alive, I swear I will never, ever, do anything this stupid again. I'll carry a cell phone, fully charged and remember my watch. And a pocket knife. Maybe a gun. I'll learn to shoot.

Leaves crunching caught her attention. Quiet steps, not thrashing like squirrels or birds. Her captors? Hunters? What if she screamed and chose wrong? What season was it? Bow and arrow? Buck? Doe? She'd had no reason to remember. She listened, straining for a clue.

"Seven point with a crossbow," someone nearby was saying.

Hunters! "Help! Help me! Over here! In the trunk!" She kicked, banged and yelled with renewed vigor.

"It's coming from over here." A woman's voice, followed by swishing footsteps closing fast through the leaves. Someone was trying the doors, which must be locked.

"In here! They locked me in the trunk."

Glass smashed, the driver's side door opened, and another man positioned behind the trunk yelled, "Pop the trunk!" Glorious morning sunshine poured onto Kingsley.

"What the hell—"

"Just get me outta here. I've got to pee!"

The hunters—two men and a woman—transmitted their location to the police and shared food and coffee with Kingsley. Within the hour, police, EMTs, and CSIs overran the area.

"This is precisely why you get your deer early," one smug hunter proclaimed to his friends. "With all this commotion, there won't be another within miles of here anytime soon."

The police did not share in their merriment. "Could have been worse. At least you found her in time. She could have been as dead as your deer."

Kingsley turned to the officer. "I left word with my friend Barrie that I'd check in at three. And if she hadn't heard from me by five to alert the authorities. Did she?"

"Around three. Said to tell you that she didn't trust you to be smart. We found your SUV and searched the cabin and garage without a warrant because you were in eminent danger."

"Did you find the killer's files? The records? I bet those license plates were stolen as well."

He sighed. "The place was cleaned out. Empty except for tools that you'd expect to find in any workshop. The evidence technicians are working the scene, but what you're describing is gone."

Finally, back in the sheriff's office where she'd begun, Kingsley held an icepack to her bare knee, having unzipped and discarded the lower-leg extension from the shorts. Stocking feet dangling from her perch on a table, she wiggled her toes and proclaimed them sore but okay, even after all that kicking. Having declined the EMT's repeated suggestion that she be transported to the local ER, she nevertheless appreciated their expert first aid. Her lip had finally stopped oozing, and her sutured scalp appeared undamaged from the ride in the trunk.

She repeated, in finite detail, the entire experience with her captor, now in the wind. She underscored how she had identified him by two different photos in addition to glimpsing him in her mirror. She felt incredibly lucky that he hadn't bothered to bind her hands behind her back. Now, exhausted by the huge adrenaline expenditure, she just wanted to go home.

"How did you find me? Did someone get my nine-one-one call?"

The sheriff grinned. "That picture—after you left, I real-

ized it looked vaguely familiar. So I compared it to the BO-
LOs we receive routinely and matched it to one we'd received from a Philadelphia detective. And knowing your
name—you've had significant coverage by the media as
have your parents. We put it together, but you'd already left.
I've got to ask—why didn't you tell us the truth?"

She shrugged. "I didn't know who I could trust. I wanted
to find him myself. Confront him. Demand answers. And
I'm still missing the most important piece of all—who hired
him."

Exasperated, the sheriff threw up his hands. "How could
you not have understood the grave danger?"

She shrugged. "My need to have answers overwhelmed
my common sense."

"We'd be happy to put you up overnight in one of our fine tourist accommodations. Give us time to go over your
story in the morning."

She kept shaking her head no.

"Of course, we could hold you on breaking and entering,
using an illegal lock pick, lying, and misrepresenting yourself to law enforcement. Let's see—that could get you, what?
Ten to twenty? Hey! Relax. I'm just kidding."

Kingsley, feeling ridiculous, wiped her eyes on her
sleeve and dug into her hip pocket to extract the murderer's
flip phones. Pretending to hand it to him, she yanked it back
before he could take it. "This is going to cost you. That bastard actually told me the attacks on my husband and me
were 'business.' He admitted that he is a hired killer! And
this phone's history appears to contain the numbers of his
clients. I have no idea whose jurisdiction this would be—
that's your problem, not mine—but those numbers should
lead to his clients, other victims or missing persons. If he
had intended to bury me locally—if he's got a burial site

near where you found me, there's that angle, too."

She unbuttoned the flap on her cargo pants thigh pocket, withdrew and unfolded the crumpled piece of paper she'd snagged when she'd heard his approaching vehicle. "Give this to the CSIs. This paper contains my husband's initials—AW with the client's' initials—SP. I believe that's Andrew Ward and Sidney Paul. He's the father who coveted my Andy's grant and hired that man to eliminate him. Cross reference that against the phone numbers stored in his phones."

The assembled people in the small office exchanged glances that begged, how often did such complicated situation befall them?

The sheriff laughed. "Okay. I'll bite. What's it going to cost me?"

From her jacket pocket Kingsley dug the keys to the rental SUV. "Would somebody please retrieve my ride from behind the lean-to near the cabin?" She unfolded the directions drawn by the man in the hardware store the previous day. She gave it to him, still clutching the phone.

"Anything else?"

"Just a place to clean up and change my clothes."

"Ah, our executive lavatory is at your disposal." She gave him the phones. "And we insist on buying you dinner. If you're intent on driving, you'll need fuel for yourself as well as your car."

Four hours later, as the miles slipped away, she addressed the unanswered question. Whoever hired that man to kill her was desperate to cover up the loan scam. But who? Jeffrey Johnston had no reason to hurt her. She hardly knew him and, in fact, she had never had a conversation with him. Nathaniel and Warren had interviewed and hired her themselves. The answers were now in others' hands. She'd done her best to quell her personal need. Her Andy was killed by someone who broke two commandments: 'Thou shalt not covet' and 'Thou shalt not kill.' And maybe the one about worshiping graven images as found on legal tender. She wished she felt relieved, but closure was only a word coined by people who thought those who mourned should shut up and move on.

Chapter 31

John Miller was furious on so many levels. Because of that Ward bitch, he'd been forced to abandon an ideal sanctuary and hide sensitive records from prying eyes. He never, ever transported incriminating evidence with or on him. And now he must find a new refuge away from suspicious eyes. Mountain men in West Virginia did that all the time, but they had kin to watch their backs and did not cotton to strangers. No, he'd stay in north central Pennsylvania where the flow of hunters, fishermen, and tourists drew little attention, except as a source of the locals' income.

Money. He needed cash. All that work, only to be stiffed by a creepy little banker who took off without paying hm. He'd settle scores later, but now he must plan for his immediate needs. He aimed his old Buick into south central farmland that stretch out in checkerboard patterns, the fertile flat valleys nestled between the Appalachian forests that he called home. From the four-lane to the two-lane to the narrow rural roads, Miller realized potential in Lancaster County when he passed a horse and buggy clip-clopping onto a dirt access road. The harvest would be in and money col-

316   Nancy A. Hughes

lected from whatever they sold. Banks. These people did
not believe in banks, or so he'd been told.

Miller invested another two hours, studying county maps,
digesting road patterns, pinpointing escape routes, and looking for farm lanes bordered by tree lines. And buggies and
wagons with those orange triangles, which meant that the
family was Amish or Old-order Mennonite. They didn't
own cars. There! Off to the right. A picture-perfect house
with a well-maintained barn and out buildings. For people
disinterested in wealth, the property looked prosperous.
Dark-colored clothing and sheets flapped on a clothesline
that extended from a back porch to well into the yard. That
would provide cover to approach the kitchen by a back door.
Maybe they were all at a prayer meeting or out in the barn.
He hoped he could ransack the house and disappear.

Even though he had no intention of shooting anyone, he
tucked a pistol into his pocket to underscore persuasion. He
slipped from the car and pushed the door almost closed. An
icy wind hit him as he hiked the short distance over corn
stubble to the back door, nonchalant as if he were dropping
in for coffee. The kitchen door squeaked as he cracked it
enough to peer inside. A woman in a long black dress,
apron, and white cap was peeling apples at an old-fashioned
draining board.

"Amos?" she asked without turning, but when she did,
she gasped, her knife clattering onto the floor.

"I won't hurt you if you keep quiet."

Panicked, she grasped her mouth with her hand, but nodded.

"Where's your money?"

Involuntarily her eyes flicked in several directions as if
she didn't know. Footsteps mounting the steps to the back
door alerted Miller. In three swift steps, he reached the

woman, grabbed her by the upper arm with his left hand and yanked her against him while simultaneously slipping the pistol from his right jacket pocket.

Spotting the weapon, she opened her mouth, but seemed too frightened to scream.

"Not one word or I'll shoot him the minute he walks in the door. You got that?" She appeared frozen with fear. "You do speak English, don't you?" She nodded vigorously.

The guy, who must be her husband, halted midstride. He said something to his wife in Pennsylvania Dutch then turned calmly to Miller. "Whatever you want, you can have it. No doubt you have greater need than we do."

Miller was stunned by his calm, not even begging for his family's safety.

A preteen boy entered through the front of the house and stepped into the kitchen. "Joshua, bring me the milk can," the father said.

The tableau of three remained rooted, listening as the boy's footsteps disappear down what must be the cellar steps. Momentarily, he returned with a five-gallon metal can. Rather than risk a catastrophe, Miller turned slightly to prevent the boy from seeing his gun. Maybe this was how the Amish paid their debts, and the boy was familiar with the routine.

The father jerked his head toward a cupboard, which the boy opened and withdrew a satchel with sturdy handles. He handed the sack to his father. "Now go help John with the milking. He is waiting for you."

The boy vanished through the back door. Miller pushed the wife toward her husband and lifted the lid from the milk can. It was stuffed with bills—tens, twenties, and some of larger denominations. He grinned.

Miller waved his gun, back and forth, between the can

and the sack. "Fill it. Her, not you," he growled at the husband.

With shaking hands, she complied. When it was stuffed to overflowing, the pair looked at him with anxious faces.

"Put the sack by the back door." They did. "Now show me the can." A few bills remained in the bottom. He grinned—that they could keep.

Motioning them toward the cellar door with his gun, Miller followed the couple at a safe distance. After they descended the steps, he closed the door. No surprise, there was no lock. He dragged a sturdy oak bench from the kitchen and wedged it in front of the door. Shoving the gun back into his pocket, he grabbed his sack full of cash. Ever the cautious survivor, he crept between the front living room windows, checking for impediments to his escape. Seeing nothing, he strode toward the back door. From its window, all he could see was the laundry whipping in the wind and the barn in the distance. The boy and that guy John would find the family when they finished milking. And of course they didn't have phones to alert the police.

The wind kicked the door open when he turned the knob, and he turned his back to grasp the knob securely to pull the door shut after him. Head bowed to the task, wind howling in his ears, Miller clutched the satchel, never hearing the approaching footsteps.

"You're under arrest." Cold metal handcuffs were slapped on his wrist before he could grasp the scene. The bag was snatched from his hand, his pistol liberated by the frisk and pat down. Rough hands turned him and shoved him against the back door.

Miller calculated how hot the water and how deep the shit. "Hey! Just collecting a debt—"

"First off, that car that you left by the road has stolen

plates. It is not a Mustang. And robbing the Amish at gunpoint. You idiot! They are not stupid people. They know how to take care of their own."

For the first time, Miller noticed a car's front bumper, peeking beyond the far side of the house that had no windows. "Hypocrites! I thought you people couldn't have cars."

"This sect doesn't, but they can accept rides. I gave Amos a ride home from the doctor's." He smirked at his collar. "And we Lutherans can drive all we want, especially when we're law enforcement."

Amos, whose son had freed him from the cellar, spoke up. "This is John. And he doesn't milk cows."

"I'll get the cash back to you ASAP, Amos. Evidence, you know."

Amos waved his hand. "We still have the big can."

ᘓᕽᘓ

"This way, Ms. Ward." The policeman directed her down corridors and around corners until she became disoriented. Eventually they arrived in a room with a large plate-glass window. Just like TV, she thought, taking slow breaths and willing her stomach to unclench.

A woman who introduced herself as an assistant district attorney and a man in a suit who gave a name that Kingsley would never remember also approached the window.

"Do you understand the procedure?" the ADA asked.

Kingsley wanted to say that any idiot who owned a TV would, but instead she simply said yes.

"Bring in the group."

Six men filed into the room and took their places in front of lines that represented their height. Each clutched a number under his chin. "Do you recognize any of these men, Ms. Ward? And if so, from where do you know them?"

Kingsley knew with one sweep of their faces that none was vaguely familiar. She couldn't tell if she was disappointed or relieved—to not have that face further etched in her brain or to relax. "I'm sorry. I do not."

She turned to exit at the same time the voice said, "Bring in the second group."

She swiveled, and before they could even face forward, she spotted him. "That's him! Number two. I'd know that face anywhere." She was shaking so violently she thought she would faint.

"From where do you recognize number two?"

"I saw his reflection in my vestibule mirror just before he knocked me out. And again when he kidnapped me in Tioga County. Please! Keep him locked up!"

♥ॐ♥ॐ

The group of friends gathered in Kingsley's apartment for a modest victory celebration, savoring the details over wine, cheese and crackers, fresh fruit, and decadent pastries. They took turns reviewing the story that was already growing exponentially. Todd, his best friend and pilot Randall, Barrie, Margaret, neighbors Michael and Isaac, and even the Philadelphia detective exchanged tidbits of information. Randall, who could not take his eyes off Barrie, remained uncharacteristically quiet.

"How did they catch him anyway?"

"Every police station in Pennsylvania received the BO-LO," the detective responded. "An officer in Lancaster had just apprehended a guy caught in the act of robbing an Amish family at gunpoint. Even in the country, law enforcement has no illusions about being crime free. Given the seriousness of Miller's crime against that Amish family, they cross-referenced everything they could find. And got a hit."

"Will he be tried here? Or in Lancaster County? Or someplace in Tioga County?"

The detective shrugged. "I don't know. Judges will have to decide, based upon the seriousness of each crime. I hope jurisdictions won't fight over him. But, Kingsley, I trust you remain willing to testify."

"Absolutely," she told the detective. "If Miller was hired to kill Andy, I hope the Philadelphia DA will not offer Miller a deal in exchange for a reduced sentence. He was hired by Sidney Paul to kill Andy because of his being awarded that fellowship instead of his son. Miller admitted that he was hired to kill me, too, but is withholding that information in exchange for a deal. I can't imagine that little mouse Jeffery Johnston being bold enough to do such a thing. But if not him, who? Who is angry enough, or vicious enough to hurt me? And why?"

"I'd vote for Manning Stoudt. You were in a position to ruin his career and send him to prison."

"Are the police combing through every bit of his life?"

"You'll have to be patient to learn those details, as the investigation is ongoing. Since you work for a national bank, the feds have an interest as well."

Todd shook his head. "I vote for Frank Ziegler. Kingsley's testimony about finding those files on his watch could destroy a lifetime of clawing and scheming to get to the top. Without her testimony, he could even keep a shit-load of money, maybe keep his job. Guess it all comes back to you, K."

"I'm in—I guess."

Glasses were raised and tapped. "To our brave, clever girl! To Kingsley!"

"No. Make that to friendship. To all of you who taught me to trust again."

Epilogue

D ays slipped into weeks without any progress on Keynote's vault murder. Speculation had been pandemic at first, as employees, locals, and the media chewed on even the most bizarre possibilities and angles. The favorite, given the half-hour timeframe and the weapon being a Keynote letter opener, was that a clever insider had committed a premeditated crime. The conundrum facing detectives, however, was that nobody could have anticipated the power interruptions and staff being sent home. The obvious suspect, her partner in crime known as Manning Stoudt, predeceased her. Ziegler had an airtight alibi, although speculation centered on his familiarity with the historic vault. How he could have tampered with the timer, however, continued to niggle the detectives' imagination. The designer of the vault had died in the forties, and the manufacturer went out of business in the 1960s, so they could not be queried about its idiosyncrasies. The case had gone cold.

In time, media attention focused on other issues rather than wasting column inches and airtime rehashing old news. As for the loan scam, white-collar crime was not sexy, and

the bank's special loans department and the feds sifting
through bank records was mind-numbing. Ordinary people
returned their attention to their bland lives, having become
bored with dead issues.

Kingsley approached the New Year with her grammy's
advice as her mantra. "Don't look back in anger or ahead in
fear, but around in awareness." She vowed not to go looking
for trouble again and not let what-ifs and suppositions spoil
her happiness. Still, her dark angel whispered the questions.
Could that killer get out of jail and wreak vengeance on her?
And what of his accomplice in the Tioga County woods?
Was a knife-bearing killer at work in her bank?

She straightened her spine, knowing she was stronger,
braver, less naïve and gullible than she had been when she
left Philadelphia. The price she had paid for her death of
innocence in solving Andy's murder was huge, but worth it.
Being oblivious had held its allure, but Grammy was right
all along. Kingsley had to move forward, into the light.

As she traveled her territory on customer calls, old field-
stone farmhouses caught her attention, as if beckoning to
her. And that led to thoughts of a future with a man who
claimed that he loved her. A new year. Another fresh start.
Bring it on!

ACKNOWLEDGMENTS

Whether dreams becomes reality often depends on special people whose faith never falters and who unselfishly share their professional and personal knowledge.

A Matter of Trust would not have been written without the love, encouragement, and critical eyes of my family and friends. My best friend—consummate banker and husband, William D. Hughes, aka Bill, Dad, and Papa—you're the best! Our son Dan Hughes and daughter Lora J H Bean cheered and willingly researched obscure details.

For decades, my dear friend Polly Brockway urged, "Hughes! Where's the book?" Polly believed, unconditionally, that I had stories worth telling. Without her, I might have given up long ago. She and faithful friends critically read and proofed early drafts with skill, a sharp eye, and humor. Linda Meyer, Connie Fegley, and Margaret Funk—I can't thank you enough. And a special thanks to locksmith Tim Ansel for sharing his technical knowledge.

I am indebted to the Mystery Writers of America's New York chapter for its boundless opportunities. Through its resources, seminars, and friendships, I've grown into the genre and delighted in our shared journey. MWA compresses the distance from small town PA to the Big Apple. Special thanks to Phyllis Halterman, Daniella Bernett, Richie Narvaez, and Sheila J. Levine.

My publisher, Black Opal Books, and my editor, Lauri Wellington, are an author's dream. Thank you for your continued confidence. I am very grateful to editors Faith and Mae for their knowledge and keen eye for detail. Artist Jack Jackson's covers convey far more than 1,000 words. Behind the scenes, Black Opal's staff tirelessly perform myriad details to produce award-winning books.

And bless you, my readers, for your compliments and well wishes. You delight and humble me. For once, I am speechless. Thank you!

About the Author

Nancy A. Hughes, a native of Key West who grew up in Pittsburgh, lives with her husband in south central Pennsylvania. Following graduation from Penn State, where she majored in journalism, she spent most of her career in business writing, specializing in media, community, and public relations for small to midsized businesses.

In recent years, Hughes turned her attention to murdering people—on paper, that is. *A Matter of Trust* is the first of a three-part mystery series. It follows *The Dying Hour*, which was released October 15, 2016. Hughes's focus is character-driven crime-solving mysteries.

When she isn't writing, Hughes is devoted to shade gardening and to volunteering at the veteran's hospital. Visit her on her website at www.hughescribe.com.